ONE MIDNIGHT WITH YOU

SHARI LOW

Boldwood

First published in Great Britain in 2024 by Boldwood Books Ltd.

Copyright © Shari Low, 2024

Cover Design by Alice Moore Design

Cover Photography: Shutterstock, iStock and Alamy

A CIP catalogue record for this book is available from the British Library.

Paperback ISBN 978-1-83518-460-8

Large Print ISBN 978-1-83518-461-5

Hardback ISBN 978-1-83518-459-2

Ebook ISBN 978-1-83518-462-2

Kindle ISBN 978-1-83518-463-9

Audio CD ISBN 978-1-83518-454-7

MP3 CD ISBN 978-1-83518-455-4

Digital audio download ISBN 978-1-83518-456-1

Boldwood Books Ltd
23 Bowerdean Street
London SW6 3TN
www.boldwoodbooks.com

To our beautiful new grand-daughter Emme...
We're so happy to have you in the world with us, little one,
and we love you beyond words... x

NEW YEAR'S EVE

OR IN SCOTLAND... HOGMANAY (HOG-MAH-NAY): THE LAST DAY OF THE YEAR, ONE OF ENTHUSIASTIC CELEBRATIONS AND HISTORICAL TRADITIONS ENJOYED BY SCOTS AS THE YEAR ENDS AND THE NEW ONE BEGINS.

ON THIS HOGMANAY, YOU'LL MEET...

Ailish Ryan, 54 – Newly divorced mum, primary school teacher, recently moved from her family home to a two-bedroom flat where she is supposed to be embracing single life. And she will – just as soon as she works up the motivation to get out of her comfy clothes and Crocs.

Eric Ryan, 58 – Ailish's ex-husband. Suave silver fox and director of a successful marketing company. Commonly known as the 'Adulterous Arse'.

Emmy Ryan, 29 – Daughter of Ailish and Eric, a nurse specialising in elderly care at Glasgow Central Hospital. Currently concerned about the life expectancy of her relationship with...

Cormac Sweeney, 32 – Emmy's boyfriend of almost a year. A firefighter who belongs on one of those fund-raising calendars because his muscly shoulders are wide enough to be June and July.

Minnie Ryan, 78 – Emmy's gran on her dad's side, Ailish's mother-in-law, married to Henry for sixty years, usually to be found with her knitting needles.

Yvie Danton, 35 and Keli Clark, 30 – Emmy's friends and fellow nurses on the elderly ward at Glasgow Central.

Rhonda Nichols, 54 – One of Ailish's best friends from high school. Owner of a chain of hairdressing salons, divorced, now living her best life and aging as disgracefully as possible.

Gwen Millen, 54 – Ailish's other lifelong friend, interior designer, defiantly dealing with major health issues.

Gino Moretti, 79 – Gregarious but stubborn founder of Gino's Trattoria. Father of Dario, Bruno and Carlo, husband of the late Alicia Moretti.

Dario Moretti, 54 – Former chef, now head of the family business, currently carrying the weight of the world on his shoulders.

Nicky Moretti, 52 – Dario's ex-wife, still close friend, work colleague, sounding board, all-round voice of reason and irrepressible sarcasm.

Carlo Moretti, 36 – Dario's lovely brother, owner of Carlo's Cafe, a trendy bistro in Glasgow, Yvie Danton's fiancé and all-round good guy.

Matty Moretti, 30 – Dario and Nicky's son, chef at the family restaurant, prone to volatility and requires work on his un-sunny disposition.

Brodie Moore, 54 – Dario's best mate since high school, now a top commercial lawyer who represents the Moretti family business in return for love and great pasta.

Sonya McGregor, 64 – Straight-talking, eternally loyal cleaner at Gino's Trattoria, gran to Ollie, the light of her life.

8 A.M. – 10 A.M.

1

AILISH RYAN

Ailish checked behind the couch for the bra that she'd tossed aside last night. In a previous era, an errant bra-toss may have been a frantic action in the throes of passion. Now it only occurred because removing the constraints of the elastic bondage was her favourite part of the day and frequently happened the moment she walked in the door. It probably wasn't ideal in case of unexpected guests, but she didn't get many of those nowadays. Actually, she didn't get many expected ones either.

Divorce did that. Empty nests did that. Leaving your home of almost thirty years for a two-bedroom flat where you don't know your neighbours did that. In moments of reflection, she conceded that these factors were also responsible for her Croc collection, her indoor, knee-length fleece hoodie and her addiction to Netflix box sets. Probably also the reason she was now bent double over the back of the sofa, peering into the abyss to see if her bra was there. It wasn't.

Bugger. She didn't need anyone to tell her that she should be handling both the bra situation and her general existence so much better. For a start, she should maybe have leapt out of bed when she'd woken at 8 a.m., instead of cosying down with the new Anna Smith crimefest for over an hour, before grudgingly getting up at the very last minute, but, well, it gave her time to psyche herself up for the day. Adjusting to a solo life after the end of a thirty year marriage was a process and she was in no rush to get to the end of it. Some women flourished when they started a new chapter in their fifties. Joined a gym. Or a dating agency. Started doing Pilates. Travelled. Got glammed up and had sex with thirty-year-old men. Or maybe that was just one particular woman close to Ailish's heart...

Her front door opened and the case in point teetered in on four-inch Cavalli stiletto boots that made Ailish's feet tingle in her Crocs. Spotting the head pop up from behind the couch, her friend, Rhonda, startled and clutched her hand to her Wonderbra in dramatic fashion. 'Flippin' hell, you scared me. What are you doing lurking in the shadows like that?'

It was hard to respond given that Ailish was being blinded by the whitest set of teeth in Europe, courtesy of Rhonda's recent trip to Turkey. It had resulted in a two-week fling with a thirty-five-year-old tour rep and a set of gnashers that a *Love Island* contestant would kill for. The thing was, much as it would be easy to cast scorn and derision in her friend's direction, no one could deny that five years after her amicable divorce from husband number three, Rhonda's post-marriage glow-up had left her looking at least ten years younger, fitter and healthier than ever before. Ailish kept telling herself she should follow in the footsteps of her friend's towering heels, but she was afraid of heights and she just wasn't mentally there yet.

It had only been eleven months since the sale of her marital home had landed her here, and exactly two years tonight since her marriage to Eric had imploded. A psychologist on one of the podcasts she listened to in the bath said a transitional event could take years to process, and there were several stages of emotions to go through. Ailish had already decided that her 'wallow and eat biscuits' era was going to last a while longer.

'Happy Hogmanay to you too,' Ailish greeted her intruder. 'And I'm not lurking, I'm looking for my bra, and last time I checked this was my living room. Is this a good time to point out that I only gave you a spare key for emergencies?'

'It is an emergency. I'm doing a juice cleanse and I need to pee on a fifteen-minute schedule otherwise my bladder is going to explode like a garden sprinkler in a drought. Rhubarb and wheatgrass juice. But it'll be worth it when I get into my dress tonight. I bloody love New Year's Eve. Anyway, hurry up, it's time to go. I'll be right back.'

As Rhonda teetered off to the loo, Ailish spotted her bra under the dining table and retrieved it, then pulled her arms out of her black jumper and using well-practised contortion moves managed to manoeuvre her 42Ds into their restraints. Mission accomplished. If Tom Cruise had to deal with this shit every morning, all that saving the world stuff would feel like barely more than a trifling inconvenience.

Now fully dressed and almost ready for the outside world, Ailish kicked off her Crocs and swapped them for her trusty Ugg boots, accessorised with the parka she'd bought last year to walk her labradoodle, Patch. The beloved thirteen-year-old pooch had passed away peacefully in his sleep just two weeks before the sale of their old house had gone through. It was as if he'd decided that life in a modern, second-floor, two-bedroom flat wasn't going to work for him after a lifetime living in a cottage with a dog-heaven of woodland right behind it. Sometimes Ailish thought that after everything that happened, losing Patch was more painful than losing Eric.

Her stare went to the brown envelope on the kitchen island.

Her official decree of divorce. Confirmation. It was done. Over. And the fact that the paperwork had arrived on the last day of the year made it seem even more poignant. At this exact time, on the morning of Hogmanay two years ago, she'd been happily married. Hours later, her marriage was done. Today, she was unhappily divorced. Maybe by this time next year she'd have found a way to get over it.

The door to the hall opened and Rhonda click-clacked back in. Ailish did a top to toe of her friend's outfit. Black leather-look skinny jeans, those gorgeous boots, a cream ribbed polo neck and a beautiful camel-hued wool jacket that reached her thighs, accessorised with a cute little camera bag. Ailish wondered if it was just her imagination or did the large shoulder bag she was pulling onto her own arm feel even heavier than normal? How did anyone actually get everything they needed for a full day in one of those tiny bags? Where would she put her banana, her purse, hairbrush, phone, glasses, spare glasses in case she lost the first pair, deodorant, perfume, a book, her Kindle, emergency plasters, the tweezers she hadn't used in a year and a half and the plethora of other things that she never left home without?

Rhonda's gaze went to Ailish's chest. 'The nips are pointing straight ahead. I take it you found your bra?'

She was rude. She was crude. And for the forty-odd years since they'd met on day one of high school, Rhonda had been infuriating her, exasperating her and making her laugh, often at the same time. This morning was no different.

The corners of Ailish's mouth turned upwards. 'Hoisted up and ready to go.'

'With those boots on?' Rhonda eyed her Uggs with undisguised disdain.

'Yep, and no judgement or I'll slash your tyres.'

'Don't worry, I don't have to say it out loud – you know what

I'm thinking. Now, let's go visit our pal, and if you could walk ten feet behind me so no one knows we're together, that would be a true act of friendship.' With that, Rhonda swayed her tight arse right out the door, leaving Ailish, still laughing, to lock up and follow her.

The cold air of the Glasgow morning hit Ailish like a snowball to the face as soon as she stepped out of the building. She would happily have turned around and gone right back inside if it weren't for the trip they had planned today. The same one they'd taken every day for the last fortnight, since Gwen, the third person in their lifelong trifecta, had been admitted to Glasgow Central Hospital.

As always, Rhonda drove, because she said hell would freeze over before she swapped the comfort of her Mercedes for Ailish's clapped-out, twenty-year-old Volkswagen Beetle. 'Only way I'm getting in that car is if I'm starring in Herbie Rides The Menopause, and I get to shag Ryan Gosling in the back seat,' she'd sneered last time Ailish had suggested that she drive them. Not that she minded today. The heating hadn't worked in her Herbie for at least a decade and it was so old it still had a DVD player instead of the fancy bells and USB whistles in Rhonda's swanky ride, so Ailish was happy to take the loss on this one.

The flash Merc was just one of the perks of Rhonda's hard-earned success. She owned three hairdressing salons – one in the West End, one on the South Side and one in the city centre – but after three decades of slogging long, back-breaking hours to build her business, she now had great managers in all of them, which allowed her to be so much more flexible with her own time.

Ailish's days teaching six-year-olds at Weirbridge Primary School on the outskirts of the city had far less flexibility, but most of the time – vomiting epidemics and the occasional insufferable parent aside – she loved both her job and the extended holidays that came with it.

There was still almost a week until the first day of next term, which meant that she could devote as much time as needed to her friends and family. Although, trying to navigate a new 'normal' on post-separation Christmas celebrations had hurt Ailish's heart. She'd had Christmas Day lunch with her daughter, Emmy, and her boyfriend, Cormac, but Ailish had left after the dessert to let Emmy get organised to go have dinner with her dad's side of the family. Tempting as the sofa, a box of Quality Street and sobbing over *It's a Wonderful Life* was, she'd refused to give in to self-pity and instead, had taken herself off to keep Gwen company in hospital for a few hours. They'd watched *The Holiday* for the thousandth time on Gwen's laptop, shamelessly made objectifying remarks about young Jude Law, sucked the caramel out of Lindt balls and made each other laugh until the ever-patient nursing staff finally announced that extended visiting was over for the day.

She'd been back every day since, usually in the company of the woman sitting next to her now.

It was a twenty-minute drive from her flat in Clarkston, on the South Side of the city to the hospital, so Ailish clicked on her seat-belt and settled into the heated seat.

'Chat or music?' Rhonda asked, as she always did.

For the first week after Gwen had been admitted, they'd talked all the way there and back, but the conversations were always on the same three topics.

Ailish's post-divorce 'moving on'. Or lack of.

Rhonda's latest escapades on dating websites, or post-date post-mortems.

Or Gwen. Her treatment. How she was doing. How they'd make her smile today and take her mind off the bastard disease she'd been fighting for months now. Surgery. Chemo. Endless tests. Bloodwork. Scans. Their hearts were broken for her. They'd talked about it all in minute detail day after day until there was nothing left to say, so now they stuck to trivial stuff when they were going there and back. What mattered most was that they walked into the hospital upbeat and positive, and ready to lift Gwen's spirits.

Ailish and Rhonda were Gwen's chosen 'framily' and her most frequent visitors. Her elderly parents now lived in Aberdeen, she was an only child, and she'd never found anyone she loved enough to marry or have children with, so she'd led a very content, successful, unattached life until now, with a few long-term romantic relationships, but none that she'd chosen to make permanent.

'Music for a bit. Unless anything mind-blowing happened since I saw you yesterday?'

'I could make stuff up?' Rhonda offered, with a teasing grin. 'Or I could tell you about my dream last night, but you'd probably disapprove. There was nudity.'

'Urgh, don't make me wish I'd brought earmuffs,' Ailish shot back, feigning horror. 'Shove some music on and spare my fragile soul.'

Rhonda pressed a couple of buttons on her steering wheel and the opening bars of 'One' by U2 and Mary J. Blige filled the vehicle. Rhonda, eyes on the road, asked the most important question. 'Do you want to be Mary or Bono?'

Ailish didn't hesitate. 'Mary. You know Bono gets right on my nerves. It's the wearing dark glasses inside thing.'

Rhonda batted her eyelash extensions. 'I forgive him for that because he contributed to the longevity of the holy male mullet back when I was starting out. There was a hairstyle that provided endless amusement, especially when it also involved squads of blokes coming in for perms, just to make the mullet extra bouncy. I think I washed the hair of the entire Scotland football team at one point or another – made a fortune in tips.'

The memory of that made Ailish smile. Back in the late eighties, before they were even old enough to legally drink, seventeen-year-old junior hairdresser, Rhonda, would regale her and Gwen with all the gossip of every famous encounter while they got ready to go out on a Saturday night. If they managed to use their flashing smiles and fake IDs to get into a club, the night would be a win. If not, they'd get chips and head back to Rhonda's house to play a Simple Minds album and have a dance party in the bedroom, because her mum worked nights in a bar.

How did they get from there to being three fifty-four-year-old women so quickly? And what would the young girls they were back then think of the women they'd become? Ailish shrugged off the realisation that seventeen-year-old Ailish would be massively disappointed with her current situation. All that optimism of youth had gone the same way as her pert buttocks, her blue eyeliner obsession and her conviction that she'd one day marry George Michael – right out of the window.

Bono and Mary kept them company for the first few minutes of the journey, before Beyoncé, Shania Twain, Madonna, and Kelly Clarkson took over and got them the rest of the way there, with Ailish and Rhonda belting out all the hits at the top of their voices. By the time they pulled into the car park, it was almost 10 a.m. and Ailish needed a throat lozenge.

'Right, deep breath, slap a smile on and let's do this,' Rhonda said, as she pressed the button to kill the engine.

It was the same battle cry that had got them through every tough moment in all their lives. *Deep breath, slap a smile on and let's do this*. Ailish had said it to herself more times than she could count in the last two years. The heartbreak of losing the love of her life. Betrayal. Separation. And then in the last twelve months, there had been divorce proceedings. The dog dying. Moving house. The loneliness that came with her new life. Gwen's diagnosis. The absolute terror that she could lose her lifelong friend. It was too much. Way too much. And yet, she didn't feel that she had a single right to be miserable because what Gwen was going through was so much worse.

That was all that mattered. Today, on the last day of the year, all she cared about was helping her friend get through the challenges she was facing.

As for fixing her own life... Well, there was always next year. Right now, she'd settle for getting out of 2024 with no more surprises.

2

EMMY RYAN

A blast of Dolly Parton singing '9 to 5' woke Emmy up and she stretched one arm out to the left and banged it up and down in random places until she hit the button that switched Dolly off for exactly five minutes until the next outburst. Yes, she still used an old-style alarm clock, because she was paranoid that she'd forget to charge her phone overnight and it would die and she'd be late for work.

Her other arm felt for Cormac, but his side of the bed was already empty. Groaning, she prised open one eye and aimed it at the digital screen on the clock: 8 a.m. Still dark outside, as it would be at this time until the Scottish spring finally kicked the gloom away in March.

Emmy hated winter. When she was on day shift on the elderly ward at Glasgow Central Hospital, she went into work in the dark, and if she finished any time after 3 p.m., the skies were already black when she left. The only bonus was the cosiness of the thick jumpers and furry boots that were her standard out-of-work wardrobe from October until the end of February.

She pushed herself up in bed and listened for signs of life. None. For a moment, she wondered if Cormac had already left, maybe headed to the gym before work, and her heart began to thud just a little bit faster. Surely he'd have woken her? But then, leaving her to sleep as long as possible was just the kind of thing that Cormac Sweeney would do, dammit. Or maybe... maybe he just couldn't be arsed waking her. A month ago, she'd have said he'd never do that, but lately he'd been so preoccupied, so distant, that it wouldn't be a surprise.

A deflated, half-hearted snap of her fingers had just flicked on the bedside lamp, when the door opened and in he walked, all six feet two of handsomeness. Not that she was biased. Even an objective eye couldn't deny this man's win in the genetic life lottery. Her mother, Ailish, was still convinced that he had such a strong resemblance to the Irish actor, Daryl McCormack, that they had to be related and fully expected some strings could be pulled to get them an invitation to next year's BAFTAs. Not that her mother would agree to a swanky night out these days. It had been pretty much impossible to get her out of the door for any kind of social interaction since... well, since their whole bloody family had fallen apart.

'Hey gorgeous, happy Hogmanay,' Cormac said, as he placed a wooden tray down on the bed with her usual winter breakfast: a mug of black coffee and a toasted, buttered cinnamon bagel. The delectable aroma of the Colombian beans mixed with the warm, oozing buttery bun stirred any remaining sleepy senses to life.

Food and her man. This should be the very best way to start the day. The only things that stopped it from being perfect were that he was fully clothed and about to leave, and that creeping suspicion that something wasn't right with them. He'd been acting strangely for days. Weeks even. And every spider sense she possessed was telling her that she knew the reason why. She just wasn't ready to admit it.

Or was she just overthinking everything because of all that had happened with her mum and dad? The complete dissolution of the one relationship she'd never doubted for a second. There wasn't a handbook for how you were meant to feel when you were a grown adult and your parents split. Or for finding out that your dad was a cheating arse who'd been having an affair with – oh, the cliché of it – his two-decades-younger assistant. Her poor mum had been absolutely blindsided, although, in hindsight, his sudden predilection for fake tan and teeth whitening should have been a dead giveaway.

Cormac hadn't done either of those things, but still, her suspicions that he could be seeing someone else, or thinking about it, were keeping her awake at night. He'd been so checked out recently. He was jumpy if he was on the phone when she walked into the room and one time when – ashamed as she was to admit it – she'd checked his phone while was sleeping, he'd changed the password. He'd come home late a few times and once she could definitely smell perfume.

Now, seeing him doing something so sweet this morning, she was wondering if she'd been wrong.

'Happy Hogmanay,' she replied, stretching over to kiss him, oblivious that the angle made the hem of her pyjama top dip into her coffee. 'I was worried that you'd gone off to work and I'd missed you.'

'I'm just going now,' he murmured, between slow, gentle kisses.

'Don't go. Stay. Come back to bed. Stuff the world, it can do without you today,' she said, already knowing what his answer would be.

'Yep, but the station can't. I'm on grub duty,' he answered, as expected. 'There would be an uproar if I didn't show today and the lads went hungry.'

Grub duty. It basically meant he was in charge of preparing the lunches for the shift. Actually, dinner too, given that he'd somehow agreed to cover for a mate and that meant he'd be doing a double shift, and would be at the station for twenty-four hours, sleeping between call-outs in the bunk room. A double shift on New Year's Eve. That was about as unlucky as it got for a firefighter on one of the busiest days of the year. Yet, he hadn't complained once, because he truly cared about his job, something she'd realised the first time she'd met him.

Cormac Sweeney had walked into her ward in his firefighter uniform almost a year ago, and by the time he'd reached the nursing station, Emmy was in lust. When he'd asked if he could sneak in to say hello to an elderly man he'd pulled out of a fire caused by a smoking chip pan, her heart was paying attention. When she took him through to the man's bedside and Cormac treated the gent with such care and respect, bits of her were already in love. Especially the bits that, despite her fears, were responding to his kiss right now.

He must have felt the heat rise between them because he broke off the snogging session and gave her one last smile as he stood up from the bed. 'I'll see you tomorrow morning, but I'll try to call you later. Sorry we're not going to be together at midnight, babe. I'll make it up to you, I promise.'

'No worries, but call me if you can. I'll be in all night. Or if I get bored, I might head over to Mum's and go wild with a bottle of wine and the box of Quality Street that's still under the tree. And I'll drop in on Gran at some point too.'

'Yeah, I'll try, but you know how it is. It'll be chaos.'

He brushed her off so easily and there was something shifty in the way he didn't make eye contact. She wracked her brain to remember the psychological tells they discussed on all those episodes of *Criminal Minds* that she used to binge on. Did the suspects look down to their left or their right when they were lying? Or did they just, like Cormac, back out before you could spot where their gaze was going? Not that she had any serial killer concerns, but there had definitely been something off with him lately.

'No worries,' she answered, trying to play it cool. 'I do know how it is. Have a good shift. And please stay safe.' He was already at the door.

'You too,' he retorted distractedly, obviously checked out of the conversation. Her shift at the hospital definitely didn't require a safety warning. The most physically hazardous thing that ever happened on her ward was an octogenarian going rogue with a Zimmer frame.

'I love you,' she said, as he went out the door. It was superstitious, an ever-present anxiety that the one time that wasn't the last thing she said to him would be the time he got injured at work. Or worse...

If he said it back, it was drowned out by the thud of his steps on the stairs.

Emmy slumped back on the bed, deflated. There it was again, the niggling feeling. He wasn't being unkind or rude or abrasive, just... distant. As if he wanted to be anywhere else but here. And it was a demeanour she recognised only too well. Her dad had perfected it when things started to go wrong with him and Mum. He'd stopped paying attention when she spoke. Stopped laughing at her jokes. Started staring into space as if he had something on his mind. Turned out it was a thirty-two-year-old called Donna. The man she'd adored above all others her whole life was now someone she barely recognised, and even two years later, there was still a lingering fracture in their closeness, one that was papered over with cordial tolerance.

After she polished off the bagel and coffee, she drifted back to sleep for a while, still knackered after her double shift yesterday. It had been midnight when she'd crawled in the door and she'd been too wired to sleep, so she'd worked her way through two episodes of *Selling Sunset* before climbing in beside a sleeping Cormac at 2 a.m., and drifting off to dream about a palatial estate in the Hollywood Hills.

Her second alarm of the morning woke her at ten minutes to ten. She had her morning routine down to perfection. One hour and ten minutes to get showered, dressed, and over to Glasgow Central Hospital in time for her shift to start at eleven.

Before she got up, she did a quick internal check and, yes, her worries over Cormac's behaviour were still there. Emmy knew she had to confront it, but even the thought of that twisted her stomach into knots. Tomorrow. The first day of the New Year. May as well get the year off with a bang and...

Bang. Bang. Bang.

It took a second to register that the noise was coming from her own front door. Someone had just thudded it with the kind of force that suggested urgency. Maybe a delivery driver, keen to get his last shift of the year over with.

She slid out of bed and trotted down the stairs, spotting the outline of a man in the opaque glass side panel next to the door. He wasn't holding any kind of parcel, so not a delivery guy. No post-person's red jacket either.

Shit. This was one of those moments when she really needed to have one of those personal safety alarms. And a bra on. Whoever it was, they were about to get greeted by a wild-haired, red-eyed woman in her pyjamas.

Cormac had already undone the overnight locks and security chain, so she only had to open the Yale at the top of the door. Trying to keep as much of herself hidden as possible, she slowly pulled open the heavy oak door and peered round it.

'Dad!' she exclaimed, confused. There was absolutely no reason for her father to be at her door at this time of the morning. Or for him to have bloodshot eyes and hair that looked like it had just come out of a tumble dryer. He was always so impeccably groomed, this sight in front of her was hard to take in. The dishevelled suit, the tie pulled loose, the unshaven face. None of this fitted on Eric Ryan. They used to joke with him that he was like one of those middle-aged silver foxes that featured in travel promos for Saga Tours and adverts for life insurance. Right now, he would be more suited to an NHS warning about the dangerous after-effects of binge drinking.

'What's happened? Is something wrong? Is it Mum?' That came out automatically, before she remembered that he would have no clue how Mum was, on account of the fact that he'd had some kind of midlife crisis, destroyed Mum's life and wrecked their family.

'Yes, love, it's Mum,' he replied, and she was surprised there was no slur to his words. Given his appearance, she'd half expected him to have got here fuelled by tequila.

'What is it?' Her blood ran cold. 'Is she hurt? Has she been in an accident?'

He immediately put his hands up as if he was surrendering. 'No, no. Nothing like that. She's fine.' He ran his fingers through his hair, exasperated.

'It's me who's not okay, Em. I need help.'

'With what, Dad?' she asked, confused and aware that this whole scene was playing out on the front doorstep and Mrs McFadden from next door was walking up her path and craning her neck so much to see what was going on that she was almost walking backwards.

Her dad's voice escalated with uncharacteristic drama. 'I've been a total idiot and I need to fix my mistake. Emmy, I need you to help me get your mum back.'

3

DARIO MORETTI

This was always Dario's favourite time of the day. First thing in the morning. When the icicles of the dawn frost were still sparkling in the air and the restaurant was completely empty. Just him and his coffee. Time to breathe. Time to reflect. Although, he was beginning to think that was overrated today. Sometimes too much reflection wasn't good for the soul.

Mug of the finest Italian caffeine in hand, he leaned against the doorway between the office and the main dining area of the restaurant, his gaze scanning the room. Gino's Trattoria, home of – according to his father, Gino, and yet to be disproved – the best food in Glasgow's Merchant City area, had been founded by his dad in the seventies.

Like several other young men in his village near Cassino in Italy, Gino had come over to Glasgow when he was fourteen to work for the summer in his uncle's ice cream shop. The week before he was due to board his return flight, two months of wages in hand, he'd met a young girl called Alicia, his first love, and Gino never went home. He'd gone to work in a family friend's restaurant, sleeping in a makeshift bed in a tiny room behind the kitchen, and he'd learned every aspect of the business by watching, studying, practising until he could do it all. Years later, by then married to Alicia and dad to four-year-old Dario, he'd inherited his uncle's old shop and his hard graft and good business sense had transformed it into a thriving restaurant that became one of the legendary eating establishments in this area of the city.

This restaurant had been his dad's world. Still was. Gino was seventy-nine now, and although he'd handed the running of the restaurant over to Dario several years ago, Gino still showed up and worked four nights a week. Dario knew it kept him going, especially since Mum had passed away a few years back. How many times had the old man said that the day he stopped serving customers in this restaurant would be the day he gave up on life?

Dario had always thought it was like looking at a premonition of his own future. He was twenty-five years younger than his dad, and he'd worked in this restaurant since he was fourteen. It had never even been up for discussion, always just expected by everyone that he would follow in his father's shuffling footsteps, just as his own son, Matty, planned to follow in Dario's.

Now, that was no longer an option. The rock his family had always stood on was about to break up into pieces and he was the only one who knew what was coming.

'Are you daydreaming or doing some of that meditation bollocks? Only I need you to move yerself so I can get this place hoovered before His Lordship arrives. He can spot a speck of dirt from fifty yards away.' Dario hadn't even heard Sonya, the cleaning equivalent of a whirling dervish, come in the back door or creep up behind him.

All pondering of his problems screeched to a halt, as an irrepressible grin crossed his face. He loved that she'd push him out of the way to get the place cleaned to his dad's standards. Or His Lordship, as she always called him, with just a hint of irreverence.

Sonya had been with them for decades, and she was the chain-smoking, straight-talking, sweary antidote to any kind of deep or spiritual reflection, believing that action and motion were the answer to all of life's woes. She'd almost worn a track in the restaurant carpet with the Dyson when she'd left her husband in the nineties. Last summer, Dario had come in to find her scrubbing the kitchen tiles at 6 a.m. Turned out her grandson, Ollie, had gone off to university the night before and she was beside herself with both pride and separation anxiety. Now she was here an hour early and desperate to get to work, so she must have something on her mind. Dario didn't like to pry, but no doubt it would all come out at some point in the day. Sonya's ability to keep a secret was up there with her ability to sit still for five minutes.

'I'm just standing here contemplating how you're my very favourite person to see at this time in the morning,' he joked. Actually, there might be some truth in that.

'Aye, right, Big Pierce...' she shot back, using the nickname she'd had for him for years, because she swore he was the absolute double of her favourite 007. 'Don't try all that smooth talking with me.' Her tone was stroppy, but there was a twinkle in her eye. 'You know I'm immune to smarmy shite, but I can be bribed with tea, so if you can flick a kettle on, I'll forgive you.'

With that, she pulled open the door of the cleaning cupboard and disappeared inside.

Dario took the hint and headed back down the corridor behind him. The swing doors into the kitchen were on his left, and on his right, the staffroom. He pushed open that door, to the small space with two medium-sized sofas and a compact dining table for four. Right next to the table was a small beverage bar area, and there, he flicked on the kettle, then pulled a mug from the wall cupboard above it. He loaded the cup up with a teabag, some milk and Sonya's standard three sugars, before backing out and shouting, 'Kettle is on. Be ready in a couple of minutes,' into the depths of the restaurant. She'd no doubt have something to say about him putting the milk and sugar in before the hot water. They'd been arguing about that for decades.

'Jesus, you've got a voice like a foghorn,' came the response. A mild insult was Sonya-speak for 'thank you', so he retreated into his office, content that he'd done at least one good thing this morning, but fully aware that no amount of teabags could solve the rest of his problems. Especially when he heard, 'And you'd better not have put the milk and sugar in first, ya reprobate,' just as he closed the office door.

He'd just sat down on the battered old leather chair behind his desk when his mobile phone rang, and the screen flashed up Jailbreak. It was an old joke, a name given to Brodie, a friend since school. When Dario had gone into the family business, Brodie had gone off to university, and was now a high-flying corporate lawyer, who had a roster of multimillion-pound clients, but still took care of anything in the legal realm for the Moretti family business, in return for unlimited free food and affection. It had always been a given that, in the unlikely event of Dario being arrested, Brodie would be his one permitted phone call. Thankfully, he'd never had to call him from the slammer. Yet. Although, right now, that phone call would probably be preferable to the one he was about to have.

'Hey, pal,' Dario answered wearily, leaning back in his chair.

'Morning. Mate. How. Are. You. Doing?' There was a deep intake of breath and then a swift exhalation in between every word.

'Are you on the treadmill? Seriously? New Year's Eve and you're up at this time and exercising? There's something far wrong with you.'

The punctuated breaths came right back at him.

'Some. Of. Us. Need. To. Work. At. It. Pal. Don't. All. Have. The. Metabolism. Of. A. Fricking. Racehorse.' It had always been an amused bone of contention that Dario's exercise regime consisted of a weekly game of five-a-side football and the occasional gym session, yet he still had a body that hadn't changed too much since his thirties. He put it down to good genes, quality pasta and a job that kept him moving all day.

Dario sighed. 'Yeah, but it's all I've got going for me right now, so hold the jealousy.'

A few deep breaths on the other end of the line, then Brodie came back with, 'You know why I'm calling. The deadline for accepting the deal is midnight tonight, then it disappears. We have to give them an answer. The Fieldow lawyers are breathing down my neck.'

Dario felt every muscle in his stomach clench. No need for sit-ups or crunchies here. The Fieldow Financial Group, a top Glasgow-based accountancy firm, were working on behalf of an American corporation who wanted to purchase the building that he was sitting in now, the one that his father had inherited from his uncle and then converted from an ice-cream parlour to a restaurant when he was barely out of his twenties. Back then, this wasn't a particularly salubrious part of the city centre, but Gino must have had the patron saint of good investments on his side, because in the eighties, the Merchant City had undergone a gentrification that had brought in high-end, designer shops, expensive apartments, trendy bars, and popular clubs, and with all that came people with money to spend, who were looking for great food. In its heyday, Gino's was steady Monday to Thursday, then packed every single night of the weekend, a party that never seemed to slow down. Until it did.

The pandemic in 2020 and the next couple of years of slow

recovery had almost crushed them. Their loyalty-fuelled determination to keep on all the staff at full salary had decimated the restaurant's capital reserves. Even when the furlough payments had kicked in, they'd still topped up all their employees' salaries, so they got exactly the same income as before. Afterwards, they'd kept everyone in a job, even when there were barely any diners to feed. On the other side of the income and outgoings scale, their costs had rocketed. Ingredients were so much more expensive and electricity, gas, water, and rates all soared. Decades of savings and profits were soon gone.

Dario had hung in there, positive that 2023 and 2024 would turn things around, but their income and footfall had never returned to pre-pandemic levels. There were a million reasons why. The health-obsessed, carb-avoiding younger crowd that socialised in this part of the city had deserted them for Nando's and Wagamama, while a massive sector of their invaluable after-office customers still worked from home. Many of their older regulars just didn't seem to travel into the city any more, their social patterns forever changed by the lockdowns. Gino's had thrived on the selling point of great-quality, family-style Italian food at a budget-friendly price, but that just wasn't a viable proposition in this high-cost, prime location now. He'd contemplated raising prices, changing direction, going more upmarket, relaunching with a new brand, increasing advertising, running promotions... There was nothing he hadn't considered. But the reality was that any price increases would risk alienating their current clientele, and any re-brand would require investment capital that they didn't have.

And all this had happened on Dario's watch.

In the beginning, he hadn't felt able to share the extent of it with his dad, because Gino was grieving the loss of his wife of fifty years. Dario had finally broken it all down for him the year before, but the old man had brushed him off. 'You'll find a way through this, son, you always do. That's why I gave you my restaurant. Speak to your brothers and work something out.'

Dario knew that was pointless. His middle brother, Bruno, had left Glasgow years ago, moved to Indonesia to run a fabulous restaurant on a five-star hotel resort. He was well paid, but he had a family to support so he wasn't exactly flush. Meanwhile, his other brother, Carlo, almost eighteen years younger than Dario and forever considered the baby of the family, even though he was now in his thirties, had opened his own café in 2021. He'd made the smart move of choosing a location just outside the city centre, but near Glasgow Central Hospital, which brought it a steady footfall. Although it was thriving, it was a new business that wasn't sitting with extra cash to spare, so Dario knew that would be a dead end. Since that last conversation with his dad, every time he'd tried to return to the topic, he'd got the same reaction. I don't want to hear it. You go sort it out. You'll fix it somehow.

But there had been no fixing it.

All over the city – in fact all over the country – great restaurants had been forced to close their doors. Gino's wouldn't be the first and it wouldn't be the last, but at least he had a chance to salvage something out of the closure.

He'd been out of time and options when the American offer had come in via the Fieldow Financial Group. They wanted the building, and they were offering a fair price, enough to let his dad have a comfortable retirement, to clear their debts and to pour some cash back into the family reserves. Dario wasn't worried about himself – someone with his length of experience in the hospitality industry would find work somewhere, and if need be, he could get his tools back out and go into a kitchen. He'd been the chef here for thirty years before Matty had taken over and Dario had moved out onto the floor. But if he sold up, he'd be destroying his father's legacy, wiping out the old man's life's work. He'd also be obliterating the future his son had always been destined for. Matty had talked about taking over Gino's since he was a boy, and that had been the whole point of his years of study to be a chef. The understanding was that it would all pass on to him when Dario was sixty. Now there was a looming probability there would be nothing to pass on.

He couldn't see any choice but to accept the offer. Legally, this was his business, and his to do with what he chose. What were the alternatives? To try to continue riding this out, taking out more loans and credit lines until the debts were worth more than the assets and they had nothing left to show for their efforts? The truth was, much as he knew that didn't make financial sense, he'd tried it anyway, but so far none of the banks would lend him any money right now because one look at the books made it perfectly clear they were in trouble and no-one wanted to lend to a failing business.

The one thing he hadn't done was take a mortgage out on the building that housed Gino's. His great uncle had bought and paid for the bricks and mortar when he'd settled here in the forties, so Dario wasn't prepared to do that. However, he wasn't prepared to leave his family destitute either.

Meanwhile, on the other end of the phone, Brodie was still, literally, breathing down his neck.

Dario exhaled as deeply as his friend. 'I know, Brodie. Listen, I'll give you the answer today. I'm just not ready to do it right at this minute.'

'Well look, I'm coming to the restaurant tonight anyway. Wouldn't miss a Hogmanay at Gino's. If I don't hear from you before, I'll speak to you then. I wish I could do something else to help, my friend.'

'Thanks, mate. Your table will be ready as always. I'll see you then if I don't call you this afternoon.' With a deep sigh, and an overwhelming feeling of desolation, he hung up.

What was he waiting for? He had no idea. It wasn't as if he hadn't already had over a week to think this through. His whole Christmas had been consumed by trying not to screw up his family's festive period, while wrangling with what to do for the best.

Now his hand was being forced.

He couldn't lose this deal.

It had to be today.

He had to make the decision, and he had to tell his dad and his son.

It was time to clean the slate, ready for the new year and the next chapter for their family.

Today was going to be the day that he changed all their lives for ever. He just hoped that he didn't lose the people he loved in the process.

4

MINNIE RYAN

Minnie heard the phone ringing, but for a moment she thought it was on the television. Then she realised that Angela Lansbury wasn't answering a call on *Murder, She Wrote*, so she pushed herself up out of her armchair and took a few steps to the phone next to Henry's chair. He'd always liked to keep it by his side. That way, he could answer it quickly or take his time to make sure he got the right number if he was voting for a smashing act on *Britain's Got Talent*. He liked that show. It didn't rile him up like *Panorama*, or *Newsnight*. Henry was the sweetest man with the biggest heart, but ineffective or lying politicians delivering or defending unfair policies always set him off. 'Clowns, every one of them,' he'd grumble as the current affairs programmes ended. 'That shower of idiots in the government should go invade an uninhabited island and stay there. That's a show I would watch.'

At which point, Minnie would pause the clacking of her knitting needles and suggest they switch over to *Strictly Come Dancing*, or maybe a Louis Theroux documentary, then she'd pick her needles up again, click-clack her way through it, until she had a

fresh batch of tiny hats for the premature baby ward at the mater-
nity hospital. Or new woolly toppers for the post boxes in the
village.

That's what she'd been doing since 5 a.m. this morning, when
she'd woken up with the birds. It was one of those strange twists
of life, that you didn't need so much sleep when you got to her
age. She could have done with extra hours in the day when she
was a young mother, juggling four boys under five. An extra pair
of hands would have been useful too. Later, she would have
appreciated more time when the boys were teenagers and she was
run ragged cooking and washing for them. Or when the grand-
children came along, and she found it impossible to spend
enough time with them all, especially as two of her sons made
their lives in Canada and one lived down in Cornwall. Four kids,
and only one, Eric, had stayed and brought his family up in the
city he'd grown up in. Visiting the ones that had left had made for
some lovely holidays over the years, right enough. Longer days
would have been lovely when she and Henry were lying on sun
loungers on a beach in St Ives.

But now? Who needed more hours when – other than chatting to Henry – it was so difficult to fill the time? What should she
be doing when she woke up at 5 a.m., and then couldn't fall asleep
again until midnight? She must have read every large-print book
in the library by now. And there wasn't an episode of *Coronation
Street*, *The Clydeside*, *River City* or *EastEnders* that hadn't been
watched at least once. In normal weeks, there were the social
clubs, the coffee mornings, and her line dancing class in the town
hall, but they had all stopped for the festive season. So now it was
almost 10 a.m. on New Year's Eve, and she and Henry were on
their third episode of *Murder, She Wrote*, while she put the
finishing touches to the post box topper she'd go fit today, in

between getting everything ready for tonight's visit to the restaurant where they'd celebrated Hogmanay for decades.

'I'll get it, Henry, love,' she said, as she picked up the phone handset and cleared her throat. 'Hello?' she answered, in the posh voice that was reserved for telephone communications and conversations with councils, customer service departments and cold callers.

The voice on the other end was female. Young. Maybe in her twenties, like her granddaughter, Emmy. That reminded her – she must give Emmy a call and thank her for the lovely Christmas dinner she'd brought over. Such a kind, considerate lass, that one. Eric had popped in too with that new girlfriend of his. Minnie never liked to talk badly of anyone, especially her darling boy, but she had plenty of thoughts on that whole situation and she'd shared them all with Henry. What was Eric thinking? After all those years with lovely Ailish, he just upped and went off with a woman young enough to be his daughter. A disgrace, that's what it was. And to break Ailish's heart like that. Minnie had been outraged because she loved Ailish like she would her own daughter. Eric had let them all down so badly. Although, the whole time she was talking to Henry about it, she knew what he was thinking. 'They're grown adults and it's not our business, Minnie. Best we just stay out of it.' Minnie had pursed her lips and knitted up a storm to take her mind off it.

The voice on the phone cut through her thoughts. 'Mrs Ryan? Hello, this is Katie from Gino's Trattoria. We're just calling all our customers who've reserved tables tonight to confirm the booking. Can I just check that you still want us to hold your table?'

'We've been coming there on Hogmanay for the last fifty years, dear. I wouldn't miss it for the world.'

'That's great. We'll see you tonight then,' Katie replied, in a soft Glasgow brogue.

Minnie wasn't sure she'd ever met this caller, but after a lifetime of being Gino's regular customers, she considered most of the staff to be family friends.

Replacing the handset, she bustled on into the kitchen, shouting, 'Right, Henry, I've told them we'll be there, so you'd better get your glad rags ready.'

There was a tug of sadness, as she thought how this year would be so different from bygone times. That's what happened when family traditions fell away for whatever reason. They'd always had one of the biggest tables in the restaurant, what with their four sons in the early days, and then Eric, Ailish, Emmy and all their friends as the years went on.

Gino's restaurant had been one of the best discoveries of their lives, and one that happened purely by accident. What year would it have been? She conjured up an image of them all in her mind that first night, and tried to picture their boys and their ages. Oh yes, the old memory was still all there. She couldn't tell you what shopping she brought home yesterday, or where she'd left her slippers last night, but she could tell you every word of her and Henry's favourite song when they were courting, 'Be My Baby' by the Ronettes. It must have been about 1972, because their eldest, Charlie, would have been around eight, which would have made the twins, Robert and Roger, seven, and their youngest, Eric, would have been six. Sometimes she wondered how on earth she'd managed to have four boys by the time she'd turned twenty-one, but back in those days... well, she chuckled to herself. She'd married Henry when they were both seventeen, they didn't have a telly or any heating in their two-bedroom tenement, and they did like a cuddle.

That night, Hogmanay, all the boys were still awake way past their bedtime, as they'd promised them that just this once they could stay up for the bells. In Scotland, they still used that phrase 'the bells' to describe the stroke of midnight on the 31st of December, but back then it actually had meaning, as all the church bells would ring out and the whole city would come alive with people in the streets, cheering, dancing and celebrating the new year. Especially in their part of town. Their two-bedroom tenement was just off Ingram Street in the City Centre, not the most salubrious of areas back then, but they made the most of every opportunity to bring a bit of cheer and joy to their lives.

Minnie didn't care that they didn't have much. They had enough to get by, and she was grateful that Henry's job as a junior planning officer gave them enough money to have the luxury of a separate bedroom for the boys. Most of their friends were living in a one-room-and-kitchen with one or two babies.

It must have been about ten o'clock, when they'd heard the music coming from outside. Other men might have moaned or gone to find the source to get it turned down, but not her Henry. Laughing, he'd pulled her up from their threadbare couch for a dance around the living room, shouting to the boys to join in. The tune was uproariously upbeat, but she didn't recognise the words that she could make out, so as they'd twirled around the room, she'd guessed where it was coming from.

'Must be from that new Italian restaurant next door,' Henry had said, reaching the same conclusion at the same time.

Roger had stopped dancing and was looking out of the window. 'Dad, there are people dancing outside too.'

Henry had still held her in his arms as he'd turned to see for himself that Roger was right. Outside, on the pavement below, a couple was dancing just as they were, and some of the people milling around them had stopped and were watching, clapping, joining in.

'Shall we go down?' Henry had asked, that familiar mischievous grin on his handsome face.

Minnie had hesitated for a second. 'But the boys... it's late.'

He'd squeezed her tightly and kissed her on the cheek. 'It's Hogmanay! One late night won't do them any harm.' Then he'd sealed the deal by adding, 'Might make them sleep later in the morning.'

Minnie hadn't needed any more persuading. This was the one night of the year that her own parents had let her stay up late for as long as she could remember.

They'd grabbed warm coats for the excited boys, hats, scarfs and gloves, and off they went down three flights of stairs, all of them giggling and trying to sing along with the tune. When they'd got outside, they formed a circle, holding each other's home-knitted gloves as they spun around in time to the music, their breath making clouds in the cold air.

When the tune had finished, the couple whom they'd seen dancing from the window stopped and the man had greeted the gathering.

'Come in, come in! The restaurant is open and a drink is on the house!' he'd exclaimed, his accent a melodic mix of Italian and Glaswegian inflections.

A few people from the crowd took him up on the offer, a few more drifted off. Breathless from the dancing, Henry and Minnie were about to do the same and return home, when the man stopped them. 'Ah, my neighbours! I see you and these boys every day when you're passing. I have a son too, but he's much younger than all your big strong lads. Come inside, meet my wife and celebrate with us.'

Henry's delighted gaze had met hers, waiting for an agreement, which, of course, she gave with an amused roll of the eyes. 'Go on then.'

The man had cheered, the boys joined in, and before Minnie could catch her breath, she was swept inside, to a room with whitewashed walls and wooden benches and tables on a stone floor, and the most mouth-watering, delicious aroma Minnie had ever experienced. She was surprised to see that the only people already inside were the ones who'd come from the street. The place must have been empty and that's why this man and his wife had gone outside to dance.

Their host began passing around glasses, helped by his dancing partner, who Minnie now realised was the most beautiful woman she had ever seen. They were probably around the same age, but Minnie could only dream of having those huge brown eyes and the jet black hair that went all the way down to her waist.

'Alicia, come meet our new friends,' he'd beckoned her, and she'd sashayed over to them carrying a tray of drinks. 'Please, tell me your names,' he'd asked them.

Henry was already holding out his hand. 'I'm Henry and this is my wife, Minnie. And these are our boys, Charlie, Roger, Robert and Eric. We live on the top floor next door and it's a pleasure to meet you.'

Their host shook his hand with glee and vigour. 'And you, my friend. I'm Gino, and this is my beautiful Alicia. Welcome to my restaurant. I hope it will be the first of many times that you come here.'

It certainly was, Minnie mused now, as she popped a splash of milk into her tea, before stirring it. As she treated herself to the last mince pie from a box Emmy had brought over at Christmas, she felt another little tug of sentimentality.

That night. they'd all sang and danced, and they'd partied until the bells rang out at midnight and beyond. And it had been the start of something wonderful. The following summer, they'd moved out of the city centre to a suburb on the South Side. Money had been tight for a long time after that, but every year, they managed to save and scrape together enough for the whole family to go to Gino's on Hogmanay. It had given them so many of the very best memories of their lives and it was a tradition she and Henry had carried on till this day.

Tonight, well, it would only be a table for two. But Minnie Ryan was determined to enjoy it like it would be her last.

10 A.M. – NOON

5
_____

AILISH

The hospital foyer was crowded with people wrapped up against the cold and had an air of damp coats and worry. The faces of the visitors were mostly set in deflated expressions, with only the occasional kind look of a passing member of staff. Ailish knew how tough it could be to work here. Her daughter, Emmy, had been a nurse for her entire career, and Ailish had lost count of the times she would come home deeply affected by someone she'd lost on the ward. It was even harder now that she'd moved to elderly care – a role that Ailish always thought had been inspired by Emmy's love for her grandparents, Henry and Minnie.

Her own parents had passed away when Emmy was too small to remember them, just a few years apart, both of them to cancer in their sixties. It was one of the many reasons Ailish felt so guilty about this lethargy that had descended on her, that she felt both unwilling and unable to shake. Surely, whether her life had fallen apart or not, she should be making the most of things and living every day to the fullest?

Right, deep breath, slap a smile on and let's do this. If only she had the motivation to apply their motto to her own life these days.

'I'm famished this morning. Plenty of time for coffees and cake,' Rhonda said, nodding to the huge clock in the middle of the foyer – 10.10 a.m. They always gave themselves time for a quick pit stop before visiting started at eleven o'clock on Gwen's ward. Both her sadness and the grumbling of her stomach gave Ailish permission to go wild and have a latte and a bacon roll. Other women might have champagne on the day their divorce papers dropped through the door, but Ailish was more of a caffeine and comfort food kinda gal. Besides, she honestly felt like this was nothing to celebrate. She had no intention of even telling anyone until she'd processed the finality of it herself.

They got their food and picked up Gwen's chocolate chip cookie to take up to the ward, even though they never knew if she'd have the appetite to eat it or not. Her cancer journey had been as tough as it had been shocking. Last year, when she'd first been diagnosed with a rare form of abdominal cancer, it had blindsided them all. Gwen was a fitness fanatic who had jogged every day of her adult life, and never suffered anything more than a mild flu. Surgery had been the first step in the treatment, followed by months of chemo. She'd been told she was in remission back in September, but then, just before Christmas, she'd fallen ill again. Unable to eat and exhausted, she'd been rushed into hospital for more tests, then kept in so she could be treated for her whole new set of symptoms.

The only family Gwen had was her elderly parents who now lived up on Skye, and she'd refused to tell them that she was unwell because she didn't want to worry them, so Ailish and Rhonda had spent every moment that they could by her side. One of the charge nurses on the ward said that she'd seen them more than she'd seen her own husband over Christmas.

The whole time they were there, they'd only uttered words of positivity aloud, but inside, they all feared the worst. As always, dark humour had got them through from day to day.

'Ailish,' Gwen had murmured on the day after she'd been brought in, when she was still too weak to stand and had barely been able to get the words out.

Ailish had leant closer, squeezed her hand. 'I'm right here, doll,' she'd said, using their pet term for each other.

'If I peg it this time, you can have my Versace bag.'

The splutter from the other side of the bed had been loud, and the outrage that followed it indignant, which was exactly, Ailish realised, what Gwen had intended.

'I don't bloody think so,' Rhonda had spluttered. 'I will rugby tackle you and wrestle it from you with my bare hands. No way is she getting her paws on that.'

Gwen had managed to smile. 'Better make sure I stay alive then. Can't be having you two fighting at the wake.'

It was just one of many inside jokes that had kept their spirits up over the last fortnight of this latest admission, as the doctors searched for the reason for her latest symptoms. Of course, the obvious answer was that her cancer had returned, but none of them vocalised their biggest fears because it was just too terrifying to say out loud. Her initial scans had been inconclusive, and the second round had been slow to come due to the hospital being short-staffed over Christmas, but in the meantime, they waited, they hoped, and they visited her every day.

'She seemed a bit better yesterday, didn't she?' Rhonda said, as they pulled up plastic chairs to the one empty table in the corner of the café.

'She did. Definitely,' Ailish replied, but neither of them mentioned what they both knew was true – they'd seen this happen before. As quickly as Gwen could seem better, it could all turn on its head again the next day. Yesterday they'd changed her medication, and they were anxiously waiting to see if that helped or inflamed her symptoms. If it was the latter... Well, Ailish refused to think about what Gwen would have in front of her.

'Okay, I'm going to change the subject because we'll just go down a rabbit hole of worry and we can't go up to the ward all teary-eyed and snotters.'

Ailish didn't disagree, but she was struggling to make her mind focus on anything else. Eventually, she settled on, 'So where are you going then? Tonight, I mean? You said you already had your dress all picked out.'

Rhonda popped the cherry off her Bakewell tart into her mouth, then held it like a gobstopper in her cheek while she answered. 'Well, since you are breaking our tradition of a million years for the second year in a row and refusing to come out with me...' That had been Rhonda's favourite dig for the last month, ever since Ailish had broken the news to her that once again all she wanted to do this Hogmanay was go to bed with a box of Quality Street, a glass of Prosecco and a box set of anything but rom coms. 'I'm going on a blind date.'

Ailish almost choked on her latte. 'A blind date? On Hogmanay?'

She struggled not to laugh as Rhonda came over all indignant, her chin jutting out defiantly. 'Yes. I think it's got an air of *When Harry Met Sally* about it. You know, all that snogging at midnight.'

Ailish put down her bacon roll, too engrossed to eat. 'Rhonda, on your last blind date, you practically commando crawled out of the restaurant while he was looking the other way. It had more of an air of *Die Hard* about it.'

Despite her very best attempt to be unamused, Rhonda crumbled into laughter. 'I know! But I'm not bloody staying in on New Year's Eve and you are the only sad git I know who doesn't have plans with their significant others or their families...' She paused, realising what she'd just said. 'Sorry if that just picked a scab.'

Ailish brushed it off. 'Yep, it reopened that wound, but carry on and see if you can make me feel worse about my life.'

They both knew she was joking, so Rhonda wittered on, 'Right then, Sensitive Sally. Anyway, unless you want to change your mind about coming with me...'

Ailish was quite emphatic. 'I don't.'

'Then I'll be spending New Year's Eve with a gentleman called Ralph, who, from the pictures on his dating profile, would appear to be an aging gym buff with thighs that look like they could crack nuts.'

Ailish's cackle made several people at nearby tables turn to stare. She gestured apologetically to them, before going back to the conversation. 'You know, I always thought I'd only have to worry about Emmy making irresponsible decisions as she navigated maturity.'

Rhonda didn't even pretend to be outraged. Her first marriage had been a spontaneous deed that she called 'a one-night stand that lasted three years'. Her second marriage, many years later, had been to a man who had come to resent her work ethic and her success, so she'd said goodbye to him around their fifth anniversary. Her third promise at the end of the aisle had lasted ten years, and she always said that for the last nine of those, it was a relationship that didn't fulfil or excite her, so she was absolutely unapologetic about living her most adventurous life now. 'And I fully plan to be completely irresponsible for at least another decade.'

Ailish didn't doubt it for a second. She just wished she had the energy or the inclination to do the same.

They finished their food with discussions about Rhonda's

frock, before Ailish checked the clock again. 'Ten minutes. By the time we get up there, they'll have opened the doors.'

They scooped all their wrappers and empty cups into the nearby bin, then Ailish picked up Gwen's biscuit, and they made their way to the elevators, both of them silent, lost in their own thoughts. Ailish's were the same every single time she did this route. *Please make her be okay. Please make her be okay. Please make her be okay...* She sent that thought out into the ether and just hoped that someone was listening.

They got stuck in the lift with a family whose tiny human pressed every single button, so they were held up by stopping at every floor. When they finally got to the right place, Ailish's nerves were frayed. As the doors opened and they stepped out, she made eye contact with Rhonda, and they needed no words to make their familiar resolution.

Deep breath, slap a smile on and let's do this.

When they reached the double doors to the ward, they stood to the side to let a nursing assistant who was coming out pushing a trolley pass them by. Inside, they made their way down the corridor, to the third door on the right, through they went, first bed on the left and there was... no one. It was empty. Gwen's bed was stripped, the machines were off, the bedside table had been cleared and there was absolutely no sign of human life.

Ailish froze, suddenly rooted to the spot. 'Rhonda, did we come into the wrong room?'

Rhonda was staring straight at the bed too. 'No. This is the right bed. You don't think...'

Ailish's stomach lurched. *No. Please no. Please don't let her have d...*

She hadn't even got to the end of that horrific thought when the door to the bathroom opened and a nurse came out, pulling a wheelchair behind her. And there, sitting up for the first time in two weeks, was...

'Gwen! Dear lord, you nearly gave us a heart attack,' Rhonda gasped.

Gwen was nonplussed by this news. 'Well, you're in the right place. Cardiac ward is on the third floor.'

Ailish held on to the end of the bed, desperate to calm her own breathing and take in the sight in front of her. 'Oh Gwen, you're up...'

'I am,' Gwen beamed.

'And you're dressed...' Ailish went on, stating the obvious.

'Always said you should have been a detective,' Gwen fired back this time, before taking charge of the conversation. 'We got the results back from the scans – it's not the cancer again. I'm still in remission. They think it could have been either the after-effects of the chemo, or a reaction to my meds. So they have very kindly...' She winked at the nurse who was now standing beside her.

'Against our better judgement...' the nurse countered.

'Agreed to let me out for now...'

'On the condition that you go home to rest and return immediately if you develop any new symptoms or discomfort. And come back in to see your consultant on the second of January for a review and a management plan for going forwards.'

'Exactly!' Gwen finished, triumphantly.

Ailish blinked back tears. This was a time for laughing, not crying, but all too often these days they got mixed up. Her face took over, breaking into the widest smile, 'You don't need to ask us twice. Nurse, load me up with her bags, and the other one' – she nodded to an uncharacteristically silent Rhonda – 'will do the driving.'

In five minutes, they were organised, equipped, Gwen's new

meds had been double-checked, explained, and they were on their way out of the ward, positively giddy with glee.

At the lift, they pressed the button, and waited, giving Gwen the opportunity to take both of their hands. 'I can't tell you how grateful I am for you two incredible people,' she said, her emotions torn between the tears that were making her eyes sparkle and the grin that was radiating joy and relief. 'But before we leave here, I need you both to make me a promise.'

'Anything,' Ailish blurted without hesitation, at the exact same time as Rhonda said, 'As long as it's not celibacy.'

Gwen and Ailish both swivelled their heads to stare at her and she flushed.

'Sorry. I don't know where that came from. I didn't realise we were being serious.'

'Sometimes your mind works in very strange ways,' Ailish told her drily, before focusing back on Gwen. 'Tell us. Anything at all.'

Gwen exhaled deeply. 'The last twelve months have been my worst nightmare. And the last two weeks have been terrifying...'

Ailish felt a piece chip off her heart. Whatever Gwen needed – round-the-clock company, her favourite foods, the assurance that they'd always support her – she would give it without question.

Gwen was speaking again. 'And there have been so many times when I've thought I might not make it. I still don't know if or when the cancer will come back.'

They all took that in.

'So what I'm saying is that I have no idea how long I could have left and I've given so much time to this disease... So I'm not giving it another New Year.'

Ailish nodded. 'You're right. We'll make the most of next year...'

Gwen cut her off. 'No, you don't understand. I'm not giving it another *New Year*. Or New Year's Eve. Fuck the bed rest – tonight we're going to do exactly what we've always done on Hogmanay. Apart from last year when you were doing the whole recluse thing,' she added, gesturing to Ailish, before resuming her call to arms. 'So tonight, ladies, I need you to promise that we're going out and we're going to celebrate.'

Ailish glanced at Rhonda, willing her to object. This couldn't be safe. It was crazy. Impulsive. Dangerous.

Rhonda got the message.

'Gwen, there's nothing else I'd rather do...' she said, voice full of regret. Ailish was about to expel a sigh of relief when Rhonda immediately switched it up and squealed, 'So if you'll give me two secs, I'll just get on my phone and cancel my blind date with a bloke with twenty-four-inch biceps.'

Half of the battle won, Gwen turned to a stunned Ailish, her eyes pleading. 'What about you, Ails? Are you in?'

6

EMMY

'Dad, are you drunk?' Emmy blurted, as she stared at him, still too sleepy to process what was actually happening here.

'No, I'm not drunk. How could you think that at this time in the morning?' he shot back, offended, as if that was some shocking stain on his character. Strange. Her outrage that he'd been unfaithful to Mum and was banging a thirty-four-year-old seemed to roll right off his back, but suddenly he was touchy about insinuations that he may have indulged in a shandy or two.

Wordlessly, Emmy took a step back to allow him to come past her and he charged right down the hall into the kitchen. For a joyous moment, she thought about pretending he wasn't there and just going to the shower to hide, but the problem would still be there when she got out.

It wasn't that she didn't love her father. For twenty-seven years he'd been a lovely, fun, supportive, caring guy. It was just that she didn't recognise this current incarnation of the man who shared her DNA, and the truth was, she was still angry on her mum's behalf. Not because they'd split up, but because of the lies and the affair and the way he'd almost broken Mum. Maybe one day she'd get over that, but right now she was still finding it almost impossible to forgive him.

Her gran, Minnie, had struggled with that too, and she just kept telling Emmy that she had every right to her feelings and the time for forgiveness would come when it was right. Emmy wasn't so sure.

'Okay, Dad, I'm due at work at eleven, and I need to get ready and get to the hospital, so you have exactly ten minutes to tell me what's going on.'

He was pacing up and down. There would be a hole in her white oak laminate at this rate.

'I've fucked up. And sorry, darling, I don't usually use that kind of language in front of you, but there's no other word for it.'

Again, slight confusion on the things that would alter her perception of him, but she went with it anyway.

'I'm scarred for life at hearing such words,' she answered drily, filling a glass of water from the tap, before taking a large slug, thinking she was going to need more than water to get through this. 'In what way have you effed up?' she asked him, going for the PG version and thinking she already knew the answer. He'd messed up in oh so many ways she didn't have long enough to list them.

'I've been a complete fool. I should never have left your mum. What was I thinking? It was the most stupid thing I've ever done. I realised it this morning when the divorce papers dropped through the door...'

That was news to Emmy. She wondered if her mum had received them too, then decided she probably hadn't because she'd have called to let Emmy know. Or maybe not. Maybe she didn't want to discuss it. Emmy thought about phoning her, but decided against it – Mum would talk to her about it when she was ready. All of those thoughts ran through her mind as her dad wittered on...

'Actually, that's not true,' he corrected himself. 'I realised it at Christmas. Fuck... sorry... but, fuck, it was awful. Excruciating. Donna and I...'

'I don't want to hear about her, Dad,' she warned him.

When he'd brought his girlfriend to Gran's house on Christmas Day, Emmy had almost choked on Minnie's sherry. In the two years that love's young dream had been together, Emmy had maintained a strict no-contact rule when it came to the woman who'd knowingly inserted herself in her parents' marriage. Not that she was trying to deflect the blame. No, that all lay with the man that was standing in her kitchen right now. He was the one that had broken his vows and trashed their family, caused the sale of their family home, then moved into a swanky city-centre penthouse he'd rented for him and his lover. She hadn't thought for a second that he'd have the audacity to formally introduce his mistress into her life on Christmas Day, in the presence of others, so Emmy would have to sit there and make polite conversation. Ho fricking ho ho ho.

'Of course. I understand. But the thing is, I only brought her because she said I couldn't leave her alone on Christmas night, and I desperately wanted to be with the rest of my family, so it seemed like... Another fuck-up, right?'

'Without a shred of doubt.' She let that one sit with him for a minute. 'The thing is, Dad, you can't be with the rest of your family, because the rest of your family includes Mum. She's always been the biggest part of it. At the heart of everything we do, every time we're together.'

He was still pacing. Hands on the hips of his undoubtedly expensive trousers, right underneath what she saw now was a

Hermès belt. Not his usual style. Donna must have been very generous with his credit card at Christmas.

'That's what I'm trying to tell you. I want your mum back. I told Donna it was over last night and we've split up. Actually, strictly speaking, I've moved out. She threw half my clothes out the window and took a screwdriver to my tyres. I had to get a taxi here. I dropped my bags off at a hotel on the way here.'

Emmy was well aware that her jaw had dropped, but she'd apparently lost the capacity to close her mouth. This wasn't happening. It couldn't be. No way was her dad standing in her kitchen, telling her that his life had descended into the kind of stuff people posted online after they'd secretly filmed their neighbours having a domestic.

Summoning all her strength, she somehow recovered her power of speech and also her anxiety about her time schedule. 'Okay, Dad, this is all too much for me right now and I really am going to be late for work, so I tell you what. You stop pacing, make a coffee, try to process your thoughts, and I'll go get ready, then you can come with me while I drive to work, and we can talk on the way. You can jump in a taxi at the hospital to get back to your hotel. There are always loads at the rank outside the main entrance.'

'Okay. Sounds like a plan.'

Satisfied that she'd distracted him and talked him down for the moment, she made for the door. She'd take the win, however temporary.

Taking two stairs at a time, she raced up to the en-suite bathroom, tied her mass of red waves back into a bun and jumped into the shower, careful to keep her hair out of the spray. She didn't have time to wrestle with hairdryers and straighteners this morning.

After drying off, she pulled a fresh set of scrubs out of the wardrobe and put them in the backpack she used for work every day, then threw on her dark grey jeans and a black Merino wool jumper. Suede boots and a leather jacket went on next, before she dabbed on a bit of lip balm and shook out her hair. No time for cosmetics this morning. She shoved her make-up bag into her backpack in case she changed her mind later, then grabbed her phone and hospital ID from the bedside table.

At the door, she stopped, running through her pre-work checklist in her mind. Okay. She had everything she required. Except perhaps her emotional equilibrium and the capacity to deal with what this day was throwing at her so far. And it was only 10.30 a.m.

Back downstairs, she grabbed her car keys from the console table in the hall, then summoned her dad from the kitchen. He seemed slightly calmer as he followed her out, clutching his mug of coffee. If he so much as spilled a drop of that in her car she'd have yet another thing to add to her current list of paternal furies.

She waited until they were out of her cul-de-sac and onto the main road that would take them most of the way to the hospital, before she could focus enough to restart the conversation.

'Okay, Dad, let's get this straight. You've split with Donna, and you want Mum back. Are you absolutely sure about this? It isn't just a fall-back plan because things aren't working out with you and your girlfriend?' Just saying the word 'girlfriend' made her cringe, but it was kinder than the more accurate 'mistress that replaced my mother.'

'No! Definitely not. That's *why* things aren't working out with Donna – it's because I've realised that the only woman I've ever truly loved is Ailish. And I still do. Honestly, Ems, I feel like I've just woken up from a two-year bender with the worst hangover ever and full of absolute horror about what I've got up to.'

'Yep, pretty much sums up how I feel about the last two years of your life. It was every bit as bad as you feared, Dad.' She had a feeling she should be going easy on him and showing some compassion and understanding, but, well, the truth was, she was running short on both of those emotions right now. He hadn't just hurt Mum, he'd damaged her too, destroyed her ability to trust. If her dependable, decent, loving dad could do something so awful to his partner, then so could anyone. So could Cormac.

She swallowed that one back down for now. One crisis at a time.

Her last comment had shut him up, and he stared out of the window for the next few moments, before breaking the silence with, 'Do you think she still loves me? Do you think she'd take me back?'

Emmy sighed, weary, then made a real effort to conjure up some softness as she answered him honestly. 'I really don't know, Dad. You know, you didn't just break her heart, it was almost like you broke all of her. She's never been the same since. Everything has changed. And you did that to her.'

'I know,' he groaned, and the angst in his voice evoked just a little more sympathy.

'I think you really need to speak to her yourself. And, Dad, I'm not getting involved. This is between the two of you.'

'I understand that, and I agree. I'm going to go speak to her. Today. Now. Do you know if she's at home?'

Emmy did a quick audit of what she knew about her mum's movements. Almost eleven o'clock. Visiting time on Gwen's ward. No doubt Mum would either be on her way to the hospital right now or already there. Shit! She was taking her ranting, distraught father right to her. This had disaster written all over it. The hospital wasn't the place for them to have that conversation.

'Erm, I think she's out with Aunt Rhonda right now. Doing a bit of shopping.' As her mum's oldest and closest friends, Rhonda and Gwen had always been 'aunties' to her, despite there being no genetic connection. 'But maybe she'll be home this afternoon. You could try her then. But, Dad, make sure you're absolutely positive about this. Don't play with her heart again, because if you do, I'll...' She switched her indicator on and turned off the road and onto the street that led to the hospital car park. As she did, something to her left distracted her and before she could even process what she was doing, she slammed on her brakes, screeching the car to a halt, throwing them both forwards and tipping the remnants of dad's coffee all over his lap.

'Christ, Emmy, you nearly killed me. What the hell did you do that for?'

Ignoring the furiously beeping horn of the car behind her, Emmy swivelled around, craning her neck, trying desperately to catch sight of the vehicle that had just passed her and turned right, heading away from the hospital.

'Emmy?' Her dad's voice was raised now. 'What's going on? What are you doing?'

Too late. It was gone. And she was pretty sure she'd tweaked a muscle in her neck. Bugger. Damn. Arse. As her dad frantically tried to brush coffee off his lap, she felt a sickening chill deep in her gut.

'I think I just saw Cormac's car. But it couldn't be him because he's at work...'

At least he was supposed to be.

7

DARIO

Dario felt weirdly detached from the world, as if all the business and action going on outside his office door was unconnected to him in some way. Usually, when they had a big night ahead, he'd be out on the floor, excited, making sure everything was set up and perfect, laughing with his staff and raising their spirits. Just like his dad before him, he never lost sight of the fact that their employees were working on the special occasions, when their families and friends would be celebrating without them, so he wanted them to feel that this was more than just a job. It was a family, and they were all part of it, related or not. He wasn't sure they'd feel that way after the news that he was going to have to deliver to them at some point soon.

He could hear Katie, the youngest member of the team, on the phone at the maître d' stand, running through tonight's reservations and calling them all to confirm the booking. Sonya was still out there, barking out warnings to 'watch that bloody floor, I've just washed it. You'll end up on your arse if you slip on it.' The sous-chefs were already in the kitchen, starting the preparations for tonight's menu. His son, Matty, would be here soon to oversee the rest of the prep and to get ready for the lunch service that would start at twelve. The foundations of their menus hadn't changed much in the last thirty years, so they had it all down to a fine art. One that was perilously close to being rendered redundant.

One more call to make. His last hope. His Hail Mary. He dialled the number of Talia Kane, the accountant who had looked after his accounts for years. She was another one who'd been at uni with him and Brodie. He might not have a business any longer, but at least he still had friends.

She answered on the first ring. 'Hey. How are you doing?'

'Fair to crap, edging further to the crap side with every passing hour.'

'Shit, Dario, I wish there was something I could do to help you salvage this,' she said, repeating Brodie's sentiments.

'So I take it the bank rejected the loan application again then?' This was the third time they'd applied for a loan, in diminishing amounts every time, and he'd held out hope that the latest application, for a sum that would tide them over just for a few months, would have come through.

'They said no, Dario. I'm sorry. I was just about to call you to let you know.'

A pause.

'Look, do you want me to speak to you as my friend or as my client?'

'Both,' he answered, knowing that some straight talking was about to come his way. That's what made Talia so exceptional at her job. She combined her brilliant brain with a strict aversion to bullshit.

'Okay, as your friend, you know that I want more than

anything to find a way to keep you going. And I could. We could go elsewhere for the money, but they would take one look at your books and they'd offer a shit deal at punitive interest rates that would just dig you deeper into the hole. That was the friend bit. As your financial advisor, I'd tell you to take the money and run. It's a solid offer, Dario, and the reality is that your business model isn't sustainable in that location any longer. I can't see a world in which Gino's becomes profitable again in the near future. The debts are way too high, and frankly, you don't have the cash reserves or the access to the kind of cash that would allow you to create the type of business that would do the necessary numbers. The sale will clear your feet and restore your financial security. Walk away, Dario. It breaks my heart to say that, but the only sensible thing to do is take the deal.'

He closed his eyes. 'I know you're right. I do. I just...'

He couldn't finish the sentence because a boulder lodged in his throat. He knew the sale was the only option that made sense. But there was no amount of money that could take away the pain of breaking his dad's and his son's hearts.

'I know. Call me back any time. Let me know how you get on. I'm always here for you, pal. Apart from tonight, because we're having a wildly expensive, romantic night away in a five-star hotel in Loch Lomond,' she said, with her usual bluntness, before going on, 'but any other time, I'm here for you.'

When his voice came back, he automatically tried to break the tension, croaking, 'Remember that when I'm sleeping on your sofa.'

'It's a two-seater. You won't fit.' As always, no bullshit.

Dario said his goodbyes and hung up, just as the office door barged open. His money would have been on Sonya, but no.

His ex-wife, Nicky, plonked herself down on the chair opposite his. She eyed him warily. 'Oh no. You didn't get the loan. Oh bollocks. I'm sorry, Dario. Sorry for me too. I'll have to get a real job. Shit, I'm screwed. I'm way too high maintenance to work for anyone else.'

Despite this being the worst morning of his life, the truth in that statement made him smile. There weren't many couples who could continue to work together after they'd divorced, but somehow they'd managed it. They'd been together since she started waitressing in the restaurant while she was at college and, corny as it sounded, they'd always been best mates. That was the problem, really. Both of them wanted passion, and fierce love, and great sex, but as the years went on, they'd realised that they just didn't want any of those things with each other. About ten years ago, they'd called quits on the marital side, but by then Nicky was his invaluable assistant manager. Confidante, too. Other than his dad, she was the only person working here that he'd shared the situation with, and unlike Gino, Nicky had listened and understood.

'So what now?' she asked. 'Roll out the timeline for me so I can let Scott know when he's going to have to start keeping me in the style I want to be accustomed to.' Scott had been her partner for the last few years, a laid-back personal trainer ten years her junior, who was so confident in himself, he had absolutely zero jealousy that his wife still worked with her ex-husband.

Dario blew out his cheeks as he slumped back in his chair. 'I didn't want to speak to Dad about it today – you know how he feels about New Year's Eve. It's his most sentimental night of the year. But this is the last day that the offer is on the table, and I'm not accepting it without trying to get his agreement.'

'Oh God, I feel sick just thinking about that. What time do you have to let them know by?'

'Midnight. Apparently, it's west coast American investors, and there's an eight-hour time difference, so that's 4 p.m. their time. That's the deadline. And Nicky... you know I'm going to have to talk to Matty too.'

She groaned again. Nicky was as close to both their kids as he was. Their daughter, Lucia, had moved to Milan straight out of college to work in fashion there, taking advantage of the fact that she was both wildly talented in textile design and spoke Italian like a native. Dario didn't get over to see her anywhere near as often as he should, because he hated to leave the restaurant for too long, but luckily Lucia came home on holiday twice a year, most of which was spent parked at a table at the restaurant window, working on her laptop while chatting to her family and the regulars who knew her when she'd waitressed here at weekends. One more person who would be sad about selling up.

'He's going to be crushed, Dario, I'm just putting that out there. And brace yourself, because you know how he'll react.'

The phrase 'hot-headed' had been invented for their son. He was exquisitely gifted, and a decent guy underneath it all, but when it came to his professional life, he was the chef that made Gordon Ramsay look reasonable and mild-mannered.

'I do. I'll make sure I tell him somewhere that there's no sharp objects.'

It was said in jest, but there was a hint of truth in there. Matty had once ejected a former food critic from the restaurant because he remembered that he'd done a write-up in the nineties saying that Dario's meatballs could be used in a game of cricket. They'd found out later he was taking kickbacks from their closest rivals.

'What are you thinking?' he asked, realising that Nicky had fallen quiet. That usually meant that either she'd done something he wouldn't like, or she was planning to.

'I'm thinking that I'm about to be the favourite parent for once.'

That made Dario smile. The truth was that the kids loved them equally, but Nicky had always professed otherwise, although he was pretty sure it was tongue in cheek.

'And I'm thinking that I'll let you break that news to him alone. I've seen the movies. The sidekick is always the one that ends up getting blamed. Let me know when you're going to tell him, and I'll go hide. It'll be just like when you did the birds and the bees chat, and I stayed in the shed until it was safe to come out.'

The thing was, he didn't blame her in the least. This was his mess, and he was the one responsible for the clean-up.

Nicky got up from the chair, came over to where he was sitting and hugged him. He held on to her for a few seconds, grateful for the human touch. It had been a while. For the last year, he'd been so busy trying to drag the restaurant out of the quicksand, he'd pretty much stopped dating, stopped socialising, stopped doing anything other than working.

'Now there's something I didn't expect to see today,' came a voice from the doorway.

Dario glanced over Nicky's shoulder to see Matty's six foot frame in the doorway. Their son. The one who had dreamed his whole life of taking over this restaurant and making it his own. And now Dario was going to have to tell him that he was snatching that dream away from him.

But, right now, Matty's mind was adding two and two and getting an answer that equalled happy families. 'Don't tell me you two are getting back together, because that'll put me in therapy. You're the most unsuited couple ever.'

On any other day, Dario would have objected to that statement, despite the truth of it, but today he let it go with, 'Nope, it's not what it looks like.'

Matty laughed. 'Said every couple in every movie when they

get caught up to no good. Okay, lovebirds, well, that's me in and I'm just going to go get started in the kitchen.'

'Actually, son, can you sit down for a minute? There's something we need to tell you.' He ignored Nicky's stare of death.

Matty glanced from Dario to Nicky and then back again. 'Shit, you are getting back together.'

'Nope, 'fraid not, son. It's something much worse than that.'

8

MINNIE

Minnie said hello to everyone she passed on the way to the shops at Clarkston Toll, just a fifteen-minute walk away. She'd lived in the same house on the South Side of the city for nearly fifty years, so she knew a lot of her neighbours, but she greeted everyone whether she recognised them or not. Some responded in kind, some didn't, but Minnie didn't mind either way.

It was cold out and she'd thought about staying home today, but she worried that giving up her daily walk would be the start of a downward spiral that would end with her joints seizing up, so she made a point of getting exercise while she was still fit. Henry no longer joined her, but that was no reason not to go. After all, hadn't she been one of those women marching for women's liberation back in the sixties? Yes, she damn well had, and if they were still marching these days, she'd be right at the front.

Anyway, the walk was essential today because she had a gift to pick up from the jewellers, and she wanted to get a packet of shortbread and a small bottle of whisky for any New Year's Day visitors, so she'd wrapped up in her favourite red cloche hat and matching scarf, and the new coat that Ailish had bought her for Christmas and set off.

Bless that woman. Minnie couldn't have asked for a better daughter-in-law. After everything Eric had put her through, Ailish still popped in to see her at least once during the week, and also took her to Asda every Saturday morning, stopping at the garden centre for tea and a scone on the way back. Which was more than that new one Eric was seeing now had done. What was her name? Minnie couldn't quite get it to the front of her mind, but then, that wasn't really a surprise. Eric popped in to visit once or twice a week, but almost always alone, so Minnie had only met her three or four times. Even when she did, the woman had barely given Minnie a second glance in her own house. On Christmas Day, when Emmy had brought over that lovely dinner, Eric had washed up afterwards, but the girlfriend had barely said two words, just sat on her phone and ignored them.

Thinking about that now, even though she'd left Henry behind at home, she still heard his voice in her head. 'Best stay out of it, love. They've all got to make their own decisions, whether we agree with them or not.'

He was right, of course, but that didn't make it any easier to button her lip, especially when she was so disappointed with Eric. 'Was it my fault?' she'd asked Henry when the affair first came to light two years ago.

He'd looked at her quizzically, his brow knitting on that face of his that was no less handsome, even in their seventies. That day, he'd just come in from having a pint at his golf club, and she was fairly sure that the lady captain there had designs on him. Probably others too. Minnie joined him for lunch at the clubhouse every couple of weeks just to let them all know she was still alive and kicking and they could all keep their illicit intentions to themselves, thank you very much.

'Why would you think that, love?' he'd asked.

Minnie had shrugged. 'Och, you know how it was when he was a youngster. He was my baby and maybe I spoiled him a bit more than the others. Indulged him. The way you're treated in childhood can shape your whole personality, you know. I saw a programme about that on Channel 4 while you were watching the football last week.'

Henry's expression had changed from confusion to a wide grin. 'So, hang on. The lad is fifty-odd years old now and you think that he got up to no good in his marriage because you gave him too many sweets as a kid?'

When he put it like that…

But still, it made her heart sore that he'd hurt the lovely Ailish and that poor Emmy had been caught in the crossfire. Minnie had tried to talk to him about it when it had all happened, but Eric could be stubborn about discussing emotional things like that. It gave her a little hope that she could see he wasn't proud of his actions though. 'Mum, I'm sorry, but…' He'd paused, struggling for words. 'The thing is, I just fell in love with Donna. And I know I haven't gone about it the right way, but I had to choose her in the end because I need to do what's right for me.'

That one had self-indulgence written all over it. Definitely too many sweets as a boy, no matter what Henry said. They hadn't discussed it after that because Henry had seen how much the conflict of loving their son, but not liking his actions, was taking a toll on her. Instead, they'd made the best of it, welcomed Eric when he stopped by, and Minnie continued to spend time with Ailish and Emmy whenever she could.

A droplet of water fell on Minnie's nose, and she looked upwards, fearing rain, but it must just have been a drip of melted ice from the tree branches above. Now that the droplet had snapped her out of her thoughts, she realised that she was at her first destination and stopped in front of the bright red post box on the edge of the pavement. From the jute bag she was carrying, she pulled out a woolly mass and shook it out to reshape it back into a circle. Putting it in its place required a teeter on her tiptoes, but after a few stretches (of both her legs and the elastic that she'd threaded around the wool), she managed to position it over the top of the post box.

She stood back to survey her work – the post box now had a hat of its very own, a bright orange knitted topper that said 'Happy New Year' along the front, next to lots of little dancing bears that she'd knitted separately then stitched on. Satisfied, she had a wee glow when she thought of how it might make the little ones that came by here smile, then carried on along the street.

The convenience store was the next stop, and in there she happily took a basket and wandered up and down every aisle, even though she only needed two things and she knew exactly where they were. It added a few more steps to her daily tally and it was nice and warm in here. There were a couple of friendly faces too, and when she reached the checkout line, she stopped to have a quick chat to one of the ladies who went to the same line dancing class on a Tuesday afternoon.

Gladys wasn't a close friend, a bit too pessimistic and concerned with her ailments for Minnie's liking, but they'd known each other for years and always passed the time of day when they bumped into each other at the dancing or the shops. As the cashier ran Gladys's shopping through the till and packed it for her, she carried on chatting to Minnie. Och, the weather was getting right into Gladys's bones and hadn't the television been rubbish over Christmas? Then over to Minnie for some joy. Yes, she'd had a lovely Christmas. And yes, she was all ready for the bells tonight. Or at least she would be by the time she finished shopping today.

'Well, Happy New Year when it comes,' Gladys said, as she paid for her shopping, then bid her goodbye. 'Let's hope we're spared for another year, although at our age, you never know the minute.' With that cheery thought, off she went, bustling out of the shop.

Whisky and shortbread purchased, Minnie made her way to the jewellery shop a few doors down the street. As soon as she got inside and the heat allowed her to remove her gloves, she pulled a ticket out of her purse and handed it over to the young man behind the counter. Actually, he was probably in his thirties, but everyone under forty counted as a youngster to her.

'I'd like to collect this please,' she said.

He rummaged under the counter for so long that she was beginning to panic that it wasn't ready, but just when she felt her body temperature begin to rise uncomfortably due to the worry of it, he stood back up and produced a square package about the size of a biscuit tin.

Relief made Minnie lightheaded for a few seconds.

Holding on to the counter to steady herself, she watched as he slid the white outer sleeve off the item, revealing a navy-blue, velvet box. He turned it as he opened it, so that she could see it was lined with silk, and nestling in the middle was a silver hip flask, the one that she'd picked out on Christmas Eve when she'd come in here to order it.

The assistant gently lifted the flask from its nest, and turned it over, to let her read the inscription she'd asked to be engraved on the back. If he noticed that some unexpected tears had found their way to her bottom lids, he was polite or embarrassed enough not to say.

Minnie cleared her throat, found her words. 'That's lovely, thank you. It's perfect.'

It absolutely was. The perfect gift, for the man who had been their friend for decades. She just hoped that Gino would love it as much as she did. Henry too. She'd told him about it after she'd ordered it, and now she couldn't wait to show it to him.

'Would you like it gift wrapped?'

Minnie nodded. 'That would be smashing, thank you.'

Off he went to the other side of the counter, leaving her to stand for a good five minutes. She glanced around to see if there was a wee chair that would let her take the weight off her legs for a minute, but there was none. By the time he came back with the square box, wrapped in gorgeous silver paper with a white ribbon around it, Minnie was warmer than ever and starting to feel a bit woozy again. With clumsy thumbs, she managed to get her purse out and hand over the three crisp twenty-pound notes that were left from the money she'd put in her purse before she left the house. Ailish was always telling her she should only use the credit card that she'd organised for her, but Minnie preferred to stick to cash. It had been good enough for the seventy-odd years she'd already been on this earth, so it would do her fine for the rest of her days.

The helpful assistant came round from behind the counter to hold the door open for her. Just a little wobbly, with her handbag over her shoulder and a shopping bag in each hand now, she stepped over the threshold, then gasped as the cold air hit her again.

Pausing to catch her breath, she'd just taken another step when a voice shouted out behind her. 'Minnie! Was that you who knitted that new topper for the post box? Och, it's lovely, so it is!'

Minnie turned her head to see Gladys grinning from ear to ear. See! It had already made someone smile today – and a tough nut to crack at that. She couldn't remember Gladys smiling since the line-dancing coach gave in to her request and introduced 'Achy Breaky Heart' into their repertoire.

All that knitting had definitely been worth it.

That was the last thing that went through Minnie's mind before she lost her footing, and felt herself falling forward, grasping futilely for something to grab on to, watching the pavement come towards her until she met it with a thud and a sickening crunch.

NOON – 2 P.M.

9

AILISH

Ailish switched on Gwen's oven and pulled a pizza out of the freezer. They'd stopped at a Tesco Express on the way back from the hospital and Ailish had run in and done a trolley dash for the basics needed to refill Gwen's fridge, freezer and breadbin. Then she'd added the two bottles of wine that Rhonda had requested and picked up three Christmas selection boxes that were reduced to half price.

Pizza in the oven, she opened a fresh tub of ready-made salad to go with the twelve-inch Margherita, then set the table with plates, napkins, cutlery and salad dressing, a smile on her face the whole time. Gwen was home. She was okay. They were all together. On a day that had begun with news that had chipped her heart, this turn of events had glued it back together again. When they'd wheeled Gwen to the hospital doors, then held her arms as she'd taken her first steps back into the outside world, Ailish had blinked the tears back. Although, she wasn't sure if that was relief, or fear over what she'd just agreed to.

'What about you, Ails? Are you in?'

How could she possibly say no and crush Gwen's expression of pure hope? But she couldn't quite say yes either, because the very thought of going out tonight, of all nights, gripped her with absolute horror. New Year's Eve used to be her favourite night of the year, but now it made her want to hibernate and ignore the world. Her own issues aside though, her natural caution that going out could compromise Gwen's health made her want to object. But she didn't have the heart to refuse her friend anything, so in the end, she'd gone for a tentative nod that Gwen and Rhonda had taken as acceptance and rolled with it.

Now that they were home in Gwen's ultra-modern, breathtakingly chic, river-front loft, Ailish still wasn't convinced. Surely it was madness? Irresponsible. What if something went wrong? What if Gwen needed medical attention? The chances of getting swift emergency services on New Year's Eve were slim to none – it was one of the busiest and most chaotic nights of the year in Glasgow. No. She was going to refuse for Gwen's sake. She'd break it to her gently over the pizza that had just pinged in the oven.

As if summoned by the bell, at that moment Rhonda and Gwen reappeared, Gwen's hair still wet from the shower. It had been the first thing she'd wanted to do when she got home, and Rhonda had insisted on sitting outside the bathroom door, just in case Gwen needed her or felt unwell.

'I'm perfectly able to stand,' Gwen had objected, rolling her eyes.

'And I'm perfectly able to do the splits, but there's always a risk that I'll end up in Accident and Emergency, so I'm coming with you.'

Gwen had surrendered, knowing she was beaten.

Ailish pressed the front of one of the gloss white kitchen drawers, searching for the pizza cutter. This whole apartment looked like it was straight out of a magazine, thanks to both Gwen's skill as an interior designer and her love of clean white spaces.

'Next drawer to the right,' Gwen said, reading her mind.

Ailish followed the instruction, and the pizza cutter was revealed. She pulled it out of the drawer and started slicing, talking as she went. 'How are you feeling now?'

'So much better. I don't think I'll be running marathons again any time soon, but I managed to stand up in the shower without feeling faint. I'll take the win.'

Relieved, Ailish slid the pizza onto the table and sat down, trying to decide whether to go for it and just blurt out her objections to Gwen's plans.

'Ailish, you have to take that worried look off your face, otherwise you'll need to hit up Rhonda's Botox clinic.'

Ailish made a mental note to check out the anti-wrinkle devices on the home shopping channels, before getting right to the heart of her concerns. 'Okay, I'm just going to put this out there. I still think going out tonight is a bad idea. Gwen—'

'Nope, I'm not listening,' Gwen cut her off. 'And besides, you promised in the hospital.'

'I didn't exactly promise. I nodded my head.'

'That was a promise. I saw it,' Rhonda interjected. There was still no doubt which side of the fence that one was inhabiting. Apparently, Ralph the body builder had taken the news of his rejection well and decided that he'd go to the gym instead.

Deciding to regroup, Ailish went for a different approach. 'How about we have a cosy night in instead? You must be exhausted and it's freezing out there. We could order food in, open some champagne and chocolates, find a good movie—'

'Nope,' Gwen answered, dismissing it without consideration.

Ailish wasn't quite ready to concede. Perhaps she could talk them out of it on practical or logistical grounds. But first, she needed all the facts.

She tried again. 'Okay, so say, hypothetically, that I did agree.'

'You did.' Both Rhonda and Gwen said that at exactly the same time, but Ailish refused to be intimidated. Someone had to be the adult in the room here. She ploughed on... 'Then where do you want to go? It'll be impossible to get a reservation anywhere tonight at this late notice, and anywhere that doesn't require a booking will be absolutely packed.'

She caught the glance that passed between Rhonda and Gwen and suddenly the worry wrinkles on her forehead were back.

'What? What are you not telling me?'

Gwen tried to go for nonchalance, mumbling, 'I want to go to Gino's,' then immediately popping a baby tomato from the salad into her mouth, as if the words had never been spoken.

Someone switched on a spin cycle in Ailish's stomach.

'Gwen, no... I can't...' Abject horror blocked any more words.

Gino's. There was a time when she couldn't have fathomed spending New Year's Eve anywhere else. But that was before... She couldn't even bear to finish that thought. All that mattered was that last year had been the first year in decades that she hadn't gone, and she had absolutely no desire to start up that tradition again. She took a breath. Then another. Tried to react calmly.

'Gwen, I can't go there. Not after what happened.'

'Yes, you can. Because we'll be with you.'

'No. If Eric is there—'

'Who cares? Not that I think for a second he will be—'

'I don't want to take the risk. That place is in the past for me.'

'But the thing is, it isn't for me,' Gwen countered gently. 'We've gone there on Hogmanay our whole adult lives, had some of our best moments there and I want to feel that again, even if it's just once more. And yes, I'm using my cancer to emotionally black-mail you. Don't judge me. Look, last year, we didn't go because it was all too raw for you, and we understood. But what it really boils down to now is that I'm not going to let your arse of a husband take away our traditions.'

'Ex,' Ailish blurted.

Her friends looked at her quizzically.

'Ex-husband,' she explained, all the fight going out of her. 'The divorce papers came through this morning. He's my ex-husband now.'

To her fury, she felt a tear slide down her face and she chided herself. She had no right to be crying, not when Gwen was going through so much worse. She brushed it away.

Gwen reached over and took her hand. 'Oh hon, I'm so sorry.'

'But you're well shot of him,' were Rhonda's words of consolation.

'I do know that,' Ailish admitted, 'but I think I'm just finding it hard to see where to go from here. Urgh, listen to me. Honestly, I'm sick of hearing myself being so pathetic. I need to pull my bloody big woman pants on and get a grip.'

'And the best place to wear those big woman pants is Gino's tonight,' Rhonda assured her. 'So come on. You know that no matter how busy they are, they'll find us a table. Dario has always had a soft spot for you, so he'll make it work.'

Ailish felt a jolt of something she couldn't put her finger on. Dario. Her first ever crush. She occasionally wondered what would have happened on a night long ago if she'd made a different decision.

And she had to admit, it would be good to see him.

Before she could mull that over any further, her phone began to ring. The screen announced that it was her Ring doorbell app. Probably the delivery of something she'd bought while she was surfing the shopping channel at 3 a.m. It had become her favourite indoor sport. In the last month, she'd bought a jewellery cleaner (still in the box), a laser device that would remove the hair from her legs forever (still in the box) and exercise bands that would transform her into a body-beautiful athlete in six weeks or your money back (still in the box eight weeks later). She'd be hanging out down the gym with Rhonda's blind date in no time. Oh, and then there was an electric mop that would apparently rejuvenate both her floors and her life. That one had yet to be delivered so she assumed this was it now. One of the neighbours must have left the front door of the building open again, because whoever it was had already made their way to her flat.

She opened the app and peered at the live footage from the doorbell camera. Whoever it was had begun to walk away and she could only see the outline of his shoulder.

'Hello? Just leave the delivery on the doorstep please.'

There were some muffled sounds as the man stepped back into the frame, then a gasp as she realised it wasn't the life-changing mop, but her second crush – the life-changing cheating husband. *Ex*-husband.

'Ailish? Ailish, it's me. Can you let me in? I need to talk to you.'

Hearing Eric's voice, Rhonda and Gwen's heads swiftly swivelled in her direction, and they were both staring at her, wide-eyed, Rhonda mouthing. 'No fucking way!'

Ailish felt the pulse on the side of her neck begin to throb. 'Is something wrong? Is Emmy okay? Your mum?'

Even without a crystal-clear picture, she could see his perplexed expression. 'What? Yes. Of course. They're both fine. Look, that's not why I'm here. Can you just bloody let me in?'

'No.'

She watched him run his fingers through his impressive head of hair – he always did that when he was stressing – as he murmured, 'Oh for God's sake...'

His exasperation was palpable, and she realised that even now her first instinct was to consider his feelings and attempt to soothe them, a little nugget of self-reflection that irritated her, so she disguised it with a curt explanation of the facts. 'I can't let you in because I'm not there. I'm speaking to you remotely. I'm with Gwen and Rhonda.'

'Oh.' That appeared to take the wind out of his sails. 'When will you be back? I need to speak to you today.'

Rhonda's eyebrows rose in irritation and Ailish was right there with her. A torrent of suppressed emotions began bubbling up inside her: rage, fury, disgust, disappointment, heartbreak, and unwavering grief for the loss of the decent, kind, honest man she'd thought she was married to for thirty years, and for the future they'd always planned together. Gwen was right. She'd let this knock her down. Now it was time to slide out from under the weight of it. She had to accept that no matter how much she'd loved him, that chapter of her life was over. He didn't want her, didn't love her, so it was time she processed that and got over it.

'Well, Eric,' she said. 'That's the thing about you having an affair and then divorcing me – I don't have to do a single thing that you want me to do. So no, I won't be back today, and even if I was, you'd still be looking at that closed door because you wouldn't be getting in. I have absolutely nothing to say to you. Go home, Eric.'

'But Ailish...' he spluttered. 'I want—'

'I'm sorry, Ailish is no longer available,' she answered before disconnecting the conversation and closing the doorbell app.

She pressed the lock button on the side of the handset, then calmly, with a confidence she hadn't felt in a long time, placed it on the table, face down. Then she ignored it when it immediately rang again. And again.

'I have no idea who you are, but I like you,' Rhonda dead-panned, pouring Prosecco into the glass that she'd just slid in front of Ailish.

Beside her, Gwen picked her moment. 'So what do you say

then, Ails? How about, instead of being sad about your divorce, we celebrate it? Are you going to let Eric Wandering Willy Ryan continue to dictate your life, or are we going out tonight to our favourite place, full of old friends, and sod whether he's there or not?'

Ailish waited for the knot in her stomach to loosen, for the huge bloody lump in her throat to go down, then she picked up the glass. Regardless of how she felt, she could see how much Gwen wanted this, and she wasn't going to let Eric get in the way of it.

'Sod him and sod it all. We're going out.'

'Yessssss!' Gwen cheered, with a smile that warmed Ailish's heart. 'Watch out, Glasgow, we're back and looking for trouble.'

Ailish's first thought was that Gwen was of course joking. Her second thought was that she might not be. And her third thought was that more trouble ahead was exactly what she was afraid of.

10

EMMY

There were many reasons that Emmy loved working on the elderly ward at Glasgow Central, but one of them was the fact that she was constantly busy, so it didn't leave any time for thinking about anything that didn't involve her patients' care and well-being. She always tried to have a chat to each patient while she was doing her rounds or administering their medications, and if she did have a spare minute, she'd spend it with the ones who rarely or never got visitors. Their solitude hurt her heart, and she would never understand the cases where families just didn't bother to come. Her grandmother, Minnie, was one of her favourite people in the world, and she spoke to her every day. She usually phoned her on the way into work, but her dad's appearance had got in the way of that, so she'd give her a call as soon as she finished work at 7 p.m.

In the meantime, she focused on her shift, until it was time to stop for a tea break at 1 p.m. She could count on the fingers of one hand how often they actually got a tea break, because the ward was always so busy, but today was quieter than usual because where possible, patients had been discharged or allowed out to spend time with their families over the holiday. Also, many of the patients who were still here had lunch time visitors.

Her closest friends on the ward, Charge Nurse Yvie Danton and Senior Nurse Keli Clark had their breaks at the same time. Yvie was first into the staffroom and had already put the kettle on when she got there. 'One step ahead of me again, Miss Danton,' Emmy teased, harping back to the fact that Yvie had got to the hospital five minutes before her this morning at the beginning of their shift. She'd commented on it because it was so unusual. Yvie was usually the one flying in at the last minute and making her start time with only moments to spare.

'It's my New Year's resolution, but I'm just kicking it off a day early. My name is Yvie, and I plan to be on time every day. Although, that whole vow thing hasn't worked with the diet, so I'm not holding out much hope,' she added, helping herself to a slice of the yule log she'd brought in with her.

Beside her, Keli helped herself to a piece too, but when she offered it to Emmy, she shook her head.

Keli put the cake down and leaned forward, elbows on the table, towards Emmy. 'Okay, spill. What's wrong with you today? You've got the worst stoic face ever.'

Yvie swallowed a chocolate reindeer. 'I thought that was me?'

Keli nodded, acknowledging that statement. 'Yep, yours is rubbish too. I'm never taking either of you to a poker game. First time you lose, you'll crumble.'

Despite her distraction and her rubbish mood, that made Emmy laugh. These two women had been an absolute joy to work with, and, in a round-about way, Yvie was one of the reasons that she was here. She was engaged to Carlo Moretti, who owned Carlo's Cafe, the bistro just along the road from the hospital that they went to most Fridays after work. It had become a bit of a tradition and a full-circle moment because Carlo's dad, Gino, owned the restaurant her parents used to take her to every New Year's Eve. That was actually where she'd met Yvie. In fact... 'I just realised we met two years ago tonight. At your father-in-law's restaurant.'

Yvie harrumphed. 'Not father-in-law yet. Despite years of undying love, and this little sparkler...' She nodded to her engagement ring, a family heirloom passed down from Carlo's grandmother. 'He's still dragging his heels about setting a date.'

Keli put her mug down. 'Oh dear. Do I detect trouble in paradise?'

Yvie took another bite of chocolatey goodness before she answered. 'Not trouble, just...' She hesitated for a second. '*Impatience*. I mean, honestly, it's been years. I'm beginning to think...' After another pause, she seemed to snap herself off that train of thought and swiftly diverted the attention. 'Anyway, enough about me.' She circled back to Emmy's comment. 'And the lest said about how you and I met the better.'

Emmy nodded silently in agreement. That had been one of the worst nights of her life. They'd all been in full-scale party mode in the early hours of the morning. It must have been after 2 a.m., but Gran Minnie and Grandad Henry were still slow dancing in the corner. Mum, Auntie Gwen and Auntie Rhonda were at their long table singing along to something by Celine Dion. It was before Emmy had met Cormac, so she was happily riding solo and had been enthusiastically joining in the chorus, until she excused herself and made her way to the 'ladies'. At that point, she hadn't even given a thought to where her dad had disappeared to. Probably off chatting to Dario somewhere. She had got to the corridor just off the back of the restaurant, where a short, gorgeous, curvy blonde maybe a few years older than her was leaning against the wall outside the row of three bathrooms. 'There's a queue, I'm afraid. But feel free to go before me, if it's urgent. I've been dancing for the last hour, so I'm just killing time until my feet stop aching.'

Emmy had decided right there and then that she liked her. 'You're Carlo's girlfriend? We've been coming here for years – our families are friends. He was telling me last year that he's off the market because of a complete babe called Yvie. I really hope that's you or I've just caused a situation.'

'Yep, that's me,' Yvie had said, laughing. 'He's a lucky man. Although, I think he's just future proofing for his old age. I'm a nurse on the elderly ward at Glasgow Central.'

Emmy's eyes had widened. 'No way! I'm a nurse in the Emergency Department at Paisley General. I'm Emmy.' Her extended hand was greeted with an enthusiastic shake.

If it had been left there, it might have been the loveliest of meetings that would have resulted in a passing acquaintance. Instead, it had gone on to be a ten-minute chat that had been interrupted when, a few feet away, Dario's son, Matty, still in his chef's whites, had opened the emergency exit door next to the kitchen, and there, standing outside in the gleam of the security light, was her father, with his arms around the waist of a thirty-something brunette whose pinched face and relentlessly moving mouth suggested she was haranguing him.

'Ouch. Wouldn't want to be in his shoes. She does not look happy.' Yvie had whistled, as Matty came back in after tossing the bin bag in the skip.

'Yeah, well, that man is about to be pretty unhappy too.' Emmy had swerved past Matty as she walked towards the door and slammed it open. Nope, she hadn't imagined it – they were still there. And now she could hear what the woman was saying.

'No, Eric, I'm not waiting. I'm sick of this. If you don't tell her now, I will.'

'Tell her what?' Emmy had interrupted them, and her dad's

face had twisted into an expression that could easily have come from being the victim of a drive-by shooting. Horror. Pain. Panic.

The woman had found her voice first. 'You're Emmy.'

'And you're Donna.' Emmy had recognised her dad's secretary from the couple of times she'd been to his office. 'This doesn't look like a work conversation.'

'Emmy, let me exp—'

'No, let me,' Donna had interrupted him. 'I'm sorry, but your dad and I have been in a relationship for almost a year now. It's better you know. Your mum too.'

Emmy couldn't absorb what she was saying, so she'd sought clarification from the man she trusted more than any other. 'Dad?'

'Emmy, I... I...' He'd run out of steam, clearly realising that there was no defence. None.

Donna had stepped back into Truth Central. 'He's been promising me for months that he was going to tell your mother, and he keeps backing down. I'm sorry, but I'm not waiting any longer. If he won't do it, then I will.'

'I think you just did,' came a low, shockingly calm voice from behind Emmy. As she'd turned around, she saw a wide-eyed Yvie first, then, just behind her new friend, was her mum, staring straight at them. Before another word had been said, her mum had turned around, gone back inside, told Rhonda and Gwen what had just happened and they'd all left.

'All these years and I never realised you were an asshole,' Emmy had spat, before banging the door shut on her dad, pretty much a metaphor for what had happened in their lives. Something closed that day. Her trust in him. And maybe a bit of her trust in life too. She'd always rolled along thinking everything would always turn out for the best. Not any more. Although, the only silver lining to the adulterous cloud was that a couple of days later, Yvie had tracked her down to check on her, invited her to

Carlo's for a coffee with Keli too, and they'd all become fast friends. The following month, when a position had become available on their ward, she'd applied for it and been delighted to get it.

However, that Hogmanay was one she definitely didn't want to dwell on right now, so she was relieved when Yvie just kept on going with, 'Although, I'm glad that it introduced us and gave me the opportunity to persuade you to transfer to this little slice of paradise,' she said dramatically, gesturing to the four-metre-square box containing a tiny kitchen area, a table and four chairs, a few lockers against the far wall, and a door that led through to a toilet and changing area.

'Indeed. I'm glad you're living the dream with us,' Keli got in on the joke. 'But let's put that to one side for a moment and go back to the original question. What's up with your face? Your frown lines have been running riot all morning.'

Emmy thought about spinning a story to brush off their concerns, but she honestly thought she was going to lose her mind if she didn't say it all aloud.

'I don't know if this tea break is long enough,' she said, 'but I'll give it a go. So... first of all, my dad turned up at my house this morning, saying he wanted my mother back...'

Their gasps shot right through her words. 'Shut the front door!' Yvie exclaimed.

Emmy nodded, the irony not lost on her. 'I only wish I had. Instead I let him in and listened to him ranting about how he's made a mistake and wants the love of his life back.'

'They're idiots. They really are,' Keli said from experience, given that she'd very publicly caught her ex-boyfriend, an actor called Rex Marino, cheating on her the previous year. But that was yet another story.

'No arguments here,' Emmy concurred. 'So yes, he wants the

woman that he betrayed back, and she is, I might add, the same woman I've been trying to prise out of her pyjamas since their marriage fell apart. I hoped when she moved into her own place it would get better, but honestly, she still never leaves home except to go to work or see her friends. Anyway, I digress. Back to my shite day, because what does it say about my life that my dad's adultery-remorse isn't the biggest issue I'm dealing with today.'

'My buttocks are actually clenching with fear,' Yvie whispered. Emmy didn't stop to check that statement.

'Because… because…' Was she actually going to say this out loud? 'Because I think Cormac is having an affair.'

It was just as well that she was sitting back in her chair, because Yvie almost spat her tea out. In the end, she managed to control it, swallow, and go with, 'What? No. No way. Why would you think that? Not Cormac. He wouldn't do that.'

Emmy wondered if her friend was okay, because she suddenly looked a bit flushed.

'I don't think he would either,' Keli offered, but Emmy spotted the slight lack of conviction in her tone.

'But?' Emmy challenged.

'But then, I'm the worst person to give an opinion because I never thought Rex would be unfaithful and then I found out he'd been living a double life and shacked up with someone else for the last three years.'

Yvie gave Keli a murderous glare. 'You're not helping.'

'Sorry,' Keli said, with a resigned shrug. 'All I'm saying is that if your gut is telling you something, it's worth checking it out.'

'No, it isn't,' Yvie blurted. 'If your gut is telling you something, it's because we're human and prone to insecurities. Most of the time, those doubts have no basis in fact whatsoever.'

Both Emmy and Keli were now facing her with the same

curious expressions. Yvie responded by lifting her mug and taking a big slurp of her tea.

Keli turned back to Emmy, checking her watch as she did so. 'Okay, we've got seven minutes left, so we'll need to be quick. Tell us what's making you suspicious and what are you going to do?'

Emmy ran through the list of factors that had contributed to her growing fears. His distance. His jumpiness when he was on his phone. The coming home late. The oh-so-clichéd smell of perfume. Changing his passwords. She ended the laundry list of weirdness with, 'Am I being crazy?'

Yvie spat out, 'Yes', at the same time as Keli countered with, 'No.'

'I've never seen you two disagree on anything,' Emmy grumbled. 'I'm sorry. My relationship quandaries have exposed a big glaring hole in your friendship.'

Emmy's attempt to lighten the mood didn't fool anyone. And they only had about two minutes of tea break left.

'What am I going to do? I've no idea.'

'Why don't you talk to him about it?' Keli came in with the obvious suggestion.

'Because if this is all in my head, that'll make him think I don't trust him and then that'll expose a big glaring hole in our relationship too.'

'You're right. I think speaking to him about it would be a mistake,' Yvie agreed. 'There's no point questioning him when you don't know anything for sure. That could be really hurtful.'

Emmy nodded. Yvie was right. Best let it be. Maybe this was just a phase and it would all get better.

'Nope, I think it's the only way you're going to get answers,' Keli argued. 'And you're entitled to have your voice heard. Look, if it's upsetting you so much, you could always nip over to the station to speak to him.'

Emmy bit her bottom lip, trying to buy time. She hadn't told them the worst of it because she didn't want her darkest fear to be confirmed. But now... well, she had nothing to lose.

'There's something else. He's supposed to be at work today...' She was starting to get hot under the heat of her friends' gazes. 'But I'm sure I saw him driving past me when I was coming into work. How could that be?'

Their ability to answer was delayed because Yvie began to choke on her tea and Keli had to get up to thump her on the back.

One minute left of the tea break.

That's when Keli came out with the zinger of a solution. 'Do you have him on Find My Friends? Could you see where he is? If he's at work, then that at least solves that mystery.'

Emmy jumped from her seat. Of course! She should have thought of that, but she'd been so harassed with all the dad stuff and then as soon as she came into work her phone had gone into her locker.

She grabbed it out, switched it on, put it in the centre of the table while it was booting up. The other two watched intently. When the screen came fully alive, she tapped her Find My Friends icon and then searched for his name. There he was. Cormac Sweeney. She clicked on it and waited for what seemed like forever until she got her answer...

Cormac Sweeney was no longer sharing his location with her.

'Crap,' Keli groaned.

Emmy's stomach sank. Why? Why would he switch that off? There was only one feasible reason that he didn't want her to know where he was. He was hiding something. Or someone.

'What are you going to do? Can we help?' Keli asked, sympathy oozing from her words.

Emmy shook her head. 'No. I think I have to do this myself. And soon, because I can't stand feeling this way.' She wasn't lying.

All the stuff with her parents, the way her dad had acted, the chaos he'd caused. It had pushed her to the absolute certainty that if someone ever cheated on her, it would be over, no questions asked.

A plan began to form in her mind. She had an hour-long break later. Cormac wouldn't for a second expect her to be anywhere else than at the hospital, so his guard would be down. The station he worked at was only a mile away, so she could be there and back in ten minutes. If he was there, she'd come up with some reason for dropping by.

If he wasn't... well, then at least she'd know if she was going to start the new year off as someone who was very definitely single.

11

DARIO

'This is a joke, right?' That was Matty's incredulous response to bombshell Dario had just dropped about the future of the restaurant. 'You're not serious.'

Dario was so desperately trying to hold it together he could barely breathe. 'I'm serious, son. We have until midnight to accept the offer, but I already know what the answer will be because I'm all out of options.'

'No way. You can't be.' The pitch and volume of Matty's voice was rising. 'Grandad would never allow it. There's no way he'll ever let this place go and you're a prick for even suggesting it.'

And there it was. His son's temper. Dario wasn't making excuses for him, but at the same time, he knew Matty's words came out of passion and love for what they had here. And for what was supposed to become his in the future.

'Matty, there's nothing you can say that I haven't said, tried or felt myself. This is where we are, and I'm devastated that it's happened, but there's no choice. This is it.'

Matty turned to his mother. 'You knew about this?'

Nicky shot a 'told you so' glare at Dario. 'See! Always the

sidekick that comes off worst.' She switched back to their son. 'Yes, I knew about it, but right up until about an hour ago, your dad was still trying to find a way to save it. I know this hurts, son...'

'Really? You know?'

There was a tone in Matty's words that Dario didn't like, so he immediately stepped in. 'Watch yourself, Matty. You won't speak to your mother like that.'

Nicky immediately put her hand up. 'Thank you, but you don't need to defend me, Dario.' She turned back to their son. 'Matty, enough. I know you're angry, but you're firing it in the wrong place and you're not the only one that's hurting here.'

'No, but I'm the only one whose whole life fricking plan has just been screwed.' He stood up, fury obvious in the blaze of his eyes and the sneer of his top lip. 'Well done, Dad. Great job.'

With that, he turned and stormed out, banging the door behind him.

There was a silence throughout the whole building as everyone stopped what they were doing and tried to work out why Matty was slamming doors, before they probably decided it was nothing they hadn't seen before and got back to work.

'You okay?' Nicky asked Dario.

Was he okay? Nope. But was there any point in saying that? Also, nope. 'Yeah. You?'

'No. I want to go kick all six foot of our son's arse for being so fricking hot-headed and only thinking about himself, but my legs won't reach that high.'

Dario tried to walk the middle line. The last thing he wanted was for Nicky and Matty to be pissed off with each other over this. 'We were all like that once upon a time.'

'No, you weren't,' Nicky objected. 'If you were arrogant and wild, I'd have fancied you so much more. Throw in a couple of hundred grand in the bank and cut your working week by about forty hours, and we'd probably still be married.'

'Good to know,' he replied, wholeheartedly appreciating that she was still trying to lift his spirits.

She stood up, unusually serious for a moment. 'I know it doesn't feel like it right now, but you'll survive this, Dario. It's a business. It's not life or death. And there will still be good stuff ahead for you.'

He was so moved, he began to feel quite emotional until she cracked and added, 'I mean, not as good as me, but at least half decent.'

With that, she took herself off, leaving nothing but love behind her. They'd been a terrible married couple and he had never regretted their divorce, but he didn't think he'd ever loved her more – as a friend and mother of his wonderful daughter and volatile son – than he did right now.

At least Nicky brought the total number of people who would stick by him through this to one. Three if he included his mates, Talia and Brodie, but they weren't family. And he still hadn't had the most difficult conversation of all. His dad would probably come in around four, so that gave him a few more hours to prepare. There was a slim possibility that Matty would try to get in there first by calling Gino to discuss this with him before Dario had the chance, but he knew his son – he was headstrong, impulsive, explosive sometimes, but there was no way he'd deliberately upset his grandfather.

Dario leaned back in his chair, closed his eyes, ran through every single facet of the situation in his mind once again. Was there a way out that he'd missed? Something he hadn't tried? A move that would delay the inevitable and give them even a shred of hope? He went over it again and again and again but came up blank every time. He had to face facts – times had changed, they'd been hit by a barrage of problems through no fault of their own, and the result was that the restaurant was failing.

Eyes still closed, he was about to go through it one more time when the door burst open so swiftly, he thought it was either a SWAT raid or Matty back for round two.

'Right, I need to talk to you.'

Sonya. Not Matty. He wasn't sure who was the most terrifying.

Slamming the door behind her – could no one just close a door today? – she marched over and plonked herself down on the seat opposite him. 'Right, Big Pierce, what's going on? And don't say nothing, because I'm never wrong about these things and I'll get it out of you anyway.'

There was a tiny temptation to fob her off, but he dismissed it immediately. It was Sonya – she deserved more than that.

'Sonya, I'll tell you, but I need you to swear that you'll keep this to yourself until the time is right because I still have to talk to my dad.'

'Aw fuckery, I knew there was something. I'll keep it quiet, Dario, but I need to know the score. Am I losing my job?'

To his surprise, he saw her bottom lip quiver and he paused. He'd known her since he was a boy and he'd never seen Sonya emotional like that. It almost made him change his mind about sharing the news, because he couldn't bear to upset her even more, but it was too late. He couldn't backtrack now, but he decided not to give her a direct answer about her job until he'd told her the full story.

'Back in 2020, when the pandemic struck, the restaurant was hit pretty hard…'

She was nodding. 'I remember. We were all shocked when you and your dad kept on paying us our full wages.' Their long-standing staff were family to them, so there had never been any question that they would do that. 'I still had my Ollie at home then and he cost me a fortune with all that Wi-Fi stuff to keep him amused. If you hadn't done that, I don't know where I'd have been.'

Dario hated that she was about to find out. She'd taken Ollie in when he was a teenager and his mum – Sonya's daughter – had remarried and moved down south. Ollie didn't take to her new husband and hadn't wanted to go with them, so Sonya had offered her spare room and her unconditional love. Thanks to that, Ollie had turned into a fine young man who was now studying architecture at university and Sonya beamed with pride every time she spoke about him.

'We were happy to do it. You know we care about every single person that works here.'

'So I'm not losing my job then?'

He hesitated and her shoulders slumped.

'The thing is,' he went on, 'when we were finally able to re-open, you know the crowds didn't come rushing back. It's taken years to get even close to the level of business we used to have, and we're still not quite there yet. And, at the same time, the cost of everything we need and use has increased in price, sometimes twofold.'

Sonya groaned. 'This is like waiting to get to the bit in the movie where the bad bastard serial killer wipes everyone out. You know it's coming but you're still hoping for the best.'

'There's no best, Sonya, I'm so sorry. I'd do anything to change that but there's no option. We're going to have to close.'

For once in all the time that he'd known her, she said nothing, just stared straight ahead for so long, he wondered if she'd fallen into some kind of trance.

'Sonya? Are you okay? Look, I know it's terrible news but...'

'I'm losing ma house,' she blurted, and Dario immediately joined the dots. The frantic work. Coming in early. The ferocious display of vacuuming fervour. He'd known she was upset about something, but not this. The knife of self-loathing that was stuck in his heart had just been given another twist. He should have found another way to save them. To save Sonya. 'The landlord is selling up because he knows he can get a packet from a developer for the land. Thirty-seven years I've lived there and he's tossing me and everyone else in the block out with four weeks' notice. And all the other rents and deposits for two-bedroom flats in the area, even in the crappiest of streets, are out of my reach. So I need this job, Dario, because I've got nothing left without it.'

Another twist of the knife.

Dario leaned forward, his arms on the desk, his wounded heart taking charge of the situation. 'Sonya, I swear to you, we will take care of you. You're part of our family, so even if that means…' He tried to rack his brains for something tangible and settled on, '…Even if that means you work helping out Dad with cleaning his house, I'll make sure that you're paid the wage you earn now for as long as you need it. I'll write you any reference you need, and I'll ask around my friends and see if I can come up with anything on the accommodation side. Just give me a bit of time on that. But consider all of it done. Like I said, we'll take care of you.'

Her forehead creased as she processed that. 'Really?'

'Really,' he promised.

This time, he really did think she was going to cry. Instead, she got up, brushing away imaginary crumbs from the front of her trousers.

'Thank you, Dario. You always were the best of your mum and dad. She'd be dead proud of you.'

The lump in his throat was back.

'And since you're taking care of me, probably time I go make myself useful and achieve the impossible for you.'

'The impossible?'

She found the strength to give him a wink. 'I'm going to the pub round the corner, and I'll drag big Matty back. We've got sixty people at lunch to feed.'

He nodded, managing a grateful smile. 'I'd appreciate that.' He really did – because otherwise he'd be dragging out his old kitchen whites and doing it himself.

She got halfway to the door, then stopped, turned around.

'You know, Dario, I'm heartsore for your dad in all this. I'm really worried that news like this will end him.'

'Me too, Sonya,' he replied, feeling the knife in his chest twist yet again as he said it. 'Me too.'

12

MINNIE

Minnie groaned as she turned over in bed, and she must have hit a sore spot in her hip because her leg involuntarily flinched. It was just one of many parts of her that were aching, but she wasn't going to complain. Could have been so much worse.

That tumble in the main street had fair taken her breath away though. Thankfully, she'd somehow managed to stick her shopping bag out in front of her, so her shortbread got the worst of it and had been crunched into crumbs. Her bag, thick scarf and padded coat had cushioned the fall, but she had an aching hip, two skint knees, two bruised palms and a whole lot of embarrassment at the fuss she'd created.

As she'd lain there, stunned for a few seconds, she'd mentally checked that everything was still working. She could still feel her arms and her legs, and she hadn't banged her head, so she wasn't worried about concussion. It was more just the racing heart from the shock of the fall. Reassured that she was still in one piece, she'd begun to think about getting up when she'd suddenly heard Gladys, who'd got to her side in seconds, screeching, 'Call an ambulance' at the top of her lungs.

Minnie had been mortified. Mortified! And she'd been like an upside-down turtle for a moment as she'd tried to right herself to assure the gathering crowd that she was fine. 'No, please don't,' Minnie had objected, as she managed to push herself up on her knees, then turn around so she was sitting on her bottom. By that time, quite a crowd had gathered, including the young man from the jewellers who'd dashed out and was on the other side of her now.

'Why don't we take you inside and get you a seat?' he'd offered.

'No, she shouldn't be moved!' Gladys had tried to take charge. 'I've seen that on *Casualty*. They always say the victims shouldn't be moved without one of those collar thingies on their necks.'

Minnie had put her hand on Gladys's arm and squeezed it, realising that the other woman meant well. 'I think a seat inside the shop would be lovely while I get my breath back,' she'd told her.

The gent from the shop, and another burly bloke who'd stopped to see if he could help, took one of her arms each. 'Now you're sure you're ready to get up? Your friend might have a point.'

Minnie had shaken her head, trying not to wince as it sent a pain shooting down her shoulder. If ever she needed her granddaughter Emmy's nursing skills, it was right then. 'I promise you, everything feels fine,' she'd fudged the truth slightly. 'The worst part is sitting on this cold ground.'

That had seemed to convince them, because, much to Gladys's disapproval, the next thing, they were very slowly and gently lifting Minnie to her feet. Another person in the crowd picked up her bags, and handed them to Gladys, who seemed to have declared herself in charge of the whole affair. Not that Minnie was ungrateful for the assistance or the kindness.

As soon as she'd been settled in a chair in a little room just off the main sales area of the jewellers, the young man who worked there had disappeared and returned with a glass of water.

Gladys had jumped right on that. 'Oh, son, I could do with one of those maself,' she'd said, and Minnie had flushed with even more embarrassment as the kind lad had gone off to get it. She really hated to create a scene.

She'd thanked the other gent who'd helped her profusely, and he'd given her the loveliest smile. All the terrible news in the world could make someone think otherwise, but people really could be so very nice.

'Now are you sure you don't want us to call an ambulance?' he checked.

'I think we should,' Gladys had interjected. 'I mean, anything could be broken in there. My husband fractured his kneecap just climbing a ladder.'

Minnie, while feeling very sorry for Mr Gladys's pain, had wanted a hole to open up and swallow her. 'I'm quite sure. I really do feel fine now that I'm getting my breath back.' Still not strictly true, but she really couldn't be going off to hospital. She had so many other plans for today.

The assistant had returned with Gladys's water. 'Is there someone I can call for you, Mrs Ryan? Or would you like me to phone a taxi to take you home?' He must have remembered her name from the order she'd collected.

She'd thought about that for a second. She really hadn't the strength to be walking all the way home with a sore hip and stinging knees, so a warm taxi had sounded just perfect. 'That would be lovely, thank you.'

Minnie had resolved to bake a delicious big cake and on the first day the shop was open after the New Year, and bring it with a bottle of wine for this chap who'd been so helpful.

'I'll just wait and get the taxi with you,' Gladys had announced. 'You know, just to get you home safe, Minnie.'

And that's what she'd done – shared the taxi home and then hadn't batted an eye as Minnie had paid for it. Not that she'd minded in the least. She'd been grateful for Gladys's assistance, no matter how loud it was.

As Gladys had set off for her own house, Minnie had walked slowly up the path and breathed a sigh of relief when she managed to get herself and her bags through the door. It certainly hadn't gone as planned, but she'd accomplished her tasks one way or another, and she had the gift, her shopping, and herself back in one piece. If you didn't count the crushed shortbread.

After setting her bags down, she'd gone into the kitchen and told Henry all about what had happened. She'd put it down to her broken sleep last night, and he'd agreed with her that a nap would make her feel right as rain. However, now, as she rolled over onto another bruise, she wasn't sure that had been completely accurate because her bones were still aching. There would be no giving in to this though. Minnie Ryan had not lived to seventy-eight years of age without learning a thing or two about the necessity to brush obstacles out of the way and just get on with things.

As she mulled that over, she realised she'd forgotten to show Henry the flask she'd bought for Gino, but she was too exhausted to get up and do it right now, and besides, it was all wrapped up. He'd see it later, she told herself, as she pulled her blanket up around her shoulders and closed her eyes, ready to let sleep take her for a little while. As often happened, that was when her memories were at their most vivid, and like the opening scenes of a movie, she saw another night come to life in her mind.

It was a few years after their first visit to Gino's and they'd already moved out to the South Side of the city. They still went to Gino's every Hogmanay, but money still didn't stretch to eating out any more than that. It was tight, what with four boys between ten and thirteen, but they were managing, mainly thanks to the promotion Henry had got when he'd finished his latest round of night school qualifications and his last stretch of training. He was a fully-fledged planning officer for the city council now, and she was proud as punch of him. She had her own job too, working as an auxiliary in the school that the boys went to, taking care of the children when they were sick and supporting the teachers in whatever way they needed. She loved that job, especially as it allowed her to be on the same schedule as the boys.

The downside, though, was that when one of the kids picked up a bug, it went round the school like wildfire, and one year they'd found that out to their cost.

Eric had been the first one to go down with the flu at Christmas, and then Roger, Robert and Charlie had succumbed to it, one a day over the next week. Minnie was next to take to her bed, in a shudder of sweats and coughs and limbs that ached even under the lightest touch, but still getting up every hour or so to check on her boys and pat their foreheads with cloths that had been dampened by cold water from the tap.

Henry had wanted to help, but she'd shooed him off. He was the main breadwinner, and they couldn't have him going on the sick and losing half his wages, so she didn't want him anywhere near them.

On the 31st, their fevers were peaking, and Minnie had spoken to Henry from the top step of the stairs, the enforced invisible barrier between their two worlds this week. He'd been sleeping on the couch since Boxing Day and she knew it killed him not to be able to share her bed and take care of her. That's who Henry Ryan had always been – the man who took care of his family.

'I'm so sorry, love, but there's no way any of us sickly ones can go out tonight. We're weak as kittens and I couldn't live with myself if I passed it on to anyone else.' She didn't say what else she was thinking. She remembered well the flu epidemic in 1968 and the lives that were taken. This time around, she'd been worried sick for her boys, and was overcome with relief that they seemed to be on the other side of it now.

They both were. 'All that matters is that you and the boys see this damned infection off, Minnie. Don't you worry about a thing, my love. There will be plenty more nights for dancing. Now, go back to your bed and I'll go over and see the Morettis tomorrow – I'll take that bottle of whisky you bought me for Christmas and share a dram with Gino.'

A few hours later, Minnie had listened as the church bells rang outside and the streets filled with people cheering the new year. She got up to shout Happy New Year down to Henry, then went to say the same to her boys. Eric was already feeling so much better, and he sang along to the music that rang out from open windows, and listened as strangers chatted as they went on their way to 'first foot' their loved ones, an old tradition that claimed if a tall, dark man bearing gifts – usually coal or cake in the old days – was the first person over the threshold after the bells, it would bring good luck to the household for the year to come.

It was about an hour later, when Minnie had heard a banging at the door and rose herself from the bed, then crouched at the top of the stairs as Henry had answered it.

She had recognised the voice of the visitor immediately.

'My friend!' the voice with the melodic accent had boomed. 'We were worried when you didn't join us tonight, so here I am. Our party is fading now, and Alicia insisted I come and check on you. Tell me everything is okay with you?'

The happiness in Henry's voice had made her heart soar, as he welcomed Gino in and explained that the boys and Minnie were sick, and that he'd planned to go over to visit the Morettis the next day. He'd poured those drams, and she'd heard Henry open the front door again, so they could share in the revelry and the celebrations outside.

'You know, Gino, it's fair moved me that you came all the way here to check on us,' her husband had told his friend.

Minnie had just been thinking the very same thing.

'And you would do the same for me,' Gino had responded. 'Because we both know that friendships last long after midnight.'

Now, years later, even as she once again lay in bed with aching bones, she knew that was true. They'd never missed another New Year's Eve in all the decades since that night. And Minnie was determined that tonight wasn't going to be any different.

2 P.M. – 4 P.M.

13

AILISH

'Okay, so there are only two rules in the Makeover Club. We don't talk about cancer or ex-husbands,' Gwen proclaimed, as Rhonda manoeuvred the car into a parking space outside the trendy new boutique that had just opened on Ingram Street, ironically only a five-minute stroll to Gino's restaurant. A whole net of butterflies let loose in Ailish's stomach, a mixture of dread and resistance, but now joined by an undeniable flutter of excitement too.

They piled out of the car, and Ailish grabbed the wheelchair from the boot. Gwen had insisted that she didn't need it, but the others argued that it would at least conserve her strength for tonight. That had won her over.

'Right, driver, expensive shops please,' Gwen demanded, as soon as she was in the chair and ready to go.

'She was less demanding when she was at death's door,' Rhonda quipped, making Gwen giggle, and Ailish felt her heart soar.

She wasn't one for swearing, but fuck it. Fuck it all. Gwen was right. No ex-husbands. No cancer. Just the three of them, having an unexpected day together, and they were going to bloody well make the most of it. If Gwen could raise her spirits and forget her woes, then Ailish could damn well do it too. Just as long as she could find something to squeeze her arse into. It had been a very real obstacle to the plan tonight.

'I have nothing to wear,' Ailish had announced earlier, after she'd finally, reluctantly, agreed to go out tonight. Gwen's glitzy career in interior design meant she already had a wardrobe full of gorgeous outfits (all of which would be way too small for Ailish), and Rhonda had mentioned earlier that she had already bought a beautiful dress for tonight. So that just left Ailish…

'Of course you do,' Rhonda argued. 'Just wear whatever you wore last year.'

'Snoopy pyjamas and socks with individual stripy toes. You all came and stayed at my house, remember?'

They did. It had been the first Hogmanay post-separation, and the removal men were coming two days later to pack up her stuff and move her out of the family home of her dreams, to a soulless box two miles away. Ailish had dug her heels in about going out and reliving the nightmare of the previous New Year's Eve, and on that occasion, they'd gone along with her. However, this year was a different story.

'Good point. Snoopy isn't exactly high fashion this season,' Gwen had agreed.

'And all my old clothes don't fit me any more since I discovered the Quality Street diet. I've gone up two sizes.'

'Only one thing for it then,' Rhonda was already scheming. 'We need to go now.'

'Go where?' Ailish had asked, playing with the crust of her pizza slice.

Another conspiratorial look had passed between Rhonda and Gwen. 'Well, the thing is,' Rhonda had begun, 'when I was up guarding Gwen against life-threatening injuries while she showered, we were discussing how maybe a trip might be in order.'

Rhonda was clearly squirming, so Ailish was intrigued. 'A trip where?'

Gwen had interjected. 'We can't drag this out. Pull the Band-Aid right off, Rhonda.'

Rhonda threw her hands up. 'Okay, fine. Right. Well, Gwen needs a wee post-hospital makeover to get her ready for tonight, so while we're there, we thought that... Aw, bugger, I'm just going to say it. The truth is, and this comes from a place of love – Ailish, you look awful. You've got roots the size of my wrists, your skin hasn't seen moisturiser in months and you're bordering on a unibrow up there. So I called the manager at one of my salons and they're fitting us in for hair and make-up at three o'clock. And while we're there, they'll take a Flymo to those eyebrows.'

Ailish's first reaction had been outraged indignation. 'What does it matter how I look? It hasn't exactly been one of my priorities over the last year.'

Gwen had nodded thoughtfully and Ailish thought she was about to get a win. Surely if anyone could understand how trivial and unnecessary all that surface-level stuff was, it would be Gwen. 'We understand.'

Ailish had wanted to cheer, until her friend went on...

'But the reality is, Rhonda and I are incredibly shallow and we're the ones that have to look at you. So we're going to sort you out and you don't have a choice in the matter. It's tough love, doll.'

'And if we leave now, we can nip into the boutique next door to the salon and pick you up something to wear,' Rhonda had said. 'I'm always in there and they've got lovely stuff. It's actually where I bought my dress for tonight, so I need to pick it up anyway.'

'Yes! Perfect plan. That's what we'll do,' Gwen had agreed. Ailish had opened her mouth to object, but Gwen spotted it and came back with, 'And you can't say no to me, because you know... cancer.'

Ailish had winced. 'Seriously? Are you still doing that? Stop with the blackmail. My heart can't take it.'

Gwen's grin had stretched from ear to ear. 'But you're going to say yes, aren't you? Because you love me?'

Ailish threw down her pizza crust. 'Aaaargh. I give in. Yes. Okay. But as soon as you fully recover, I'm getting new pals.' Two could play at that game. And, of course, Gwen knew she was joking and let out a cackle of triumphant laughter.

That's why, at half past two in the afternoon, they were now trooping into a way too trendy boutique, with Ailish panicking because she was going to be trying on clothes, and she knew she was wearing huge, grey knickers and a bra that she'd fished out from under the dining table this morning. She couldn't help thinking that wasn't exactly the usual attire of this place's clientele.

As soon as they got in, Rhonda took charge. It was absolutely no surprise that she'd been in here many times, given the immediate proximity to her salon and a shopping habit that bordered on requiring therapy.

'Chanel!' she greeted the owner with a hug. 'These are my pals, Gwen and Ailish. Girls, this is Chanel.'

The very tanned, glamorous Chanel flicked her waist-length platinum hair back from a face that had impossibly full lips and cheekbones like sausages, and extended a hand past her voluptuous double-G chest and miniscule waist as she greeted them. Ailish felt her grey pants curl up and die.

'Right, Chanel, I need to pick up my frock for tonight. But that aside, and much more importantly, you're on a mission. This one here,' Rhonda gestured to Ailish, 'Size...'

'Sixteen,' Ailish replied. Her weight had fluctuated all of her life, so she didn't mind in the least that she was bigger than before. She'd spent her whole life encouraging Emmy to have a positive body image no matter her size, and she truly believed in that.

'Size sixteen, and she needs something fabulous to wear tonight. She wants to look like a goddess.'

'I don't,' Ailish clarified. 'I want to stay on my couch. But these two are forcing me to go out. It's getting close to a hostage situation at this stage. However, if I'm going to go, I may as well look like a goddess, apparently.' She knew she was rambling. She always did that when she was nervous.

Chanel scanned her from top to toe, and Ailish began to sweat. Just when she was sure she was about to be written off as a lost cause, Chanel clapped her hands. 'I've got just the thing. Come with me.'

Ailish was outnumbered and too defeated to object, so she did as she was told. Chanel led her to a very glamorous changing area, then disappeared and came back two minutes later with a red sequinned dress.

The problem was immediately obvious to Ailish. 'There's no way I'm fitting into that.'

'Trust me. I'll leave you to change into it, but shout when you need me to do up the zip.'

Off she went, and Ailish rested her forehead against the wall of the changing rooms. This was going to be embarrassing. Humiliating. But she was worried that if she didn't try, Rhonda and Gwen would storm the cubicle, so, reluctantly, she stripped off her jeans with the elasticated waist, and the jumper that had seen better days, averting her eyes from the underwear calamity underneath.

She took the dress from its hanger and carefully, terrified she'd rip something – maybe the fabric or a hamstring – she stepped into it and pulled it up. There was no denying it was gorgeous. It had the kind of shoulder pads she'd worn in the eighties, and a deep V at the front, then a body-skimming A-line skirt that dropped from right below her bust. So far, so good... if it weren't for the fact that when she turned around, there was a ten-inch gape where the zipper was supposed to close.

'How are you getting on in there?' Chanel chirped from the other side of the curtain.

'It doesn't fit, Chanel.'

'Okay, coming in.'

Ailish took a step backwards as Chanel entered, her enhanced boobs arriving a solid second before the rest of her.

'Right, turn around and let me zip it...'

'There's no point, Chanel. It'll never close and I don't want to damage the dress.'

'There goes the words of someone who's never worn a dress with inner corsetry before. Right, turn around and put your hands on the wall.'

'Am I under arrest?' Ailish fought off an urge to giggle. This was ridiculous. But she did it anyway.

Chanel stood behind her, Ailish felt an almighty tug and then a miracle happened. An actual miracle. The zipper rose, and parts of her body sucked right back inside her torso. She was fairly sure her belly button was now nestled beside a kidney. As she turned around and stared in the mirror, Ailish gasped. It fitted. Not only that, it was spectacular. Stunning. She still didn't want to go out tonight, but that was now because she just wanted to stand here for hours and look at her reflection in the mirror. How long was it since she'd worn something that came even close to making her look as good as this?

'Holy Kardashian,' a new voice exhaled, and Ailish realised that both of her friends were now peeking round the curtain.

Rhonda went on, 'If you don't take that, I'm giving up on you altogether.'

'There's no way I can afford—'

Chanel got in there quickly. 'It's 60 per cent off in the sale because it was Christmas stock. No one is going to be wearing red dresses in January. And I'll throw in some gorgeous lingerie to wear under it for free.'

There was nothing else to be said.

Ten minutes later, Ailish and her grey undies were on the way out of the shop, clutching the most expensive wardrobe purchase of her life – even with the 60 per cent off! Come to think of it, her wedding dress had been more expensive and look how that turned out. Hopefully the divorce-day dress would have a happier ending.

'Okay, Makeover Club, stage two,' Rhonda announced as they entered her glam, gorgeous salon next door.

The manager, Alexis, was ready and waiting for them. 'Hi boss,' she greeted Rhonda first, before turning to Gwen and Ailish. They'd met a few times over the years, so there was no need for introductions. 'Great to see you, ladies! We're all set up for you. If you want to head over to the hair chairs, I'll organise drinks. Cocktail or mocktail?'

'Mocktail,' Rhonda answered first. 'I'm driving. You, Ails?'

Screw it, Ailish decided, her resistance to this whole plan swept away by the hem of a sparkly red frock. 'Cocktail,' she announced to a cheer from the others.

'Me too,' Gwen requested, then spotted Ailish and Rhonda's surprise.

'What? It's one drink. The doctor didn't say I couldn't. It's not going to kill me. Do I need to play the C card again?'

'Don't you dare,' Ailish warned her, shaking her head. 'If I'm playing by the Makeover Club rules, so are you. One more attempt at emotional blackmail and I'm going to start listing all Eric's pros and cons. Wait until I get to the bit where he picked his toenails in bed.'

Gwen feigned a gagging motion, and Ailish knew they'd reached a truce. For now.

Beverage orders placed, they followed instructions to a row of three leather chairs.

A stylist who introduced herself as Roxy, appeared behind her and immediately began studying Ailish's hair. 'What would you like me to do today?' she asked.

Ailish had absolutely no idea, so she was resigned to her fate when Rhonda broke off from the discussion she was having with a handsome stylist called Kaden about the look she was going for, and piped in with, 'Colour, cut and take ten years off her.'

Roxy giggled, 'Not sure that's on the price list, but I'll give it my best shot.'

Ailish liked her immediately. 'You know what, Roxy, just do whatever you like. I'm going to leave it completely up to you.'

'Ooooh, I love it when a client says that. Let's get you all over to the basins.'

Ailish did as she was told, no longer even pretending to object. At the basins, the three of them chatted away to the juniors who washed their hair, before heading back to the big leather chairs, where their drinks were waiting for them.

Roxy got to work on her, while Kaden combed out Rhonda's waves, and Alexis began working her magic on Gwen. They made small talk for a while, before Alexis hit on the all-important question.

'So, where are you ladies off to tonight, then?' she asked, as she sliced Gwen's hair into sections with her comb, then pulled the strands up and cut into them with speed and precision.

'Gino's. Just along the road.'

Alexis nodded. 'I know it. We used to go there sometimes on the weekend after work, before...' She thought about it. 'Before the pandemic, I guess. Not sure why we haven't been for a while. Out of the habit, I suppose. And plus, half of the younger ones in here haven't eaten a carb in years. They'd probably faint at the sight of pasta. We did love it when we went there. It was always a great night.'

Gwen agreed with her. 'It always is. We've gone there on Hogmanay almost every year since we were teenagers.'

'Really? Oh, you must have some great stories,' Alexis teased, grinning.

Rhonda got in on the act. 'Yeah, there was the year that...' And off she went, for a good ten minutes, sharing stories of their nights out and exploits, with Gwen chiming in. They were laughing so much, it wasn't until the story of the time that Rhonda had been dancing on a table at midnight and by 2 a.m. was in the X-ray department of Glasgow Central because she'd fallen off it and broken three toes, that they realised Ailish hadn't joined in.

Gwen rounded on her. 'What are you thinking about, Ailish? Tell me it's not that bloody ex-husband.'

'It's not, I promise. I was just thinking about...' She stopped, suddenly realising that she didn't want to put this out there. It was stupid. Embarrassing.

'About what?' Gwen pressed.

Ailish desperately tried to come up with something else that was on topic but drew a blank. She shouldn't have had that cocktail.

'Okay, it may have crossed my mind how different life might have been if I'd made a different choice on that first night we went to Gino's.'

'I think about that too,' Gwen agreed. 'I think you might have lost your mind, to be honest.'

From the third chair in the row, Rhonda emitted a confused, 'Lost her mind about what?'

Gwen turned to her in surprise. 'Dario!'

Rhonda was clearly none the wiser. 'Nope, I still have no idea what you're talking about. What happened with Dario?'

Ailish felt the rise of the red rash that always crept up her neck in times of embarrassment. 'Och, it's a long story. There's no point dragging it all up again.'

Rhonda leaned forward. 'Is it gossipy, surprising, and does it end with a sexual encounter?'

Ailish mentally ticked all of the things on that list. 'It is.'

'Then I'd like details please. Alexis, I think I'm going to need another mocktail.'

14

EMMY

The time between her tea break and her mid-shift break had felt like a week and a half, and it had been made even later by Mrs Bennet in bed four going for a wander that resulted in every member of staff on the ward searching for her for twenty minutes. In the end, they played back the cameras at the doors of the ward, and spotted that she'd managed to sneak out by loitering at the door until someone was buzzed in. Then she'd gaily swerved past them and done a runner. Or rather, a particularly nifty slow shuffle in her furry slippers. After some very anxious minutes, Emmy had had a hunch, and headed to the hospital café on the ground floor, where, yes, there was Mrs Bennet, in her dressing gown and slippers, enjoying a nice cup of tea and a ginger slice.

She'd gently steered her back upstairs, just in time to referee a disagreement between two patients about what they should watch on the TV in the day room and then speak to a concerned relative who'd called in for a progress report on their grandmother. Emmy never rushed family members off the phone, taking all the time they needed to feel reassured, because she knew just how upset she would be if anything happened to Minnie.

In the end, it was almost half past three by the time she managed to get away, and she went straight to the staffroom for her car keys and phone. She switched the handset on and shoved it in her pocket.

Yvie's and Keli's breaks were staggered, so Yvie came in right behind her, while Keli was just about to go back onto the ward.

'You're not actually going to check up on him, are you?' Yvie asked, and Emmy felt real gratitude for the concern that was written all over her friend's face. However, she still had to do this because the suspicion was eating away at her. This was the first time in her life she'd ever felt this kind of emotion and she was hating every second of it.

'I am. I need to, Yvie. And I know that makes me a terrible person, but there it is. If I'm wrong, then I'll eat humble pie...'

'And if you're right?' Keli asked her, clearly just as concerned.

'Then I'll cry. For a long time. And maybe slash his tyres, but it depends if there's witnesses.'

Her attempt to make a joke was fooling neither of them.

'Look, I'll come with you,' Yvie offered. 'I don't want you to do this on your own and if I stay here, I'll only eat the rest of that yule log, so you're saving me from myself.'

Emmy appreciated the offer more than she could say. 'Really? You don't mind? Okay, well...' She was about to say 'Let's go,' when the phone sprang to life in her pocket. For a split second, she hoped it was a message from Cormac, saying something that would set her mind at ease, quell all her fears and put her back into a bubble of bliss and security about their relationship.

But no, it wasn't Cormac.

'Oh bollocks,' she murmured. 'It's a text from my dad.' Her first instinct was to ignore it, but she couldn't bring herself to blank him.

'Honest to God, this day...' she said, as she clicked to open it.

HEY LOVE IM DOWNSTAIRS IN THE CANTEEN
IF YOU GET A MINUTE CAN YOU POP DOWN
VERY URGENT LOVE DAD

He had obviously taken to using the caps button these days. Quite a surprise that his thirty-four-year-old mistress hadn't taken a moment to point out to him that CAPS were the equivalent of shouting. Or maybe she had, and that was the point.

'We're going to have to hold off on the boyfriend check,' she told Yvie. 'My dad's downstairs and wants to talk to me. The man has spent the last two years avoiding any kind of meaningful conversation with me and now he wants to be my best friend and needs me to sort out his problems with his love life. When did my father become a needy teenager? I feel like I'm stuck in one of those movies where the kids and adults swap places.' She tossed her car keys back into her locker and then, as she walked past them, kissed Yvie on the cheek and then did the same to Keli. 'You're both awesome and thanks for listening to me today. But if I don't come back, it's because I'm tired of all my fricking drama and you'll find me in a beach hut in Hawaii.'

There was only a half joke in that. Emmy wasn't predisposed to emotional turmoil. All her life, she'd had lovely, stable, sweet grandparents who'd made so much time for her. And she'd had happily married, maybe a little unexciting, parents who never made her feel anything but loved and secure until exactly two years ago today when it had all gone to shit. All this craziness today was making her want to run for the hills. Or some beach hut by the ocean.

The elevator doors on her floor were just about to close when she stuck her hand in, reopened them and jumped in, much to the annoyance of an elderly gent, who rolled his eyes and sighed. Emmy wanted to point out to him that if the worst thing that happened to him today was his lift getting held up by two and a half seconds, he had hee-haw to moan about. Instead, she clamped her mouth shut and said nothing, her stomach churning with the anxiety of it all.

When she reached the canteen on the ground floor, it wasn't too busy, because it was between the lunchtime rush, the dinner rush and the pre-afternoon visiting rush, so she spotted her dad at a corner table straight away.

On the way to him, she stopped at the counter, where Joanie, the lovely canteen supervisor was placing a Victoria sponge under a glass dome.

'Joanie, can I have a cappuccino, please?' Emmy asked. 'And a tuna sandwich, please.' The realisation that she hadn't eaten since breakfast had just reached her stomach and it was rumbling.

Joanie was already on the case, and it was only a couple of minutes before she handed over Emmy's order. 'There you go, pet. Just tap your card on the machine there. And Happy New Year when it comes. Anything nice planned?'

It was the same conversation that half of the country would be having today and Emmy appreciated the normality of it. 'Nothing exciting. Just... family stuff. What about you, Joanie?'

'We've got the karaoke machine set up at my sister's house and she's been making sandwiches and sausage rolls since dawn. If the whole street doesn't turn up, she'll be gutted.'

That made Emmy laugh. 'Well, if they don't, it'll be their loss.'

'Aye, that's what I said because her and I are like Beyoncé and Miley Cyrus when we get started on that thing.'

'I bet you are. Have a brilliant night, Joanie, and thanks for this.'

Heart rate reduced a little by Joanie's chat, she took her coffee and sandwich over to her dad's table. He had his back to her, so he didn't spot her until she came up beside him and then pulled out the chair opposite him.

'Dad, what are you doing here? You know I don't want to get in the middle of this situation with Mum.'

'I know, but, Emmy, you're the only person whose opinions mean something here and I need help on what to do. Clearly, I've messed up so much and I don't want to do the wrong thing again.'

The sight of him made her feel a twinge of compassion. He was still undeniably rocking the silver-fox thing – as witnessed by the fact that Joanie's gaze had been fixed on him since Emmy left the counter, and now she was out on the floor, on the pretext of wiping tables, trying to get a better gauge of what was going on. This whole hospital ran on care, compassion and gossip and Joanie excelled in all three.

However, dashing looks aside, she couldn't help notice that her dad's forehead was etched with deep lines, he was still unshaven and the stress was almost seeping out of his pores.

Emmy immediately slid several notches down the irritated scale. 'Okay, well, I've only got another half an hour on my break, Dad, so I don't have long.'

'Right.' He took a deep breath. 'I went to your mum's new flat. It was the forwarding address she gave when we sold the house, so I knew where it was.'

No wonder he looked stressed.

'I'm scared to ask, but I take it by the fact that you're sitting here, it didn't go well?'

'She wasn't in.'

Oh. That was a bit of an anticlimax. Her emotions were struggling to cope with the peaks and troughs of this meeting, and she'd only just sat down.

'But I spoke to her...'

'I thought you said she wasn't in?'

'She wasn't. I spoke to her through the doorbell.'

Emmy closed her eyes for a second of reprieve. This was unbelievable. What should have been a cataclysmic point in her parents' relationship, and it was conducted via doorbell. Great.

'So what was the upshot of that then?' she probed.

'Well, she said she was out with Rhonda and Gwen, so I asked her when she'd be back and told her I needed to speak to her and she basically told me to sod off.'

Emmy felt the corners of her mouth begin to twitch and there was a tiny swell of admiration for her mum there. The old Ailish would never have done something like that. Throughout their entire marriage, her mum had been absolutely devoted to her dad, and she'd always put him first. This was Ailish Mark Two, and Emmy wholeheartedly approved. Besides, if she was with Aunt Rhonda and Aunt Gwen, she must still be on Gwen's ward in the other wing of the hospital, not, as her dad clearly imagined, out gallivanting somewhere getting fired up for a big night out.

Her dad put on his best 'taking action' face. 'I think the only answer is to go and sit outside her front door until she comes back.'

'You can't do that, Dad. That's stalking. You'll get arrested.'

'Exactly. Which is why I need you to call her to find out where she'll be tonight.'

Bugger, she'd walked right into that one.

'No. I'm not getting involved. I told you that you need to sort this out for yourself.'

'I understand. I do. I'll just wait it out at her apartment right enough then, because this is a conversation I want to have face to face and I need to do it today.'

Ah, the manipulation. Emmy saw it loud and clear, but at the same time, she didn't relish two of the possible outcomes of that decision: either Dad getting hoicked off to the slammer after some concerned neighbour reported him for suspicious behaviour or – more importantly – Mum getting ambushed when she got home.

'Okay, I tell you what. I'll find out if she'll be around later, and then you can call her and ask to see her. That's as much as I'm doing, Dad, so don't ask for any more and don't you dare tell Mum I helped you. I'm not taking sides in this, although, if I was, it would obviously be Mum's.'

Much as she loved him, she still wasn't letting him get away with what he'd done.

Putting her tuna sandwich down, she pulled her phone out of her pocket and texted...

> Hey mum, hope Aunt Gwen is doing well today. I was thinking about popping over tonight while Cormac is at work. Are you going to be in?

She tried to tell herself she wasn't doing a terrible thing, because she'd already tentatively suggested that she might join her mum on the couch later if she didn't have other plans and wasn't too tired after work.

Her mum's reply was almost instant.

> Spooky! I was just about to call you. Gwen got discharged and we're in the hairdressers' because we've decided to go out tonight. Very welcome to join us? Xx

What? Now she was intrigued. And also, obviously, very happy that Aunt Gwen must be out of the hospital. Her mum must be so relieved.

> I don't think I'll make it, Mum – I don't want to go out to party in case Cormac gets finished early. Where are you going?

Okay, so it wasn't strictly true, but it was close. Kind of.

> You'll never believe it – they've talked me into going to Gino's. Reluctant, but actually quite excited now. Love you. Will call you at midnight. Xx

If her mum had walked into the canteen right now and did a duet to 'All the Single Ladies' with Joanie behind the counter, Emmy wouldn't have been more gobsmacked. She never thought her mum would ever step foot in that restaurant again – not after what had happened there.

'What is it?' Her dad's voice cut through her thoughts and almost made her jump. She'd been so focused on her mum's texts, she'd forgotten he was there.

'Okay, Dad, bad news I'm afraid. Mum won't be back home tonight. She's going out with Rhonda and Gwen.' That was all he needed to know.

'Going out where?' he shot back, clearly as surprised as she was. He was fully aware that her mum had lost her zest for life since the divorce.

'I don't know,' she lied.

But he knew her too well to get away with that.

'Darling... There's only one place the three of them would go on New Year's Eve and after what happened, I don't think they'd go there.' He was staring at her intently as he spoke. 'They wouldn't, would they?'

He hadn't even asked a clear bloody question, but they both knew exactly what he was referring to. Jesus, he was using reverse psychology on her and it was working. She was rubbish at this. And she must have blinked or something because the next thing, his eyes widened.

'They are. That's where they're going. Well, I'll be damned, they're going to Gino's,' he exclaimed.

How the hell did he do that? This was next level Paul McKenna mind-reading stuff. Urgh.

Annoyed with herself, although she didn't quite understand how that had just happened, Emmy tried to pull back some girl-code credibility. 'Dad, I'm not going to tell you where they're going. But even if you find out where they are, I want you to promise me that you won't go. Let Mum have her night out. She deserves it.'

'Of course, yes. I promise.'

As she got up to leave, her break over, she decided that she didn't believe him for a second.

15

DARIO

The lunch service in the restaurant had been busy, mostly with workers from nearby offices that had knocked off early because it was the last day of the year, and tourists that had travelled to the city to revel in the celebrations tonight. There were still a few stragglers sitting at tables, making the most of their afternoon off, but Dario knew from experience that they would drift away soon, taking advantage of the interlude before the parties started.

When he and Bruno were kids, his mamma, Alicia, had always insisted that they sleep in the afternoons on New Year's Eve so that they would have the energy to stay up way past their bedtimes. Years later, when he and Bruno were teenagers and Carlo came along, she did the same with his youngest brother. His father used to say it was the only day of the year that the Scots adopted a Mediterranean schedule: a siesta in the afternoon, followed by dinner late in the evening, usually around 10 p.m., which geared them up for their riotous celebrations at 'the bells' and the parties that would last long into the early hours of the new year. For those hours before dawn, they didn't have a care in the world. His mother would spin around the room, laughing and dancing with everyone she passed. His dad would climb on a chair and sing at the top of his voice. And everyone would vow that the days to come would be better than the ones that went before.

Over the years, timings had changed a little, but the restaurant's dinner sitting was still later than usual on the 31st, starting at 8 p.m. instead of six o'clock. That gave plenty of time for food, for drinks, and for Gino to get the music cranked up and get the guests on their feet to dance their way into the New Year. And it never got old. Not one minute of it. Somehow, Dario's mind still refused to accept that tonight would be the last time he watched his dad in his element like that. The only way to get through this and hold back the waves of devastation that had been ebbing and flowing all day, was to stay busy, keep his mind occupied.

Dario had spent the busiest part of the lunch service out on the floor, but when the buzz died down, he'd sought refuge in the office, checking and rechecking the figures from every angle. The days to come definitely weren't going to be better than the ones that went before, but he was going to do everything he could to ease the pain for those around him. He'd meant what he'd said to Sonya. He'd make sure she had a job and an income for as long as she needed it, even if he was paying it out of his own pocket. As for the rest of their employees, the waiting staff were mostly students who worked here part-time, so he knew they'd have no problems picking up other work, and he'd give them stellar references and a month's wages to tide them over until they landed new jobs.

In the kitchen, Matty ran a pretty tight ship, with just two sous-chefs and a pot washer who kept the place gleaming. Again, there were always jobs out there for reliable, talented workers with good references, so he knew that closing down the business wouldn't change their lives.

Matty was another story. Sonya had managed to get him back in the kitchen as promised, but Dario knew that the storm wasn't over. There was a whole lot of banging and swearing coming through the wall that separated the kitchen from the office, so Dario was avoiding him for now, grateful that the main restaurant was too far away for the noise to be heard.

He put his pen down on the desk, and shoved the calculator away, then picked up the mug of coffee Sonya had brought in just a few minutes before, on her way out the back for a cigarette.

'Here you go, big yin. If you want me to shove a couple of shots of something strong in it, I won't judge you,' she'd said, as she placed it down on the desk. As always, especially when she was worried about something, her perpetual ranting was on overdrive. 'If you're looking for me, I'll be outside the back door, chain smoking and plotting ways to force my landlord not to sell my flat. In the old days, I'd have offered sexual favours, but I think that time has passed. He's about 106 and it would kill him. Actually, maybe that's worth a go.' She'd flitted seamlessly from one train of thought to another. 'Anyway, what time is your dad coming in?'

Dario had glanced at the clock on the wall. 'I'm not sure but probably about four o'clock.' Gino didn't keep him informed of his schedule – just came and went whenever he pleased.

'Right, well I'll go and have my breakdown over him being devastated now, and then I can put a brave face on when he needs me,' Sonya had said, before going out as she came in, at Road Runner speed and trailing a cloud of nervous energy behind her.

Peace restored now, Dario took a sip of the warm liquid and then reached down to his bottom desk drawer and opened it. There was a picture there. His mum and dad, next to him on the day he left school.

He could remember it all like it was yesterday. He'd been about seventeen, and he'd already worked in the restaurant for years, first washing dishes in the kitchen, and then, when he hit his teens, he was allowed out on the floor to serve guests. Dario had soon realised he preferred the seclusion of the kitchen and the artistry of the food. When the time had come for him to make his life choices, there was never an option to do anything other than carry on the legacy that his parents had created from nothing but dreams and graft.

All his life, he'd heard Gino tell everyone who would listen that he was the luckiest man in the world. He had his restaurant, his family and the most gracious woman on earth. What more could he ever want in life?

Only one thing, Dario realised now. For his blessings to last until the day he died.

The door opened again, and Nicky popped her head in. 'That's the worst of the madness over out there, so I'm going to nip home for a couple of hours to restore my fabulousness. How're you holding up? Anything to report?' She spotted what he was holding in his hands and came all the way into the office, letting the door close behind her. 'Bloody hell, it's a long time since I saw that photograph.'

'I was thinking the same thing,' Dario told her, with a sad smile, as he placed the wooden frame down on the desk, glad of the interruption from his thoughts.

'You all looked so happy there. And your mum...' Nicky peered at the image. 'I've always thought she looked like Sophia Loren. Your dad definitely got lucky the day he found her. And look at you, all smiles and skinny legs.'

'Yeah, I still had them when we married, so they must have worked for you,' he teased, before his eyes drifted back to the photo. 'You know, I'm not sure that I was really happy that day. All my mates were going off on holiday or to start jobs and figure their lives out, but mine was all a foregone conclusion. Choices didn't factor into any of it.' He paused, surprised at himself. 'I don't know that I've ever said that out loud before.'

'So let me ask you,' Nicky said, moving from standing beside him, back to the chair she'd been sitting in earlier. 'If you had to go back, would you do it all again? Make all the same decisions?'

'Some of them. Maybe not all.'

They let that sit between for a few seconds, until Nicky let out a slow, meaningful sigh. 'Want to know what I think?'

'I don't think so. The freedom to ignore your thoughts was one of the perks of the divorce,' he joked, trying to cover up an uncomfortable feeling that he wouldn't like what she had to say.

'True, but being allowed to piss you off is one of my perks, so I'm going for it anyway.' She took a breath. 'But I want you to remember that all this comes from a loving place in my heart.'

'Oh God. I've never wanted someone to press a fire alarm more than I do right now.'

That didn't dissuade her. 'I think that you've spent your whole life doing what was expected of you, Dario. I think you trained as a chef, because it was what your parents wanted. I think you went into the family business because it was always taken for granted that you would. I think you worked harder than was asked of you, because you didn't want to let anyone down. And I think you've sacrificed so many other things along the way, including our marriage and time with our kids. I don't think any of that was ever a conscious choice, but that was the way it all turned out.'

He thought about arguing, but he didn't have to dig too deep to know that there was some truth to what she said.

'I really hate it when you're even partially right,' he shot back, making her smile.

'I know,' she said, her grin getting wider. 'Another perk of the divorce for me. I get to be way smarter than you and I don't have to pretend otherwise.'

Even as the barb made him wince, he knew that he'd miss this. Not many people got to see their best mate every single day, and have her point out his flaws in a way that made him laugh, even in the shittiest of times.

'The thing was I didn't see any of it at the time. I just went with it all, told myself that it was just the way it was. I'd grown up with a dad that worked day and night and it was just bred into me. That's just the way it was done. My brothers are exactly the same.'

'I know. And I worry about them too. Bruno is on his third wife...' Bruno was the middle brother, the one who'd moved to Asia a decade ago to manage a fabulous restaurant on an island resort, '...and Carlo is lucky that Yvie has the patience of a saint. I don't think any of you ever learned that there's more to life than work. It was okay for your dad, because him and your mum were true partners in it all, but for you... You just worked a million hours a week and we all had to fit around you. Around this place. Sometimes I used to wish that you came home late and skipped out on holidays because you had a bit on the side. At least that I could compete with.'

'For what it's worth, I'm sorry,' he admitted.

'I know. I am too. But maybe... don't shoot me... maybe this is a chance for you to make some of your own decisions, Dario. Start living life on your own terms. At the risk of sounding like one of those shite notepad mottos, life's too short to waste.'

He took in the poignancy of her words, the sincerity in her voice, right up until she added, 'And at this rate, you're going to die a lonely old man who hasn't had sex for decades, so maybe it's time you started prioritising finding someone to spend your life with. Have a bit of fun. Live a little.'

'It's been so long since I thought about anything else but keeping this place going that I don't think I remember how.'

'It's easy. I'll draw you pictures,' she quipped, before adding more seriously, 'Look, it's not too late for you to start another life, one that makes you truly happy. Just promise me you'll think about it.'

Before he could answer, the moment was broken by a familiar booming voice out in the restaurant. Dario knew that the owner of it would be greeting the waiting staff and the guests and that any minute now he would work his way back towards the office.

His dad had arrived.

His personal life and his decisions about his future priorities were going to have to wait, because Dario couldn't hold off on breaking the news, or his father's heart, any longer.

16

MINNIE

Friendships last long after midnight...

The memory of Gino's words to Henry were still going around in her head when Minnie woke up after her nap, and for a moment she was back there again, at the top of the stairs, watching her husband and his friend bring in another New Year together. Those had been the best years of her life, when she had her little family all under one roof and all she had to do was love them and take care of them. Why did they have to grow up and leave? Two of her boys were on the other side of the world now, one was hundreds of miles away on the south coast and Eric... Well, that man was still here, but he'd lost direction and she wouldn't admit to anyone except Henry that sometimes she worried he'd never find his way back to being a son that she was proud of. She knew that Henry still had faith in him and that had to be something, because he'd always had a sixth sense about these things.

Just as that thought crossed her mind, she felt a breath on her face and realised Henry had slipped in beside her. A hand reached for hers and she closed her eyes and held it, while his breathing slowed and she sensed that he'd fallen asleep. She'd been about to get up, but this felt too good, too safe and warm, so she was tempted to stay under the blanket for a little while longer, letting her mind go back into the vault of her memories. Sometimes that felt like all she had left. She wondered if Gino felt the same way.

Friendships last long after midnight...

Henry had quoted the same words back to Gino a couple of years later, when he'd broken all the rules of his job for his friend.

It must have been at the end of the seventies, and Henry had done even more years of night school to get another qualification so that he could get promoted within the planning department. 'A senior position would set us up for life, Minnie. We won't have to scrimp the way we've been doing and we might even have a bit extra every month that we can save up for a holiday. And, Minnie, there's a good jump in the pension too. Imagine that. I mean, who'd have thought it, my old dad died when he was fifty-nine, and there's me, I'll have a good pot of savings for when I'm sixty-five. Bloody years away!'

He loved his new role, thrived on the complexity and the responsibility of it, took every decision seriously. Every night he would come home and tell her all about the plans that had crossed his desk that day and she'd happily listen to him all night, as he talked her through the pros and cons of every case.

She was surprised then, a couple of months later, when he'd come home with a frown on his face, his eyes dark with worry.

He'd waited until the boys had their dinner and went off to bed, before he shared the reason why. A new planning application had come to him that afternoon...

'A councillor brought a planning application to me on the hush-hush today. Nothing official, but he wanted it checked out and made it clear that if it was to go ahead, he'd look favourably on it getting passed through quickly. It was from a London-based national restaurant chain. Worth a fortune. They want to build a complex just off Ingram Street, with four or five restaurants in the same building. The thing is, it's a huge bloody place. They'll pack them in.'

Over at the sink, where she was doing the washing up, Minnie brushed the Palmolive soap bubbles off her hands and turned to face him. 'And I'm guessing by your face that you don't approve of this one?'

Henry took a sip of the lager shandy he'd poured just as soon as the boys went upstairs. He never drank on a weekday, so she knew this was serious. 'It's a monstrosity that's totally out of keeping with that part of the city. But more importantly, it's next door to Gino's, love. And to half a dozen other family businesses in that area. It'll ruin them all.'

Minnie fully understood now. She had dried her hands on the dish towel on the hook on the wall, then went to sit next to him, tangled her fingers around his free hand. 'And you don't want that to happen.' It wasn't a question.

He shook his head. 'No. And the way it came to me... well, they've clearly got friends in high places. Whole thing stinks.'

'So what can you do?'

He had stared into his beer for a moment. 'That's the thing I'm torn over. If I push against it, I'll make enemies where I don't want to make them. But on the other hand, if I don't say anything and they somehow manage to find a way to get this through, I'll never forgive myself. I just keep thinking that the businesses that will be affected, well, they deserve to know about this as soon as possible so they can get ahead of it and do everything they can to block it.'

'But you'd be giving away information that should be confidential?'

'I would. I could lose my job if it got out and they knew it was me who'd leaked it.'

Minnie had reached over, traced her finger down his cheek, then leaned in and kissed him. 'You'll do the right the right thing, Henry Ryan. You always do, love.'

Not one bit of her had been surprised when he'd got up about ten minutes later, took his coat from the back of the chair. 'I'll be back soon.' He didn't even have to tell her where he was going.

'Say hello to Gino for me,' she'd told him, with a kiss, as he left.

There had never been any doubt in her mind about what he'd do, but she just had to let him figure it out for himself.

Over the next few weeks, there were reports in the newspapers over the devastation that a rumoured new development would wreak on local businesses in that area, there were petitions with thousands of signatures, and one Gino Moretti, owner of Gino's Trattoria, the man who was leading the campaign to object to the proposals, was even interviewed on the six o'clock news.

Much to the councillor's disgust, the plans were thrown out. A probe into the exposure never ascertained who was responsible for the leak, and everyone went back to their lives and their businesses. And the following Hogmanay, at midnight in Gino's restaurant, after Henry had kissed her and his boys, Gino had come over to him with a glass of whisky and they'd raised a toast to the new year. 'Thank you, my friend. I'll never forget what you did,' he'd said, and only Minnie knew what he was referring to.

Henry had raised his glass. 'What is it you said before, Gino? Some friendships last long after midnight. You're welcome, pal.'

Neither of the men had ever spoken of that again, but every year since, they'd raised the same toast. Now, in the dim light of her bedroom, a tear slid from the corner of Minnie's eye and she brushed it away, chiding herself for being so sentimental. If Henry saw her, he'd kiss her nose and call her a daft old fool.

A pain began to twinge in her hip now, because it had been pressed into the mattress in the same position for too long. Her own fault. She'd tried to stay so very still because she hadn't wanted to disturb Henry, but the soreness was beginning to radiate down her thigh. Reluctantly, she very gently moved her legs off the mattress and found the floor with her feet.

The room was chilly and the blinds were still drawn, so she fumbled for her housecoat, and found it hanging on the back of the door, then slipped it on over her clothes.

Slowly, she went down the stairs, holding on to the banister to steady herself. When she got to the bottom of the stairs, she stayed there for a few minutes, waiting for a sudden wave of light-headedness to pass. Had she eaten today? She really couldn't remember. It was so easy to forget these things when one day blended into another. There were sausage rolls in the fridge. She'd heat up a couple of those and have a cup of tea with them and she'd feel right as rain.

She'd only got halfway there when the peace was suddenly shattered by the persistent ring of the doorbell and she spun on her slippers, desperate to make it stop before it alerted the whole street. Henry would definitely have something to say about that.

Hobbling as quickly as her aching legs would take her, she got back to the front door in just a few seconds, but before she even opened it, she saw the outline in the glass door and realised immediately who it was.

The door frame creaked as she pulled it back. 'Hello, Gladys.'

'Minnie, I was just making some sandwiches for a wee party we're having tonight at the bells, and I realised that I hadn't so much as cracked a light about it to you. So I said to my Fred, "I'm just going to pop back round there right now and tell Minnie that she's welcome." So here I am. Can't have you sitting in the house when we're all over there having a great old time.'

Minnie thought about inviting her in, but she had her house-coat on and, well, she had other things she needed to be doing. Gone were the days when she could get ready for a big night out by just dabbing on a bit of lipstick and changing her frock.

'Gladys, I really do appreciate the offer, but I'm afraid I have plans tonight already.'

'Oh. Is your Eric coming over then? Must be difficult at all these special occasions after what happened with him and Ailish. Nothing like families, eh? I was just saying to my Fred that when our Wynette split up from her man – we named her that after Tammy and she says it's a curse because people are always singing to her about standing by her man – not ideal when you're on your fourth husband. Anyway, where was I? Aye, that's right. When our Wynette split up from her man…'

Another wave of light-headedness swept in with no warning and Minnie gripped the door handle tighter.

'Gladys, I…'

The other woman wasn't even listening, so intent on ploughing right on with her story. '…Well, it caused all sorts of problems, so it did. Not that I liked him right enough. He was probably better than the second husband, but nowhere near as nice as the first. Liked a drink and didn't know when to stop. Anyway, are you sure you won't change your mind? I've made my soup and my special steak pie – I put sausages from the butchers in it and my Fred says…'

Minnie never did get to hear what Fred said, because before she heard the rest of the story, or had a chance to comment on the wonderment of Gladys's steak pie with sausages, she felt herself begin to slide down the door frame.

And her last thought before everything went dark was that she really hoped Henry wasn't hearing all this commotion.

4 P.M. – 6 P.M.

17

AILISH

Ailish prayed that there wasn't a hidden camera in the salon recording them, because the parents of her pupils definitely did not need to hear that once upon a time, her twenty-one-year-old self had consumed so many Slippery Nipples before 6 p.m. on New Year's Eve 1991, that she'd fallen into a bush singing 'I Wanna Sex You Up' by Color Me Badd. The spelling alone was atrocious.

Beside her in the chair, Rhonda squealed with laughter. 'Oh lordy, I remember that. You'd come into the salon I was working in because there was a rumour that my last appointment of the day was going to be Marti Pellow from Wet Wet Wet. We sneaked you in, but he never showed up. Some of the stylists who'd already finished for the day decided to drown their sorrows by making cocktails in the staffroom and you got pished pished pished.' Rhonda was hooting now. Actually hooting like an owl because she was laughing so hard. 'And then I gave you a boob tube and my favourite silver trousers to wear...'

'And I looked like I was about to re-enact the moon landing,' Ailish giggled, trying to hold her drink steady and failing miserably. Not that much different from 1991.

'I'm seeing a whole new side of you lot,' Alexis chuckled, as she continued to shape Gwen's short grey pixie cut. Her hair had regrown with a salt-and-pepper hue after her last round of chemo and it looked fabulous on her. Over on the other side of Gwen, Kaden was working product into Rhonda's mass of curls before her blow-dry, and Roxy was currently loading Ailish's hair up with more tinfoil than a roast chicken. It would have been a natty accessory to the silver outfit back on the night in question.

'Anyway, yes, I won't dispute that I was slightly on the inebriated side of sober, and may have fallen into a large, misplaced plant pot when exiting the salon, but if you two had been sensible enough to take me home at that point, then it would have been a sliding doors moment.'

'I think that was my fault,' Gwen joined in. 'I decided that we should go to this little Italian place I'd been in the week before, because I'd totally fancied one of the waiters.'

'But you didn't tell us that,' Ailish countered. 'You just said something about pasta being the best thing for sobering me up.'

'I may have slightly manipulated that situation,' Gwen conceded and Ailish forgave her immediately because it was just so bloody amazing to be sitting here with her and to be watching her come alive again for the first time in ages. Today was turning out to be the best medication for all of them.

'So you two took a very tipsy me – I still can't handle any more than three drinks in a twenty-four-hour period – along to this gorgeous little Italian place that turned out to be Gino's. And that started something that lasted for decades.'

Ailish tried to wrap the story up there, because whatever was in her cocktail had suddenly, out of nowhere, caused her chin to wobble and her windpipe to tighten. Decades. All wasted. Because Eric had decided to take a wrecking ball to their lives. Sometimes she wondered if there would ever be a time when she didn't think of him and feel devastated about what he'd done. She'd just begun to drift back down that wordless path to grief and regret, when she realised that everyone had gone silent. Raising her gaze, she saw five pairs of eyes, all staring at her questioningly.

'What?'

'We're waiting for the bit about the life-changing choice and the sexual encounter,' Rhonda informed her, harping back to the checklist that had sparked this conversation.

Gwen was leaning forward, eager for the details. 'And don't leave anything out because I haven't had so much as a snog for the last two years and I might need instructions.'

Ailish felt her toes curling. Why was she the centre of attention in this little cabal right now? That was Rhonda's natural habitat. Maybe Gwen's when she was feeling up to it. Ailish had always much preferred the side-lines and the 'here for backup only' position.

'Also,' Gwen went on, 'I remember this night very clearly, so don't think you can skip over anything. We want all the gory details.'

Ailish sighed, cornered, with no weapons to shoot her way out of this.

'Okay, so we get to the restaurant and it's pretty quiet because it's only about seven o'clock. Obviously now we know that things get going there much later on New Year's Eve, so that's why there were only a few tables taken. Anyway, we had dinner, and, of course, the most handsome guy I'd ever seen brought our pasta out.'

'Dario!' Rhonda sniggered. 'That man has aged like a fine wine. He still sets my ovaries spinning.'

'And mine,' Gwen piped up.

Ailish barrelled on, desperate to get this over and done with.

'Correct. Anyway, so you were right, the pasta did help to make me feel a little more sober...'

Rhonda looked very proud of that. 'Told you.'

'However, the bottle of wine Gwen ordered for the table counteracted that pretty quickly.'

Gwen gave an apologetic shrug. 'Sorry, but we were twenty-one, and I just wanted any excuse to make the handsome big guy keep coming back to our table. I'm only human.'

'I'd still do that now and I'm thirty-seven,' Alexis said with a wink. The manageress had reached the end of the styling stage of Gwen's hair transformation and had taken a break to fill up all their glasses with their chosen beverages. Ailish was very aware that they were getting preferential treatment due to hobnobbing with the salon owner. She took a sip from her refilled cocktail glass and psyched herself up for the next bit.

'Next thing we know, the whole place began to fill up – honestly, it was like someone had stopped a bus outside and everyone had piled in. An older man, who turned out to be Gino, the owner of the restaurant,' she added that in just in case the hair squad weren't aware of that. '...turned the music up, and within a couple of hours, it's the maddest, most fun party ever. Everyone was having a great time, and even if I was seeing double, I was loving it.'

'It hasn't changed. Still the best time ever. Always has been,' Rhonda sighed, smiling. Then she suddenly realised what she'd said and blurted, 'Apart from the year before last, obviously. That was a shit show. But... but... fuck it, let's not talk about that. Let's stay in happier times. Keep going, doll.' She prompted Ailish again.

'Hours later, everyone was on their feet and mingling and a conga line was working its way through the tables, and I don't quite remember how or why, but I'd somehow ended up standing at the bar. There was another guy there already – around my age and handsome in a too-good-looking, Don Johnson from *Miami Vice* kind of way.'

'Who's that?' Kaden asked, pulling his phone out to google him, to much eye-rolling from Gwen, Rhonda and Ailish, until he blurted, 'Holy shit, I'd fancy him myself.'

'Exactly,' Ailish agreed. 'I'd caught eye contact with him a couple of times and I think he thought I was interested. Actually, I was just seeing double and trying to focus because I figured he was way out of my league. But, anyway, Dario had come back with a tray of empty glasses and somehow we got talking. I had my glass in my hand so I was still drinking and swaying, and the next thing, Gino was up on a table and all I heard was ten, nine, eight...'

'I'm on a knife-edge here,' said Roxy, who had finished the foils and was now staring at Ailish's reflection in the mirror, waiting to hear the rest.

'I was on a knife-edge back then too,' Ailish admitted. 'It was almost midnight, I was standing next to two of the most attractive men I'd ever seen – and we were just about to get to the bit where it hits midnight and you kiss the first person you see. The count-down kept going. Five... Four... Three... And then, before I knew what had happened, Mr Suave Stranger, Don Johnson-lookalike, at the bar had moved around so that he was in my eyeline too...'

'It's like watching a train crash in slow motion.' Kaden winced.

'And then it hit midnight, and the place went wild, and I had two choices – kiss the totally gorgeous waiter or the totally gorgeous stranger beside him and... well...'

'You kissed the stranger,' Gwen stole the punchline.

'I did! What was wrong with me?' she said, with a dramatic shrug. 'I kissed bloody Eric Ryan.'

'Hang on, who's Eric Ryan?' Alexis asked, missing the link.

Gwen filled in the blanks. 'The stranger. The man she then married. And divorced.'

Ouch, that still stung. Which, Ailish knew, was pathetic. She should be way past that stage by now.

'And then?' Rhonda was on a mission to get to the juicy bit.

'Well, then I spilled the red wine that I was holding all down the front of my borrowed boob tube, so I went off into one of the bathrooms to wash it. They have three individual unisex cubicles in the back,' she explained to Kaden and Roxy. 'And somehow I happened to take Eric Ryan with me. The next thing I was taking my top off to wash it in the sink, and I flashed my boobs at him, and we stayed in there snogging for half an hour.'

Ailish felt her face begin to burn, and she couldn't believe she was saying this aloud, but she was in too deep to back out now.

'And there may or may not have been some fondling, but I can't possibly confirm,' she said, trying to restore some dignity, while the others found much hilarity in her discomfort.

'So what happened to the big sexy waiter?'

Gwen sheepishly raised her hand. 'I think I might have swooped in and kissed him. I was pretty fast on my feet in those days,' she chuckled.

Ailish could actually feel tears popping onto her bottom lids, but for once they were tears of laughter. Or joy. Or maybe just huge bloody relief that Gwen was still here to reminisce with them.

'So there. That's the story. That night, I chose to kiss Eric. And do a few other things. The next morning, I was so absolutely mortified at what I'd done, I agreed to go out with him again. I think I just wanted to show him I wasn't the kind of girl who got up to no good in restaurant toilets. Also, I was very hungover and in no state to make a sensible decision. If I had decent pals, they'd have intervened,' she added, feigning side-eye at the other chairs.

'Not long afterwards, we got hitched and we were married for over thirty years. The end.'

There. That was it. The story of her life.

Roxy was almost as invested in the story as she was in Ailish's hair make-over. 'Did you ever regret it? Choosing your husband, I mean.'

Ailish thought about that for a moment. Did she? It would be easy to say yes, given what had happened over the last two years, but the truth was that up until then, she'd honestly thought they had a great marriage. She'd fallen madly in love with Eric, and she'd stayed that way for many years. They'd been truly happy. And, of course, the biggest factor of all was Emmy. There was not a single thing she would do differently, if it meant she wouldn't now have her favourite person in the world.

'No,' she answered honestly. 'Because we had a good life and a really happy family for a long time.'

'Okay, I get that,' Roxy said. She'd taken a step back from her foil mountain and was talking to Ailish via the mirror again. 'But don't you ever wonder, just for a minute, what it would have been like to be with the other guy? The sexy waiter?'

Ailish dropped their eye contact as she felt a red heat begin to tingle in her neck again.

'Well, maybe once or twice...'

18

EMMY

Emmy tossed her phone on the desk of the nursing station, then stretched back in her chair and groaned.

'I swear on all that is fricking holy, I. Am. Having. The. Worst. Day. Ever.'

'Not as bad as Mrs Leckie in bed number six,' Yvie deadpanned. 'She's just discovered that her dog bit her neighbour's arse when he went in to feed it because she's stuck in here. The poor man is down in casualty waiting for a tetanus.'

'And Mr Catterson in bed 14 has just got the results of his tests back,' Keli said, not even glancing up from the chart she was writing on. 'Syphilis. Apparently, there's been a four-way romance situation going on over at the care home and he had no idea. Poor man is distraught.'

In the middle, Emmy looked from one of them to the other. 'You know, you two are really taking the jam right out of the middle of my doughnut today. Couldn't you just have let me have my moment? I'm trying to be seriously pathetic here, and you keep snapping me out of it. You're terrible friends.'

That pulled Keli from her chart, and she looked up, smiling.

'We are. Forgive us. Carry on, please. Tell us all the reasons your problems are worse than syphilis.'

Sometimes it was hard to keep a straight face around these two, but Emmy appreciated that they at least tried to make her laugh in times of high-level irritation. It was just as well that the nursing station was out of earshot of the rooms on the ward and all the patients, because there was very little that didn't get discussed there.

'Fine. Maybe not exactly worse than syphilis, but everyone who's still in here is beginning to feel a bit sad because they're not going to be with their loved ones tonight, we almost misplaced a patient, my dad's lost the plot and may be contemplating stalking my mother, my mum has finally got off the couch and appears to have decided it's time to party, I'm deeply suspicious that my boyfriend is having an affair as he's now hiding his location from me and I nearly rear-ended my car this morning because I thought I saw him somewhere he shouldn't be, and now I've been trying to call my granny, the one sane person left in my universe, and she's not picking up her phone. The world hates me.'

'But at least...' Keli began, and Emmy immediately put her hand up to stop her.

'I know. I don't have syphilis.'

Keli grinned. 'Exactly!'

Yvie stretched over her to reach the stapler. 'Are you worried about your gran? Does she usually answer?'

Emmy shook her head. 'No more than usual. She's terrible for not picking up the phone if she's busy, and if she goes upstairs for an afternoon nap, she can't hear it. She refuses to have a phone upstairs because she says it'll just interfere with her relaxation if it rings and disturbs her.'

Keli was back on chart-writing again but still engaged in the conversation. 'I love your gran. We should all be more like

Minnie. Bugger the world – if we don't want to be disturbed, then we won't be.'

'Exactly. Although she does also think that the Rolling Stones should make another comeback, that you should wear a natty knitted scarf at all times and that all ailments can be cured by a sausage roll.'

'That's me won over too,' Yvie concurred. 'I'm for making Minnie Prime Minister.'

'I'll try her again in a few minutes. If she's sleeping, then I really don't want to wake her. In the meantime, I'll select one of my other issues at random and ruminate over that for the next half an hour.'

The buzzer to Emmy's left suddenly went off, making her jump, and all three of them swung their heads to the security screen.

Keli got there first. 'Em, I think one of your issues may be standing at the door.'

By this time, Emmy had spotted it too, but she wondered if she was hallucinating. Cormac. There. Waiting to be let in. She reached for the button to open the door, mind whirring. What was happening? What was wrong? She could count on the fingers of one hand the number of times he'd popped into to the ward. There was the first time they'd met, when he'd visit one of her patients, and once when he'd been brought into A&E downstairs, to be checked out after a smoke-inhalation situation. He'd come up after he'd been cleared just to let her know about it and tell her he was fine. The only other occasions were when she'd forgotten to bring something in and asked him if he could drop it off. None of which applied here, so it was with some trepidation that she buzzed him in.

It only took him a few seconds to cover the distance from the door to the nursing station, by which time, Emmy was on her feet and got in first with, 'Hi. Is everything okay?'

Cormac gave her the smile that had won her over the very first time that she'd met him. 'Yeah. I was literally just passing and thought I'd say hello since I won't see you until tomorrow morning. How you doing, Keli? Yvie, all good?'

He was always so lovely to her friends, who returned the greeting, then moved discreetly to a desk a few feet away and carried on with their work.

Emmy's brain took that very moment to start working overtime. This was odd. Out of character. Why was he doing this? And why was she completely terrified to just take him somewhere private and ask him straight out what was going on?

Instead, she was channelling some kind of rom com fake sweetness. 'Aw, that's really nice,' she said, with the smile that he said had won him over the very first time he'd met her. She then tried a minor ambush with, 'How come you're out of uniform?' He was still wearing the clothes he'd left in this morning. Usually, he changed as soon as he got to the station, and even if he was nipping out to Civvy Street, he'd normally keep on his uniform trousers and T-shirt, and just throw a jacket over them.

He obviously hadn't been expecting the question because he looked a little startled. 'Oh. We were out on a job and I got manky. Changed back at the station afterwards.'

'Ah, that makes sense.' The rom com sweetness was wearing off, so she let that sit there, wondering if anyone else was sensing a slight awkwardness, or if this was all in her mind?

'Anyway,' he went on, 'I had to nip to Asda for supplies for the lads' dinner...'

Fair enough. The supermarket was right opposite the hospital and that was perfectly plausible.

'So just thought I'd swing by and bring you this.' From the

pocket of the black padded Barbour jacket she'd bought him for his birthday, he pulled out a little clear plastic tub and inside was a cupcake with a heart in the middle. 'It's the ones you like. The red velvet. I feel bad that I'm not going to be with you at the bells tonight, so I thought this could be the second best thing.'

That fired straight into her chest and tugged at a heart string. It was the kind of sweet, considerate thing he used to do when they started seeing each other. She'd fallen madly in love with all the contrasts in his personality. On the one hand, he was a real lads' lad, who played football and basketball and liked a game of snooker with his mates. On the other hand, he loved lying on the couch with his head on her lap, watching old episodes of *Friends* because it was her favourite show.

On one side, he could be a party animal who loved a night out and a good time, and acted like he didn't have a care in the world, but on the other, he would – quite literally – run into a burning building to save someone.

He was this big strong guy who wasn't the best when it came to talking about emotions, but then... well, then he would bring her cupcakes to let her know he was thinking about her.

'That's the loveliest thing, thank you.' She almost held it in. Almost. In the end, she dressed it up as a joke. 'Unless you're doing it to soften me up because you've done something terrible. In which case, I'll need a bigger cake.'

Her suspicions took over, suddenly convincing her that she saw him flush a little and then commit the heinous crime of blinking too quickly.

'Nope, not guilty,' he acted as if he was in on the joke. 'Anyway, did you decide what you're doing tonight? Are you going out or staying in?'

Why did he need to know? To what purpose? Was he projecting something? Didn't psychologists say that cheaters were the most paranoid about being cheated on? Or was that a line from a documentary about the Tinder Swindler?

'I'm not sure yet. My mum got a better offer. Aunt Gwen got out of hospital and, believe it or not, they've decided to go to Gino's. They're at the hairdressers right now getting ready.'

He was as surprised as she'd been. 'Gino's? That's the last place I thought she'd go.'

'Yep, me too. And, in other news, my dad's dumped Donna and wants Mum back, but that's a story that'll require a lie-down in a dark room, so I'll tell you later. It's been quite a day.'

'Sounds like it.'

'But as for tonight... I'm not sure. I've been trying to call Gran, because I wanted to see if she fancied some company, but I haven't got her yet. I'll probably do that though. Or, if she's having an early night, I'll just go home.'

He seemed pensive as he absorbed that. 'Okay, well, drop me a text and let me know.'

Why text? she wondered. She would usually give him a call on his night shift, and if he was out on a job, he'd just phone her back when he was free. Why did he want to switch to texting all of a sudden?

After glancing around to check there were no patients in sight, he leaned over the desk and gave her a very quick, workplace-appropriate peck on the cheek. 'I'd better get back. I'll try to give you a call later, but it just depends how busy we are. I've got a feeling it's going to be crazy.'

'No worries at all. Thank you for the cupcake. First lovely thing that's happened all day. I'll see you in the morning...'

'You will,' he said, flashing that cute grin again as he backed away from the desk. 'See you later, ladies,' he raised his voice so Keli and Yvie would catch it, although Emmy was almost 100 per cent positive they'd listened to every word. 'Happy New Year when it comes.'

The two of them snapped their heads up and chirped their goodbyes, returning the most used phrase in Scotland today.

Emmy watched his back as he went all the way down the corridor, then gave her a wave before going out the door.

Yvie came over to stand beside her. 'Aw, that was lovely. He's a catch, that one. Has that put your mind at ease and squashed all your worries?'

Emmy paused. Thought about it. Weighed it up. Looked at it from all sides.

'Nope, I'm even more sure now that he's up to something.'

And she was absolutely positive that she wanted to find out what it was.

19

DARIO

Gino came into the office, arms wide, greeting Nicky and Dario in his usual way, with hugs and kisses on each cheek. As always, he was dressed impeccably, in black trousers and a formal shirt, with a silver cravat around his neck that matched the hanky in the pocket of his dark grey blazer. He still had an exceptional head of hair that was white now, but always perfectly combed back from a face that belied his years. If Dario didn't know him, he would guess that he was a man ten years younger, but when he looked closer, he could see the shade under his father's dark eyes. Dario didn't think his dad had slept properly since his mum passed. He'd definitely never regained the sparkle in his eyes, or his zest for life, but at his heart, he was an incredible host, and coming to work every day meant that it was time to put on a show and lift the lives of everyone around him. He'd been doing that for decades and Dario was well aware that he didn't know how to act any other way.

The only time he'd ever seen the mask fall was after Mum died and for two solid weeks Gino had refused to leave the house, ignored their visits, locked himself away, almost as if he couldn't stand to be around anyone when he couldn't be the enthusiastic, gregarious man he'd always been.

On the fifteenth day, he'd called Dario over to the house. His parents had bought the semi-detached bungalow when the restaurant began to make a profit, allowing the two of them and their three sons to move out of the one-bedroom flat above Gino's, which they'd converted into a private dining space for small functions. When Dario got to Gino's house that day, his dad was already sitting at the old mahogany table in the kitchen, so he'd poured a coffee from the cafetière that was always beside the stove, and joined him.

As Gino slid a sheet of paper towards him, Dario's heart had ached for the broken, brutal grief that was etched on every line of his father's face.

'What's this, Dad?' Dario had asked, thinking it was maybe a list of things the old man needed.

A quick glance had told him otherwise.

A contract. Or some kind of deed. With a line for a signature at the bottom.

'I've had my lawyer draw this up, son. It's the restaurant. It's time for me to step back and make it yours.'

Dario's jaw had dropped, horrified. 'Dad, no. No way. I'll run it for you for as long as you want, but it will always be yours. I don't need a piece of paper that says otherwise.'

'Dario, listen to me.' His voice was deathly calm, a wild contrast to the joyful, convivial man he'd been before Mum took her last breath. 'This is not a request. It's already done. I need to be free to take a step back, because right now I don't know that I'll ever be able to spend a moment inside the restaurant again, when I know my love will not be there. To me, she was in the walls, in the flowers, in every dish that was placed on a table. Maybe one day that will be a comfort, but now it is just another way to break my heart. So take it... please. It's what she would have wanted and what I want now too.'

'But my brothers...'

Gino was one step ahead of him as always. 'They'll be compensated in other ways. We've never had much savings, but Bruno and Carlo will get this house and the proceeds from my life insurance policy. It's all there in the document too.'

On a purely practical level, Dario could see it made sense. Bruno had been happy to break free from Gino's when he'd moved abroad, and Carlo was already searching for premises to house the café that he'd always dreamt of opening. Matty was out of catering college and was more than capable of taking over from Dario in the kitchen on a permanent basis, allowing him to take his dad's place managing the other aspects of the business. But still, it had made him ache inside.

'Dad, I can't...' He didn't see why things couldn't just stay as they were, without the need for legalities. He could make the transition, take the burden off his dad, but leave the option open for Gino to change his mind.

However, the most stubborn man in Glasgow was taking no arguments. 'And yet I'm asking you to do this for me, so you will.'

There was no budging him. For the next few weeks, Dario had worked until he was exhausted, making the necessary changes, covering every responsibility and overseeing the new structure, getting Matty up to speed and learning the things that had always been in his dad's domain. And he'd got there. So when his dad had walked through the door a month later, his pressed suit back on, his debonaire appearance no different than it had been before, Dario had been happy to have him there. His reappearance was never discussed, because Dario understood.

'To me, she was in the walls, in the flowers, in every dish that was

placed on a table. Maybe one day that will be a comfort, but now it is just another way to break my heart.'

His dad had reached the stage where being in the restaurant brought him comfort, where the joy in the memories outweighed the pain and the distraction of the place he loved soothed his soul. Gino had changed his role, becoming only the host, doing what he did best, entertaining and serving his guests with joy and love, and then, only when he went home, did he lock the door and mourn his Alicia.

It had been that way from that day until now, and here he was, a seventy-nine-year-old man, who still came here every afternoon with a smile on his face. A smile that only dropped a little when he registered the mood in the office.

'Why the long faces? It's New Year's Eve, we should be starting the celebrations.'

Dario felt his chest tighten, and wondered if this was how it felt when a heart attack was coming on.

Before he could reply, Matty stormed in behind his grandfather, still in his chef's whites, his long black hair tied back from his face.

'Have they told you yet?'

'Matty, wait... Let your dad do this,' Nicky intervened.

'Fine. But let's do it now,' he said, leaning against the back wall, arms folded, but one finger tapping against his other forearm, showing his impatience.

Dario inhaled. Exhaled. 'Dad, I need you to sit down. We need to talk.'

Gino waved him away. 'Today is not for talking. Today is for dancing and eating and showing everyone a good time.'

Dario almost fell for the naivety, but there was a look in his dad's eyes, a pucker in the lines on his forehead, that told Dario he knew exactly what was going on here and he had no intention of facing it. This was the same reaction his father had pulled out every single time Dario had broached the issues and challenges that they were facing. Trouble was, now there was no getting away from it. This was crunch time.

'Dad, you need to listen to me. Give me five minutes of your time. Five minutes. I'm asking you because I have no other choice.'

Gino's face tightened and Dario recognised the look that had occasionally come the way of the brothers when they were younger and up to no good. Mum had always been the strict one. The disciplinarian. But if Dad made that face, then they knew that they'd crossed a line. Now Dario was a fifty-four year-old man and about to reveal just how far across the line they were.

Gino reluctantly sat down on the chair across the desk from his son, and Dario began to lay it all out again, just as he had before. The state of their accounts. The debts. Their costs. Their options. Gino's jaw set into a hard line and he said nothing, but at least this time he was listening, and not brushing the problems off.

Next, Dario went into detail about the offer. Only when he'd finished, did his father finally speak.

'I know nothing about this. I need time to consider it.'

'Dad, that's not true. I warned you about this last year. And I told you about the offer when it first came in. You just chose not to listen. I've been trying to talk to you about the deadline all week. I even printed a copy of the offer and gave it to you.'

'I don't read paperwork. That's your job now.'

If the situation wasn't so resoundingly shit, Gino's obstinance would be almost amusing. The truth was, he didn't read it because he didn't want to know. That was it. No more or less.

'I know this is my responsibility, but the time has come for a decision that I don't want to make without your consent, because I understand the importance of it. So I won't do it without you.'

It was a dangerous gamble, but Dario meant it. If it was a choice of losing the shirt off his back, or his father, he would start undoing the buttons.

He carried on pleading his case. 'You have to understand that if we do this, we will be fine. There will be enough left over to clear our debts and for you to have a comfortable retirement.'

'I'll retire when I die,' Gino repeated his long-held stance on the matter.

'Well, maybe you could retire before that and go enjoy your life. This will give you the financial freedom to do that.'

'And what will you do in this fairy-tale world?' Gino's eyes were blazing and Dario knew his dad well enough to understand that the fire came from passion more than temper. A trait he'd passed down to his grandson, who was standing behind the family patriarch right now, silent, but with the same furious expression.

'I'll work. I'll go back in the kitchen. I'll do something different. I really don't know what I'll do, but I do know I'll be fine. Matty...' He moved his gaze to his son. '...You'll be fine too. You're a great chef and there's a whole world out there. There's nothing you couldn't take on.'

Matty didn't respond, so Dario turned back to his dad. 'What's important is that this offer expires tonight. And I think the only option that makes any sense is to sell. I'm so sorry. I really am. But it's the only way.'

'Mum?' Matty didn't need to ask the whole question.

Nicky's sigh came from her boots. 'I'm not involved in this decision, but I've seen the figures and I think your dad is right. I don't see another option, Matty.'

Before Matty could reply, Gino had something to say.

'The restaurant belongs to you, so I have no power to change where we are. And I understand what you're saying. But over the years I have faced many challenges...'

'Not like these ones, Dad.'

'Perhaps, but challenges all the same. And every time, I worked my way out of it.'

'And we worked with you too,' Dario countered. It was true. The global crash of 2008 had made numbers plummet and forced them to cut staff and run on the tightest budget, but they'd managed it because when things were lean, Gino and Alicia, Dario and Nicky, Bruno, young Carlo and teenage Matty had worked obscene hours and taken meagre wages to get them through. This was different. Now, there was nothing else to cut, and with the extortionate rise in costs, the seesaw between the outgoings and income had slammed down on the wrong side. There was no pulling this back. Because even if they were at capacity every single night of the week, an impossibility in itself, there would still not be enough profit in this location to cover the inflated bills and the payments on debts they'd incurred during the pandemic.

'Why can't we take out a loan? Sell my house? Sell yours?' Gino challenged him.

Dario flushed. 'Because I've already mortgaged my home, Dad, and put it all back in here.'

That made Nicky's eyes grow wide. 'Dear God. If you'd done that when we were married, I'd have murdered you.'

Dario decided this wasn't the time to debate that point, but he could see both his dad and Matty registered it. He ploughed on, 'And your house, Dad? Really? You know that you told me that had been left to Bruno and Carlo, so it would kill me to touch that. In in the meantime, you want me to sell and put you out on the street? No. Because the thing is, it won't be enough. It'll never be enough, because any attempt to inject cash and keep it going is just throwing good money after bad. In six months, a year, two years, we'll be right back here again. That didn't stop me from trying though. The reason we're at crunch time today is because I found out this morning that my last-ditch attempt to get another loan failed. It's probably not a bad thing, because for all the reasons I just listed, it's a terrible idea. I just need you to know that there isn't an option I haven't explored.'

'I don't want to discuss this any more,' Gino answered stubbornly. 'Not today.'

Damn it. If avoidance was a sport, Gino would be on the podium. Not for the first time, Dario wished his mother was here. She had always been shrewd. Sensible. Able to handle the tough stuff.

'I don't either, Dad, but the offer to buy the building and the land it sits on expires at midnight...' he spelled it out one more time, '...and it's a take it or leave it. And I really don't think we'll get another deal anywhere close to this. Like I said, it's crunch time, Dad.'

Gino stood up, and Dario knew the conversation was about to be over.

'Not for me. I don't want to talk about this any more. Dario, you do what you have to do, but I don't agree, and please don't ask for my blessing because I won't give it.'

With that, the father that Dario adored walked out and left him firmly wedged between a rock and a hard place.

20

MINNIE

The first voice she heard when she started to come around on the floor of her hallway was Henry's. 'Minnie, love.' He sounded worried, spoke with urgency. 'Minnie. Come on, ma darling. Open your eyes. Minnie!'

The anxiety in that last word reached somewhere right inside her and brought her all the way round. As her vision began to clear, the first person she saw was Henry, holding her hand, then he pushed her hair back off her face and kissed her forehead.

'You had me worried there for a moment, ma girl. I'll go put the kettle on and let your friend take care of you.' He gently rested her hand on her hip, then disappeared out of her field of vision, and in his place... Gladys!

Oh my word, the woman was terrifying. Her face came down so that her mouth was only inches away from Minnie's ear, and she had a voice that could raise the dead.

'Minnie! Jesus, you scared me there. One minute I was talking to you and then the next you went down like you'd been shot by a sniper. Never seen the likes of it. I was terrified out of my wits. And I'm not a woman that scares easily. My Fred is always saying that… "Gladys," he says, "you're made of steel, so you are." But you've given me two shocks in one day, and well, I think I've aged ten years.'

Minnie wondered if her own ears were actually bleeding. Maybe that was a side effect of fainting.

She began to push herself up on her elbows, and tried not to wince with the discomfort of it, then cleared her throat to check that she still had a voice.

'Gladys, I'm fine. I'm sorry I scared you. I think it was just a wee faint, that's all. It can happen sometimes if I forget to eat and if I'm not sleeping well. This last week, over Christmas, has had me all out of sorts. If you could just help me get up onto the couch…'

'Second time today I've had to get you up, Minnie. We're making a habit of this. If this carries on, I'll be scared to let you out of my sight in case you go down like a stone and I'm not there to catch you. You hear of that, don't you? These old folks that lie on the floor for days and then get eaten by their Yorkshire terriers. Sends a chill right down the spine.'

For the second time today, Minnie was hugely grateful to this lady. She really was. But she was also considering playing dead so Gladys might stop talking to her. She immediately chided herself for being so uncharitable. She'd tell Henry about her thoughts later though. It was the kind of thing that would make him roar with laughter, especially as he was obviously staying out of the way while Gladys was here.

Gladys held out her arm, and Minnie used that to pull herself up to a seating position, with her back against the hallway wall. One step at a time. This aging process thing was a piece of nonsense. One minute you've got your leotard on and you're singing 'Xanadu' with Olivia Newton-John at the church hall aerobics class, and the next thing you're an elderly lady who is fainting and can't go from lying down to standing up without a two-minute warning.

Minnie wasn't giving up though. Eighty was knocking on the door and she was going to face it and ride that wave all the way to ninety. Although, it would be helpful if she didn't keep forgetting to eat or sleep, and then maybe she'd stay upright a tad longer.

Gladys was still chattering away when the front door, just a few feet away, was rattled by someone banging on it. And, oh my, there was the phone ringing too. What was this like? Emmy called her every day and Ailish phoned every second day or so, but other than that, she and Henry could go days without speaking to another human being, yet all of a sudden it was like the January sales in here.

'That'll be the paramedics. I'll let them in.'

What? For a second, Minnie thought that Gladys had said paramedics. Now her ears were going as well.

'I called them as soon as you fainted. They must have been just round the corner. One of the perks of living near a hospital.'

Minnie didn't have time to reply because the damn phone was ringing again. In two seconds, Gladys had opened her front door and in came two paramedics, a woman and a man, both of them in their yellow jackets with their medical bags by their side.

'I'm afraid you've had a wasted trip,' Minnie informed them straight away. 'I just had a wee faint, that's all. I'm right as rain.'

'I think they should be the judge of that, Minnie,' Gladys overruled her, before turning her attention to the new arrivals. 'That's the second time today that she's fallen and I was there for both of them. What's the chances of that? I mean, thank goodness I was there. My Fred said the same thing...'

'This morning, I tripped on a step. It could have happened to anyone...' Minnie began, but the young female paramedic had heard enough.

'Okay then, Minnie,' she said, coming down onto her knees on the floor beside her. Minnie guessed she must have been about Emmy's age, with her dark brown hair pulled back into a ponytail, and a kind but no-nonsense demeanour. 'I'm Lauren and this is Danny.' She nodded to her partner before going on, 'Why don't you tell us what happened while we just run a couple of checks. First, though, is anywhere sore, do you feel like you've damaged anything?'

Minnie shook her head and tried to cover up her wince due to the ache that was coming from her shoulder. It was nothing she couldn't handle. 'No, I don't think anything is broken. As I said, I tripped this morning, so I have a couple of skint knees, but then this afternoon was just a faint because sometimes I lose track of time and I forget to eat. I've got low blood pressure too, so that doesn't help.' She didn't mention the pain in her hip. No point in adding to the list.

'I'll just check that out now for you,' said the other paramedic, who was now kneeling by her too. He opened his case, then rummaged inside and brought out a blood pressure cuff, a thermometer and one of those oxygen test thingies that they always put on her finger when she went for her annual check-up with the GP.

The woman continued to ask questions, while she checked out Minnie's head, then did all the tracking tests with her fingers to check her vision, then on to her arms, legs, looking for any obvious damage, even though Minnie had already assured her there was none. She appreciated the thoroughness, though.

'Your blood pressure is definitely low, and I think you're a bit dehydrated too.'

That reminded Minnie that Henry had said he was off to put the kettle on. Must be staying out of the way to let these good people do their work.

'Do you think you could give my blood pressure a check with that thing too because what a fright I got,' Gladys inserted herself. 'I'm sure my heart could power a train, the way it's thumping right now.'

The male paramedic, Danny, gave her a sympathetic nod. 'We'll have a wee look at you in just a sec. Let's do what we can to get Minnie off the floor first, shall we?'

Gladys nodded. 'Absolutely. I was just saying earlier to my Fred, I should have called an ambulance this morning when she fell up at the shops, but Minnie would have none of it. I shouldn't have listened. I mean, anything could have happened to her after that. She could have one of those blood clots that kill you instantly. I'm sure that's what happened to Elvis, wasn't it? Or was he the one that got stuck on the loo?'

'Earmuffs. Please give me earmuffs,' Minnie whispered in Lauren's ear and the young woman's face creased into the loveliest smile.

For the next ten minutes, the paramedics worked quickly and efficiently, checking off concerns, until they were confident that Minnie was fit to be moved. Only then did they help her to her feet, and after pausing for a second or two to let her head settle, she was steady enough to lead the way through to the living room. There, she took a seat on the couch, and Lauren sat down next to her.

'Right, Minnie, we have a couple of choices here. Your blood pressure is a little on the low side, but not at a level that suggests any immediate treatment is required. Other than that, there's nothing in any of the tests we've done that's causing me concern, although I do have a slight worry about the fact that you've fallen twice in the same day.'

Minnie was very calm, but direct. 'But I did tell you that was a trip this morning. I was going from a very warm room out into the cold, and I just got a bit flustered and missed my footing.'

'Okay,' Lauren said sympathetically. 'And I just want to check again that at no point in either that fall or this afternoon's faint did you bang your head?'

'She definitely didn't,' Gladys interjected from Minnie's armchair, where she had seemingly taken residence.

'I definitely didn't,' Minnie repeated, trying her best to be patient.

Lauren made eye contact with Danny, and a subliminal agreement passed between them, evident with two almost indiscernible nods of their heads.

'Okay, well, in that case, we can either take you in with us so that the doctors can check you over again, just to be of the safe side—'

'Absolutely not,' Minnie countered.

'I had a feeling you were going to say that,' Lauren replied, her voice kind and understanding. 'The other option is that I can get you to sign a form, saying you're refusing care, and that you understand the risks of that.'

Minnie didn't need to be asked twice. 'I'll sign the form.'

'Are you sure, Minnie? You definitely feel well enough and there is nothing you're not disclosing to us?'

'She doesn't drink, if that's what you're insinuating,' Gladys said, with just a touch of indignation.

'I don't think they were insinuating that at all, Gladys,' Minnie assured her, while also thinking a wee sherry wouldn't go amiss right now.

Minnie suddenly realised that she had an ace up her sleeve that would settle this. 'Anyway, my granddaughter is coming over. She's a nurse at Glasgow Central on the elderly care ward. She'll be here within the next hour and she'll be staying here tonight.

You can't get better care than that. And I promise we'll be doing nothing more than sitting on the sofa.'

Out of the corner of her eye, she spotted Gladys's interested gaze, and knew she'd want to question every detail of her plans. Minnie hoped, for once, that she'd say nothing.

'You're absolutely right – that's definitely the kind of care you want on hand,' Lauren agreed. 'Okay, I'll note that on the form as well.'

It took a couple of minutes to get the paperwork all done, and then Minnie walked them to the door, feeling even more steady on her feet now.

'Thank you for coming so soon. I feel very lucky that you responded so quickly,' she said, as she opened the front door.

'You definitely were,' Danny said, patting his jacket, before pulling a set of keys out of his pocket that Minnie assumed were for the ambulance she could now see was parked at the end of her path. 'We just happened to be passing on our way back to the hospital after a false alarm. And you got us in the calm before the storm too. It'll be chaos tonight and God knows how long you would have waited. We do what we can but... cutbacks.' He let the words trail off with a shrug.

'Anyway, nice to meet you, Minnie, and you take care of yourself and take it easy. Especially tonight. Make sure you get plenty of rest,' Lauren instructed her.

'I certainly will,' she assured them, as they went off down the path. She was sure Henry would hear them going and feel much better about the situation. He must have been worried sick.

She closed the door behind them. Right, only Gladys to deal with now.

'Gladys, thank you so very much for taking such good care of me. I really do appreciate it. You've been an absolute godsend today and I don't know what I'd have done without you.'

Gladys beamed, bless her, and Minnie sensed that the need to be seen and appreciated was at the very heart of this woman's ceaseless chat.

'You're ever so welcome, Minnie. Just glad I was here. Again. I could just give my Fred a call and tell him I'm going to wait here with you until your granddaughter comes along...'

Minnie decided just to cut to the quick. 'Gladys, that was a bold-faced lie, because I just wanted to give them the confidence to leave me here.'

Gladys's mouth gaped open. 'But, Minnie...'

'And I'm so sorry to be blunt, but I really do need to get on. It's Hogmanay and I've got to get myself dolled up because I've got a party to go to.'

6 P.M. – 8 P.M.

21

AILISH

Roxy had turned Ailish away from the mirror, while she blow-dried her hair, and Kaz, one of the salon's make-up artists got to work on her face. At the next chair, Alexis, who was, it turned out, skilled in both hair and beauty, was now applying Gwen's foundation, while Rhonda was doing her own make-up because she said she was too much of a control freak to delegate.

The last hour had been utterly blissful, as the foils had come out and her hair had been rinsed and cut, all the while sipping on a cocktail and reminiscing about a hundred different wonderful times they'd had since the first day they'd walked into high school. Or rather, in Rhonda's case, danced in – she was the only one whose parents could afford a Walkman and she'd worn it everywhere for the entire duration of the eighties.

Ailish still had huge reservations about going to Gino's, but she'd blocked them out of her mind for the time being. Right now, she was sticking with all those corny modern-day sayings that she usually mocked. Focus on the present. Don't worry about what you can't control. Live in the moment. Live, laugh, love. And drink cocktails with your pals. That last one she'd made up herself and it was her favourite.

The salon was completely closed now, with all the other clients gone, and the only staff remaining were the ones who were working on the VIP guests. The luxury of that wasn't passing Ailish by because she'd never been a VIP anything. That was probably why – despite Rhonda's million attempts to give her a make-over – she'd had the same hairstyle for thirty years and it had taken a good fifteen minutes with tweezers and wax for Kaz to de-bulk her eyebrow forestry situation.

'Good thing is, heavy brows are in right now, so you're bang on trend. Just need a bit of tidying up,' she'd told her. Ailish realised she was just trying to make her feel better, but she was grateful for it. Even when she'd been facing the mirror, she'd avoided looking at her reflection, because what was the point? The whole 'high-maintenance grooming' thing just wasn't for her. Although, she could definitely see the merits of making it an occasional treat, especially in this company.

Gwen already looked completely transformed from the exhausted, worried friend that they'd been visiting in hospital for the last two weeks. Her short, silver grey hair was stunning, her eyes were bright and she had that enthusiasm in her voice that had been swallowed up by fear, pain and struggle for a long time now. Ailish would have been happy just to sit here and appreciate the boost to her pal, but there was no denying that getting a bit of pampering herself was an extra bonus. Roxy was now twirling Ailish's hair around an implement that she didn't even recognise. Apparently, it was going to give her 'beach waves', despite the fact that it was minus two degrees outside, and her typical beach look had always been 'pulled back in a ponytail, slightly sweaty and smelling of SPF 50'.

'So, tell me then, what are your New Year's resolutions?'

Rhonda asked. 'I'll go first. I'm going to live every single day on my own terms, do whatever the hell I please and look into getting a Brazilian butt lift.'

'Is that not just a normal Monday for you? And a Tuesday. And a Wednesday...' Ailish teased her.

'Exactly. That's the point. I honestly don't think I want to change anything.'

Ailish noticed a flicker of a shadow go across Gwen's expression as she contemplated that. 'You okay, Gwen?'

Her friend nodded, causing Alexis to yelp, as she was in the process of drawing on Gwen's eyeliner flicks with intense precision.

'Shit, sorry,' Gwen cringed. 'Do I look like a goth with eyeliner out to my ear now? Only that was my gig for half of the eighties, so I know I can rock it.'

Alexis was already correcting the blip with a cotton bud. 'Nope, I can salvage it. I've got talents in this department. I once did my pal's eyeliner when we were driving in the back of a transit van. It's a long story.'

'Were you being kidnapped?' Ailish asked, intrigued.

'Nope, going to a party. Our car had broken down and a pal who's a plumber picked us up. There were ten of us in there.'

Ailish was dying to hear more, but first, she wanted to find out what had perturbed Gwen. Was she starting to feel unwell? Too exhausted to do this? Having second thoughts about going out?

'Gwen? Sure you're okay?'

'I am. I'm just...' She cleared her throat. Took a moment. Then spoke with sad, but determined clarity. 'I'm just thinking about that whole New Year's resolution thing. You know, I always used to buy into that. Lose ten pounds. Start doing Pilates. Declutter the junk drawer in the kitchen. But if you asked me over the last year, I'd have said I was happy just to go for staying alive. That was it. None of the other stuff mattered. But now...'

She paused again, and everyone in the room was hanging on her every word, conscious and grateful that all their trivial, bull-shit worries had just been put in perspective.

'Now I think I'd like to do more than that. I don't just want to *be* alive, I want to *feel* alive too. I want to make plans. Prioritise the right things. I've dedicated so much to my career for so long that now I think I want to dedicate myself to me. To my friends. To living life. And... I feel so corny for saying this out loud, but I want to love again. Real love. The kind that sets your knickers alight and makes your heart race. I want that.'

Silence. Not a single sound. All of them were still, pensive, moved, heartsore for second, after second, after second, after...

'Well, that blows my Brazilian butt lift out of the water then, doesn't it?' Rhonda said, with a dramatic sigh.

Meanwhile, right next to Ailish's face, Kaz began wailing, 'Oh no, oh no, no, no. no... Roxy, help me out here – you get the other side.'

It was only when both women began frantically dabbing Ailish's cheeks with sponges that Ailish realised tears were streaming down them.

'Ailish, doll, I think I've seen you cry more today than I have in the last forty years,' Gwen said, gently cajoling her.

'I know!' Sniff. 'I'm sorry.' Sniff. 'It's just that... Argh, I want all that for you. I really do. You deserve everything. And the fact that you're still open to starting over and taking risks with your heart just blows me away. In case I haven't told you lately, Gwen Millen, you're fricking spectacular and I love you.'

Gwen reached over and squeezed her hand. 'I love you right back, hon.'

'I promise we're not always like this,' Rhonda said to the

others while wiping tears away. 'We're usually fairly emotionally repressed and prone to covering up feelings with superficial chat and wine.'

As always, Rhonda's way with words lifted the mood again.

Cosmetic applications resumed and Ailish took a large sip of her cocktail, before realising that Gwen had more on her mind.

'Right then, Ailish Ryan, it's your turn. Resolutions?'

Ailish thought about it. 'If you'd asked me ten minutes ago, I'd have said I had none, but now I don't know. I think I've been in a bit of a hole since Eric... well, you know what he did. And to be honest, I've been happy there in my bubble of nothingness. Hurts less. But maybe it's time to start thinking about finding something that makes me happy too.'

'Or someone?' Rhonda asked.

Kaz took that moment to apply lip liner and then lipstick, so Ailish had time to formulate an answer. It just wasn't a great one.

'Maybe. I don't know. Perhaps. Or maybe not.'

'Good to know you're decisive there,' Rhonda chuckled. 'But while we're getting all deep and meaningful here for once, tell me something. What about Eric? If he ever came knocking on your door again, how would you feel? Would you consider taking him back?'

'Oooh, good question, Rhonda,' Gwen took over. 'I've wondered that too.' She turned back to Ailish. 'Don't hate me, but I've always thought that maybe you've been shut down for the last couple of years because... like I said, don't hate me... But maybe a part of you is still in love with him? I mean, you had a lifetime together and right up until he had a midlife crisis and screwed everything up, you were always so fricking happy – it would be totally understandable.'

Ailish felt all the muscles in her stomach tighten and her palms begin to sweat. The truth was, it hurt to even think about being with him again, because then she had to remember how great so much of their lives had been. Somehow, it was so much easier to demonise him as the Adulterous Arse, and that was true, but for almost thirty years before that he'd been a different Eric altogether. One who loved her. Who made her laugh. Who she couldn't ever imagine being without, because they made each other so incredibly happy. And it wasn't just the big moments, like the day he asked her to marry him. Although, that was, without doubt, one of the happiest moments of her life.

Of course, it had been at Gino's. And it was just before midnight. Rhonda was with the man who would be husband number one, Gwen was with a guy who looked like the lead singer from A Flock Of Seagulls. Minnie and Henry were there as always, but so were her own parents, Duncan and Vi. Eric had invited them along, but she had no idea it was because he'd already asked her dad's permission to propose. It would have been easy to do the big public thing of asking her in front of everyone, but that thoughtful, considerate Eric, the one she was madly in love with, had known she would hate being the centre of attention. So just before midnight, he'd taken her hand and, as the party went on around them, he'd led her into a little alcove at the side of the main dining area, where Gino kept the restaurant's dessert trolley.

'Ails,' he'd said, rubbing her cheek with his thumb. 'I know you said you won't get married until you're thirty...' She'd vaguely remembered saying that in a moment of acting cool and independent one day, but she hadn't actually meant it. 'But I love you more than anything and I don't want to wait that long to call you my wife. I mean, I will, if you insist. But I'd really much rather marry you now – today, tomorrow, whenever you'll have me. So will you please—'

'Yes,' she'd blurted. 'Yes, yes, yes!'

That's when he'd realised he hadn't even had a chance to get the ring out, and he'd fumbled for it in his pocket. But the jewellery wasn't important. Their love was. Their family.

That happiness came around again the night Emmy was born and the three of them had lain on her hospital bed for hours, while Eric told his new daughter all the wonderful things they'd do in their lives together.

But Ailish had adored him for who he was in all the small moments of their day to day existence too. The way he'd tug her down on to the couch after she'd had a bad day and he'd stroke her hair while he listened to her. Or the way he'd ooze enthusiasm for weekends and holidays, and he'd persuade her to walk along the beach with him at sunset, while he told her how much he loved her. He'd buy her flowers for no reason at all, other than to make her smile. He wasn't perfect, but he was honest and kind, and he adored his family. It was almost impossible to reconcile that man with the person who'd cheated on her, because it was so incomprehensibly out of character that she still found herself wondering how it could possibly be true. Sure, he was an adrenaline junkie who thrived on new and exciting things, but he'd always taken her and Emmy along for the ride. Until the last time. That was an adventure that he'd gone on with someone new.

That thought snapped her back to the present, her mind replaying Rhonda's question. How would she feel if he came knocking on her door now? Well, he'd done that earlier today, but she was 100 per cent sure it wasn't because he wanted some windswept reunion. Probably realised she'd got his Elton John CD collection in the split and wanted it back.

No, reconciling with Eric was the last thing she wanted to think about. The very last. And yet... Gwen wasn't wrong. She had loved Eric with everything she had, been so sure that they would grow old together, that he was the one person she could trust with her heart. It wasn't him being with someone else that hurt the most, or the fact that it was with a thirty-something who had yet to discover the joys of middle-age spread and hot flushes. It was that he'd made her wonder if she'd ever truly known him, and taken away the future they'd planned together. If you couldn't trust your best friend, the person who'd promised you the world for thirty years, then who could you trust? How could you live with that person again? But then, clearly she was doing a terrible job of living without him too.

Before she could answer, Rhonda had a light-bulb moment. 'Actually, I've just realised something. Today must be the anniversary of the day you got engaged, as well as the anniversary of...' She stopped, diplomatic enough not to mention it. 'Oh shit, Ails, I'm sorry.'

It was the other kicker in their story. They'd got engaged on the 31st of December. Over thirty years later, she'd found out he was cheating at a party that began on the 31st of December. And today, her divorce had become official. On the 31st of December. There was some kind of deep, twisted poetry to that.

Gwen's forehead creased with concern. 'Wow, so it is. What's the chances of your divorce dropping today too? I bet you just wanted to stay in bed this morning.'

Ailish gave a half-hearted smile, then shook it off. 'I did, but not now. I'm so glad we did this and I wouldn't swap it for anything. Although, strictly speaking, I found out he was cheating in the early hours of the first of January, so, technically, you can strike that one off the anniversary list.'

She could see both Rhonda and Gwen's shoulders relax a little when she said that. And, in front of her, Kaz stood back, scrutinised Ailish's face, then broke into the sweetest grin.

'My work here is done,' she announced. 'You're now 100 per cent babe.'

It was the very best interruption at the very best time. Ailish just wished she could turn around to view her newly proclaimed, and undoubtedly wildly exaggerated 'babe-ness', but Roxy was still at work with the curling thingy. Instead, she thanked Kaz profusely and made a mental note to give her a whopper of a tip.

'I'll be another five minutes or so,' Roxy promised. 'Nearly done.'

Gwen and Rhonda were already completely finished, both still just relaxing with their drinks next to her. Ailish hoped the interruption to the conversation would have jumped them on to a different subject, but apparently not.

'You still didn't answer the question about Eric?' Dammit. Rhonda wasn't letting that one go.

It was the question she'd asked herself a dozen times. 'I want to say absolutely not, no way, not in a million years.'

'But?' That came from Gwen.

'But the truth is,' she braced herself for the backlash, then winced as she admitted, 'I really don't know.'

It took her a second to absorb that she'd really said that out loud.

Thankfully, she was saved from her friends' questions, push-back or outrage by the magnificent Roxy, who, right at that moment, put the twirly thing down and began shaking out Ailish's hair with her fingers. A spray of some divine-smelling mist came next, then Roxy stood back, surveyed the scene, smiled. 'All done. Are you ready to see?'

'This is like one of those makeover shows on TV,' Ailish giggled, mostly because everyone was staring at her and, well, the whole aversion to being the centre of attention was kicking in. She was sure Roxy and Kaz had done a perfectly lovely job, giving the constraints of the canvas they had to work with.

'Absolutely,' she confirmed, ready to smile, to say thank you, and then leave here with her beautiful pals.

Roxy beamed, as she whooshed her around to face the mirror. 'Here you go then. Pure stunner.'

Ailish got ready. Smile. Say thank you. Then...

Something wasn't right. Wasn't computing. She was staring in the mirror straight ahead, but... Who. The. Actual. Hell. Was. That. Staring. Back?

It was Ailish. But not fifty-four-year-old, exhausted, brow-beaten, recently divorced Ailish. It was pre-heartache Ailish. Pre-grey Ailish. Pre-neglect Ailish. Years younger. Years brighter. Years of pain and stress all rubbed out by Kaz and Roxy's magic.

And oh, if she did say so herself, for the first time in recent memory, in fact, maybe since the nineties, she was indeed 100 per cent babe. Fifty-four-year-old babe, but still.

If it wouldn't ruin Kaz's artistry, she'd willingly succumb to tears of happiness.

A swell of something she didn't recognise came right up from her toes and it took her a minute to realise what it was... Optimism. Hope. A tiny tug of excitement.

In the last few hours, it was more than just her physical appearance that had experienced a makeover. Something on the inside had changed to match the outside.

'What do you say then, Ails?' Gwen asked. 'Are we going to leave here feeling fantastic and ready to conquer the world?'

The woman in the mirror gave her a silent push. If Gwen, after all she'd been through, was ready to open her heart to life and to love again, maybe it was time she did that too.

Deep breath, slap a smile on and let's do this.

'Yes,' she said, to everyone in the room, but most of all to the woman staring back at her in the mirror. 'I think we are.'

22

EMMY

'Is it just me, or has today been the longest day ever?' Emmy sighed, as she plonked herself down on one of the chairs in the staffroom. She pulled her white New Balance trainers off one by one, glad the old days, when nurses had to wear proper shoes, were long gone. Today had been bad enough without adding sore feet to her troubles. She still hadn't been able to get Cormac's weirdness out of her head and his visit this afternoon had only made it worse. She quickly checked her location app again to see if maybe there had been some kind of blip earlier. Hopefully, Cormac was on there again, showing at the station, exactly where he should be. When the app gave her the same answer as earlier, her stomach sank. Still no Cormac. However, there were three missed calls from her dad and a text asking her to call him back. She deleted it.

On the other chair, Keli stretched her hands up. 'Yep, but it's over now and we're off for two whole days, so my dancing pants are ready to get going.'

'Oooh, I like the sound of that. What are you doing for the bells?'

'Party at Noah and Tress's house.' Noah was Keli's brother, a paediatric consultant down on the third floor. 'I think most of Weirbridge is going. My mum's in charge of the food, I'm in charge of drinks, and two of his neighbours, Nancy and Val, are in charge of entertainment. They've got a bit of a thing for Tom Jones, so anything could happen. Their moves to "It's Not Unusual" are a sight to behold. If you're at a loose end, come along. The more, the merrier.'

Emmy appreciated the offer, but for once, she wasn't up for party central. 'Thanks, but I think I'm just going to have a chill night tonight. In fact, let me try my gran again. I still haven't been able to get her.'

Emmy retrieved her phone from her locker, while Keli was lacing up her bright red Doc Martens, getting ready to leave. She dialled Minnie's number and listened to it ring. And ring. And ring.

'Still no answer?' Keli asked.

Emmy shook her head, unconsciously chewing on her bottom lip. 'Nope. I was thinking about going over there to keep her company tonight anyway, but maybe I'll just go now. Feels like something isn't right. Or maybe I'm just overthinking my granny as well as my boyfriend.'

Anxiety rising, she was just about to disconnect the call when she heard a faint, 'Hello?'

'Gran!' she blurted, relief coursing through her. 'I was beginning to worry there. I've been trying to get a hold of you all day and it's been ringing out. I was about to summon a search party and come find you.'

'Emmy, love, I'm sorry – I've been a busy lady. I had shopping to do, and then a friend dropped by and I had a wee nap in the afternoon. It's been all go here.'

Emmy felt her heart rate begin to return to normal. Gran was fine. She could deal with pretty much anything in life, as long as Minnie was okay.

'Aw, I'm glad you've had a lovely day. You deserve it, Gran. Especially today. I know you've always loved New Year's Eve.'

'I certainly have. Not the same any more though, is it, love?'

Emmy heard the sadness in Minnie's voice and she could have cried for her. For as long as she could remember, Christmas had always been at Gran and Grandad's house, and Hogmanay had been at Gino's with her grandparents and her parents. Her gran and her mum would both spend all day cleaning their houses – it was an old tradition that decreed it bad luck to go into the new year with a home that wasn't spotless – and then they would down their mops when it was time to get ready for the night out. They'd dress up in new frocks, Gran would have on her favourite pearls, they'd all go to Gino's, and at midnight, every single year, Grandad would kiss Gran, Dad would kiss Mum and Emmy. Then they would all hug and wish each other a Happy New Year and Minnie would tell Ailish that she was the best daughter-in-law she could ever have wished for. After the affair, their family was fractured, and they couldn't even continue to socialise together, because Dad had screwed things up so badly. Her poor grandparents had been caught up in the fallout, as it took away their lifelong traditions. It was just another of the reasons she found her dad's selfishness so hard to forgive.

'Actually, Gran, that's why I was phoning. I thought I'd come over tonight and see in the bells at your house.'

There was a pause, and Emmy wondered if Minnie had dozed off mid-conversation. Wouldn't be the first time, and it had given her such a fright on the couple of occasions it had happened before. Eventually, she heard a quiet exhalation on the other end of the line and wondered if Gran was crying. Please, no. She couldn't bear it.

'Gran, are you okay?' she asked, so softly that Keli glanced over, concerned.

'Oh yes, dear, I was just taking a bite of my sausage roll,' Minnie said breezily. 'I'm trying to make sure I eat, so I don't get all that light-headed way.'

Emmy sagged as a second wave of relief swept over her. The sausage rolls were out already. Gran was fine.

'But about tonight,' Minnie went on. 'Thank you for thinking of me, but I'm actually just going to have a wee chat with your grandad and then an early night. As I said, it's been a busy day.'

'Gran, are you sure? Because, honestly, I'd be so happy to come over...'

'Och, love, I can barely keep my eyes open. *The Steamie* is on the TV...' *The Steamie* was a much-loved, classic old TV show about working-class Glaswegian women doing their family's laundry in the communal washhouse on Hogmanay 1950. 'And you know that's always been Grandad's favourite programme. I think it's the perfect way to finish the year. So you have a lovely night, sweetheart, and don't you be worrying about me at all. I'll be just fine. Goodnight, my love, and Happy New Year when it comes.'

The next thing Emmy heard was the click of the call ending. Almost in slow motion, she took the phone away from her ear and stared at it, just as Yvie came into the room.

'What's up? Why have you got that face on?' Yvie questioned, warily.

Emmy sat back down. 'Because I just called my gran to say I'd come spend the night with her and she blew me off. Says she'd rather go to her bed.'

Yvie pulled out a chair and slumped down just as Emmy had

done, hands going immediately to her trainers to get them off her feet. It was like the end-of-shift standard ritual. 'Maybe she's just sad and can't face it?'

'That's what I thought too, but to be honest, she seemed perfectly chipper. Says she's had a busy day, so she'd rather just watch *The Steamie* on TV and then call it a night.' It was difficult to tone down the incredulity in her voice. She ran over the conversation in her head one more time, questioning herself and coming up with the same answer – no, Gran definitely didn't sound sad. Not a bit, actually.

'Well,' Yvie said, pulling on a pair of bright pink moon boots that were a natty contrast to her blue scrubs. 'Maybe she's just changing things up. She's almost eighty, Ems. I guess the things she felt like doing at seventy or sixty or fifty can change, especially when the dynamics in a family shift. Maybe this is just a new phase for her.'

'Yeah, you're probably right,' Emmy concurred, unconvincingly, as she pulled her jeans out of the bag that lay next to her. 'Guard the door a sec please, Keli.'

Keli immediately did as she was asked, leaning against the white wood. They were supposed to change in the staff locker room next door, but no one was likely to walk in during the next five minutes.

As soon as Emmy had buttoned up her jeans, Keli released the door and came over to kiss them both goodbye. 'See you on the third, lads. Love you both and Happy New Year.'

Yvie and Emmy returned the wishes and they fell into a group hug that ended with Yvie saying, 'Right, break it up before I start getting emotional and telling you that I'm going to name any future children after you. It's the whole New Year thing. Gets me right in the sentiments.'

Laughing, Keli headed out the door, leaving the other two behind.

'Yvie, I've just realised you haven't told us what you're doing tonight. Usual place, usual time?' Emmy asked.

'Yup. Usual place, usual time, usual fiancé. Carlo closed the café at 4 p.m. today, and he's heading over to Gino's now to help out tonight. I'll be propping up the bar there as usual, waiting to get snogged at midnight.'

'Don't complain about that,' Emmy laughed. 'We'd never have met if I hadn't got talking to you at Gino's. And if we hadn't met, then we wouldn't have become friends, and then I might still be working over in Paisley ED, blissfully unaware of the joy that was waiting for me up here.' She wasn't kidding. The Emergency Department had been tough and relentless, but although she'd loved it, she was so much happier in this role.

'Ah, you know how to sweet-talk a girl,' Yvie said, nudging her playfully on the shoulder. 'Why don't you come with me to Gino's? I'm going to stop by my apartment to get changed on the way, so we could have a wee Prosecco there first.'

Yvie and Carlo lived in a flat about two hundred yards from Gino's restaurant, so it was always handy for pre or post-dinner drinks.

'Thanks, but I'm...' Emmy thought back to earlier, to the plan she'd abandoned when her dad had shown up at the hospital, then her mind flashed with the image from the app.

Cormac Sweeney's location is unavailable.

It was so distracting, she almost forgot that Yvie was waiting for an answer. 'I'm just going to go home and do exactly the same as Minnie. Watch a bit of TV and go to bed.'

She'd leaned down to pull on one of her biker boots, so it was only when she sat back up that she saw Yvie was staring at her, one eyebrow raised much higher than the other.

'Emmy Ryan, I think you're lying to me.'

'I'm not!' Emmy lied. Again.

'Swear on the Holy Ryan Reynolds that you're going home and you are not, in fact, going to spy on your boyfriend at his place of work.'

Emmy tried desperately to deflect the conversation. 'What's Ryan Reynolds got to do with this?'

Yvie shrugged. 'Nothing, but if you're lying I won't watch *The Proposal* with you ever again and it's your favourite.'

Despite everything, that made Emmy giggle. 'You're ridiculous, you know that?'

'I do. And I also know when you're fibbing.'

'Okaaaay!' Emmy conceded, hands up in surrender. 'I may drive past the station on the way home. Just to see if his car is there. He came to my work today, so I might just drop in on him. Purely as a loving girlfriend. Not to check up on him. Nope. Definitely not for that. Absolutely not.'

'Why would you do that?' Yvie challenged her. 'Don't you trust him at all?'

'I do!' Emmy insisted. 'But then... I trusted my dad too.' There it fricking was. It all came back down to that every time, and she could see how unfair that was. Cormac was a good guy and she shouldn't be doubting him. Cormac loved her and she loved him. The end. 'You know what, Cormac isn't my dad and I just need to remember that and trust him. This is so stupid and fricking ridiculous that I'm twenty-nine years old and letting my parents' split affect me like this. I need to get a grip. You're right, it's not fair and I've got no business doubting him. So no, I'm not going to the station. I'm going to go home, get into bed, and watch the holy Ryan Reynolds in *The Proposal*.'

'Are you sure? That's definitely what you're going to do?' Yvie asked, doubtfully.

'It definitely is,' Emmy replied, with utter conviction.

However, it was utter conviction that she definitely didn't feel.

She would go home. She would go to bed. She would watch a movie.

But only after she'd made a slight detour on the way.

23

DARIO

Dario did a final round of the restaurant, checking that everything was in order for the celebrations tonight. He didn't miss the irony of the fact that he had never felt less like celebrating. His son was working in the kitchen, and refusing to even engage in a discussion with him. And right now, his dad was sitting alone at a table over by the window, having his favourite meal of pollo alla cacciatora, even though he said every time that it wasn't as good as Alicia used to make it. Dario chose never to pass that feedback back to Chef Matty.

It struck Dario how frail his father now looked. Since he was a child, he'd viewed his dad as this irrepressible, joyous force of nature, the very essence of life itself, but now, to see him over there, he was a shadow of his former self. It was as if, when his mother died, she'd taken Gino's soul with her, leaving the outer shell of the man, but not the passion for life that fuelled him.

It broke Dario's heart. Not for the first time, he wondered if he was looking at a snapshot of his own future. Alone. In Dario's case, it would feel like every chance for a normal life had been sacrificed, albeit for a job that he loved.

'You look deep in thought there, *fratello*,' said a new arrival, who had just come in the door.

Despite everything that was weighing him down, the sound of Carlo's greeting made Dario smile. *Fratello*. Brother. Carlo was the baby of the family, the surprise, born eighteen years after Dario, and stereotypes would say that he should be a little spoiled or indulged, but the truth was far from that. Like Dario, he had worked in the restaurant from when he was old enough to wash a dish without breaking it, and he'd been a natural. For many years, it was truly a family business, with Gino and Alicia running the show, Dario in the kitchen and Nicky, Carlo and Bruno out on the floor. It was the best of times... but times changed. Death. Divorce. Leaving for faraway shores. And in Carlo's case, breaking off to set up on his own, but with his family's blessing.

Even after only a few years, Carlo's Cafe, over by Glasgow Central Hospital, had already gained a reputation as one of the best eateries in the city. It had a consistent flow through of hospital staff, families of patients, tourists. Unlike the city centre, it didn't come with crippling rates and a reduced footfall, and unlike Gino's menu, which, on his dad's insistence, had barely changed for decades, Carlo had a far more flexible approach, allowing him to work round seasonal price hikes. It had been a great move by his *fratello* and Dario respected him immensely for it.

Dario hugged him, then grabbed two bottles of Messina lager from the bar and beckoned Carlo to follow him.

In the office, Dario sat in his usual chair, while Carlo flopped down on the couch.

'I want brother of the year award for working here tonight,' Carlo joked, although they both knew there was nowhere else he would even dream of being. It had been their dad's one request when Carlo left here to open his own place – that he come back to work with them every Hogmanay. Carlo had never missed a shift, closing his café early on this day every year, and then reporting for duty with his family.

'You always have brother of the year award with me. Just don't tell Bruno, because I say the same thing to him.' Dario took a sip of his beer. 'How's Yvie doing? Still telling you that you work too much?'

'Every day,' Carlo chuckled. 'But I wouldn't change it for anything.'

'I hope you tell her that, bro. Takes a lot of patience to be in a relationship with people who graft like us and sometimes we don't realise it. At least, I didn't. And look what happened.'

Dario noticed Carlo's quizzical glance, which settled into a curious frown. 'Okay, what's happening, Dario?'

Sighing, Dario put his bottle down on the table. 'You remember a few months ago I told you how financially rough things were here?'

'Yeah. I'm gutted I couldn't help you out, but we're still paying off our start-up loans and the cash just isn't there yet. But if you could hold on for another year or so, I should be able to...'

Dario put his hand up. 'There's nothing left to hold on to, Carlo.'

For the third time today – first to his son, and then to his father – he laid the whole thing out. The debts. The costs. The end of the line. And he watched Carlo grow paler with every detail of the story.

'Oh Jesus, Dario, I'm so sorry. I didn't realise it had got this bad. Dad must be devastated.'

'He is. But he's pissed off with me too.'

'But why? You've worked your ass off to keep this place going.'

Dario gave that a nod of acknowledgement and appreciation. 'I know, but he wants to keep going. Hope for a miracle.'

'They're in pretty short supply in our business,' Carlo said, now looking as helpless as Dario felt. 'Sometimes no matter what you do, you have to take the hit and move on. How bad is it going to be?'

'That's the thing... There's a solution, but Dad doesn't like it. Neither does Matty.'

Dario went on to explain the offer from the American developers, told him what they'd get out of it and what it would leave them with. A clean slate. Money in the bank. Enough that Dad would never have a day of worry.

'I've got until midnight tonight to accept or decline, and if I knock it back, I'm not going to get another shot at it because they'll move on to something else.'

'Fuck,' Carlo said, blowing out his cheeks as he sighed. 'Maybe for the first time ever, brother, I don't want to be you.'

Dario was about to reply when a knock at the door interrupted them.

'Come in,' he shouted, figuring it was probably one of the staff, probably looking for change for their till float, or maybe keys to the cellar to change a beer barrel.

He was wrong on both counts.

His best mate and lawyer, Brodie, joined the party.

'Hey,' he greeted them, Dario first, then Carlo, with one of those shakes of the hand that morphs into a hug.

Dario passed over his bottle of beer and Brodie took it without question. They'd been sharing drinks, food and secrets for a million years, so this was nothing out of the ordinary.

Brodie displayed the intuition that had made him one of the city's top lawyers, by reading the room perfectly. 'You're talking business?' His comment also displayed the kind of discretion that had made him one of the city's top lawyers.

Dario nodded wearily. 'Yeah. Spoke to Dad today and finally

got him to listen to the whole story. He's a definite no. Told Matty too – he was a definite "no fucking way".'

Brodie was in gentle lawyer mode. 'Don't they get that this is the Hail Mary? It's this or you close the doors with nothing, because we both know that you've only got enough cashflow to last another couple of months. Look, I've got no skin in this. I'm not taking a fee and there's no vested interest, but I'm just acting as your mate here. You tell me to take the deal, I'll take it for you. You knock it back, I'll do everything I can to help you find another way.'

As always, it was the kindness that hit Dario square in the chest. Problems he could deal with. And he would face any fight. But love and kindness? Touched him every time. That was in the DNA stream that came directly from his mother. 'I appreciate that, Brodie.'

'Any time.' Brodie turned to Carlo. 'What do you reckon, Carlo? Any words of wisdom, because we'll gladly take them.'

Carlo leaned his head back, thinking. 'Look, I can help with your staff, find them jobs where I can...'

'I might need to take you up on that. I promised Sonya that somehow we'd keep her on.'

Carlo's face creased into a grin. 'Now you're talking. You know she's my favourite woman on the planet after Yvie. She once bollocked one of my teachers for giving me detention. Told him he was a fascist and that she'd be reporting him for being a dick. She got removed from the school, but it was worth it.'

It was the light relief they all needed.

Carlo went on, 'And if this is about Dad having a purpose, you know he is always welcome to come hang out at my place. I guess it's not the same, but the customers would love him.'

Dario didn't want to say that he didn't think that would ever happen. This was Gino's spiritual home, it was part of his soul.

That was the problem. It was so much more than bricks and mortar.

'And the deal? Yes or no?' Brodie asked Carlo the direct question. His mate had known his brother since he was a kid, so it was pretty cool to see that he valued his opinion.

'I'd bite their hands off. It's a no-brainer to me. But then, I'm not Dad.' Carlo stood up. 'Listen, I'm going to go check on him, see how he's doing. The tables will be starting to fill, so I'll keep everything going while you two speak. And, Dario, whatever you decide to do, I'll back you.'

Dario thought how proud his mum would be to see the guy that her youngest son had become. 'Thanks, bro.'

As the door closed behind Carlo, Brodie put his beer down on the desk. 'How are you holding up? I'm so sorry you're dealing with this shit.'

'Me too. Thing is, I know there's only one answer, but I just need to think some more before I pull the trigger.'

Brodie stood up. 'I get it and there's no rush – we've got a few hours before the deadline. I'm going to get out of your hair and let you get your head round all this. Just give me a shout when you're ready to make the call.'

24

MINNIE

Minnie leaned in to get a better look at her reflection in the mirror as she applied her lipstick, ignoring the twinge in her hip from this morning's fall. She always wore bright red lippy on New Year's Eve and Henry had always loved it. 'Here comes Ruby Lips,' he'd say as she came down the stairs. And it didn't matter if she was twenty-five or seventy-five, he'd add, 'The most beautiful girl that there ever was,' and then he'd pull her close and they'd slow dance for a moment whether there was music on or not.

He was quiet tonight though, ever since she'd come off the phone to Emmy.

'I know what you're thinking there, Henry Ryan. I shouldn't have lied to the lass about staying home tonight. But you know fine well that if I was honest about where I was going, well, it would have caused all sorts of issues. And, let's face it, you're not exactly squeaky clean in all this. You were party to the lie we told them last year too, when you and I were sneaking into Gino's but didn't want to tell them about it.'

Minnie had felt terrible about that, they both did, but they were caught between a rock and a hard place.

The year before that, two years ago now, they'd been having a wonderful time as usual at Gino's. Eric and Ailish were there as always, and Emmy too. Of course, poor Alicia had already passed, and you could see the heartache on Gino's face, but, goodness, he made an effort to cover it up, putting all his energy into being the host that made sure everyone had a fabulous night. Dario was there too, such a lovely man, who made her heart stop when he looked at her because his eyes were the same gorgeous almond shape as his mother's.

Who else was there? She tried to think. Carlo! Yes, the youngest son was over at the bar, keeping the drinks flowing. And Gwen and Rhonda were providing endless entertainment as usual too. It was before Gwen got sick, and they had no idea what was to come for the poor soul. You just never knew the minute. Anyway, it was all going smashing right up until the early hours of the morning. All the happy new year kisses had been exchanged, there had been much jubilation, a smashing singalong, and then some slower music had come on for another round of dancing. Minnie hadn't even noticed that Eric had disappeared, because she was too busy having a wee sway with Henry to something by that lovely Celine Dion, if she remembered correctly. Next thing, well, all hell broke loose. Ailish rushed back from the loos, grabbed her things, and she was off, Emmy chasing after her. Turned out poor Emmy had caught Eric with his... Minnie hated the word mistress, but that was the truth of it. Ailish had seen them too and that had set it all off.

Shocking didn't even begin to cover it. Minnie had been devastated and crushed that a son of hers had acted that way. Henry had been furious. Livid. In fact, she wasn't sure Henry's relationship with Eric had ever recovered.

Not surprising then that she'd felt uncomfortable telling the family that they were going back to Gino's last year, but as Henry said, there was no point in them losing a tradition they'd shared with friends for fifty years, over an act of stupidity by a son who'd been brought up to know better. Emmy was working anyway, Eric was away with that floozy of his, and Ailish didn't have the appetite for going out. He'd broken her heart, so he had, and the lass didn't deserve it after being a devoted wife to him for all those years. So yes, last year they'd lied about going to Gino's because they didn't want to hurt anyone by admitting they were returning to the scene of the crime. They'd said they were staying home, having a quiet night, but, in truth, they'd eaten delicious food, sang their hearts out and danced until they were breathless, putting another memory in the vault of their lives together. And Minnie would always be glad of it.

Make-up done, she picked up her brush, and styled her hair into the same look she'd worn on special occasions for most of her life: a middle parting, her hair swept back into a low, twisted bun at the back, like a ballet dancer. A chignon, it was called. Alicia had taught her how to do it when they were just young mums, and Minnie had always felt it was so sophisticated, even when they didn't have a bean to their names.

A blast of Elnett hairspray kept it in place, and then she picked up the atomiser from the dressing table and added some scent to her wrists. Estée Lauder's Youth Dew. Henry's favourite.

As he often did, Henry left her to get ready. Her burgundy silk dress was already hanging on the front of the wardrobe, so she swapped it for her robe, glad that it covered her newly skint knees, then, wincing just a little with her aches and pains, slipped her feet into her low-heeled, silver shoes that were smart enough for a party but comfortable enough for a dance. She never did see the point of those towering heels the young ones wore – one wrong move and you could break an ankle in them.

As she came down the stairs, she heard 'Moon River' playing

and there Henry was, waiting for her, handsome as ever. 'Here comes Ruby Lips,' he whispered. 'The most beautiful girl there ever was.'

When she reached him, she felt his arms go around her and they swayed to the music, and Minnie knew, as she always did, that this was the most perfect moment of her year. She savoured it for as long as she could, before the beeping horn of the taxi outside interrupted them.

'Come on, love, time to go,' she murmured to him, then chided herself for the tears that were making her eyes glisten.

Henry noticed them too. 'Hey, hey,' he soothed her, stroking her cheek. 'This is our happy night, ma darling. Another year. More memories to make.'

'More memories to make,' she repeated softly, before slowly pulling her hand away, their fingers sliding apart until only the tips were touching, then letting go.

The taxi beeped its horn again, but she still took her time, careful not to unsteady herself. After her fall this morning, and then that faint this afternoon, she didn't want to add a 'third time unlucky' to the day.

In the living room, she picked up the box that she'd collected from the jeweller's shop that morning, a gift for their oldest friend and for the man that her husband loved like a brother.

The front door creaked as it opened and closed, and then Minnie walked slowly, carefully down the path, Henry right beside her. The taxi driver spotted her, and jumped out of the car with an apologetic shrug. 'Sorry about beeping the horn there like that – it's double time tonight and I'm just trying to get as many fares in as possible so I can get home for the bells.'

'No apologies needed, son. I'd be doing exactly the same thing if I were you and so would my husband. Nothing would ever make him miss midnight with his family.'

The driver opened the door and offered an arm for her to hold on to while she climbed in, happy to have redeemed himself for his impatience.

She gave him the address for Gino's and they pulled off.

'I take music requests if you have one, missus. This app on my phone has got just about every song you could think of.'

As always, Henry had quietened down, happy for her to chatter away, but she didn't have to ask what he'd want to hear.

There was only one song on her mind too.

'Can you play "Moon River"? It's an oldie, a bit like myself.'

She got the fright of her life, when he suddenly shouted, 'Siri, play "Moon River"' in an American accent.

He caught her eye in the rear-view mirror.

'It disnae do great with the Scottish accent. Best shout at it as if I'm born and bred in America. Works a treat.'

And it did. The opening bars of 'Moon River' began to play and Minnie and Henry smiled all the way out of the street.

From the South Side to the city centre, every time a song finished, Minnie told the driver the name of another old favourite and the next thing it was playing for them. Magical things, those Siri machines. She decided she was going to get Emmy to set one up for her in the house.

By the time she saw the twinkling lights outside Gino's restaurant, she already had her money out and an extra tip for adding a delightful trip to their night.

For the second time, the driver jumped out and held the door open, and Minnie took her time, stepping out carefully to ensure she didn't have a repeat of the gymnastics from this morning. 'Hold on to me, Henry,' she said, quietly. 'I can't be getting this far and then not make it.'

The taxi drove off, the driver grateful for his tip, and Minnie paused on the pavement for a moment to glance up at the third floor of the building next door – her and Henry's first ever flat. The place where she'd given birth to all her boys, and where she'd loved the man who'd made her happy her whole life.

'There it is, Henry,' she told him. 'It'll always be ours.'

The spell was broken by the opening of Gino's front door, as two giggling ladies, maybe in their thirties, came out, as friendly and carefree as could be.

'Are you waiting to go in?' one asked her cheerily, holding the door open.

'I am indeed, dear,' she replied, stepping forward, and even before she crossed the threshold, Minnie could smell the familiar, delectable aromas of the food inside. This was the best tonic she could have for her throbbing bones, and the excitement of it washed all her aches away.

'Thank you so much,' Minnie said as she passed them. 'And Happy New Year to you when it comes.'

'You too! Have a lovely night.'

'Oh, I'm sure we will,' Minnie told her with a grateful smile.

Inside, at the greeting stand, a young woman she didn't recognise, met her with a beaming smile. 'Good evening, and welcome to Gino's. My name is Katie. Can I just check if you have a reservation?'

'I do, dear. Minnie Ryan is my name.'

On the clipboard in front of her, the girl made a tick with her pen.

'I have you right here, Mrs Ryan. Table for two.'

Minnie took a breath, her smile tainted with every sadness that had come her way since she had last stepped into this restaurant a year ago.

In her mind, she saw Henry take a step back, and then blow her a kiss goodbye.

'Ah, no, dear. I'll only be needing a table for one. I'm afraid my husband passed away at the beginning of the year.'

8 P.M. – 10 P.M.

25

AILISH

'How do we look?' Gwen asked, as they did one last check in the mirror in the hallway of her riverside loft.

'Like Charlie's Angels,' Rhonda beamed, and Ailish was pleasantly surprised about the generosity of that statement, until Rhonda added, 'The Menopause version. Wearing well, a few hot flushes, and we'd kick the shit out of the bad guys if they catch us in a mood swing.'

If the taxi driver who picked them up two minutes later wondered what they were laughing about, he didn't ask. And if he wondered why the car fell silent after a few moments, he didn't ask about that either, but Ailish knew.

All afternoon, the three of them had been riding a wave of excitement, adrenaline, nostalgia and emotion, but now it was the moment before the curtain went up and a whole different set of feelings were setting in. Gratitude. Trepidation. And if she were honest, a niggling worry that this could all turn out to be just a sad reminder of the rejection and devastation that had been her constant companions since the night, exactly two years ago today, that her world had been blown apart.

Before she could dwell on that, Rhonda broke the silence.

'I hate to be the harbinger of doom here, but has anyone considered that we might get here and they won't be able to fit us in? I mean, what if Dario isn't there to pull strings for us? Or if he is, and the place is packed and there's nothing he can do?'

Ailish wasn't sure she had an answer for that question that didn't involve a tiny touch of relief. They could go to another bar, one that came without memories she wanted to forget. Or they could go home and get into their comfies, then sit up all night reminiscing, just like they'd been doing all day. And no, she wouldn't get to see Dario, and that would be a shame, but now that she was off the couch, she could always pop in next week, or next month, or never...

Her deliberation of the other possibilities was derailed when Gwen suddenly blurted, 'Okay, I have a confession to make, so I'm just going to say it quickly and you need to forgive me.'

'I love it when it's not me that's having to 'fess up to things,' Rhonda gloated. 'Tell me it's something awful that they'll make a documentary about?'

Ailish had the feeling Rhonda wasn't taking this situation seriously.

Even in the dim light of the back of the cab, Ailish could see Gwen looked a little sheepish.

'Okay, shoot,' Ailish prompted. 'Although, I'm not sure I want to hear.'

'The thing is...' Gwen began. 'Today isn't the random event that I've led you to believe all day. I booked this table at Gino's months ago. Looking forward to coming here tonight, to seeing everyone and being in the place we've always loved, has kept me going even in my darkest moments. I wasn't sure how I was going to get you both here, especially you, Ailish, but I knew I'd talk you into it somehow. Please don't take offence. But I didn't tell you before now because I was waiting for the right time. And then when I got sick again a couple of weeks ago, I thought we were screwed, but here we are... And the only reason I'm telling you all this is because when we walk in the door, there will be a reservation in my name.'

Ailish wondered if there was a cap on how many times today she was going to be gobsmacked and speechless.

'Are you mad at me?' Gwen asked her.

Ailish sighed, taking a minute to formulate how best to describe how she felt right now. 'I'm disappointed. I feel manipulated. Coerced. Betrayed...' She let that sit there for a second before adding, 'But thank God you're a cunning old boot because I've had the best day ever and I wouldn't change it for anything.'

Gwen was still grinning and squeezing her hand when they pulled up outside the restaurant. Ailish – her purse now transferred from the bag she'd taken to the hospital this morning to an evening clutch she'd borrowed from Gwen – paid the driver and they stepped out into the cold, dark night, yet she didn't feel a single shiver.

They heard the music pounding through the pavement, smelled the intoxicating aromas of Gino's food, but it was only when they opened the door that Ailish felt, as she always did here, that she was walking into another world. Only half the tables had people sitting at them so far, but already the room crackled with energy and elation and hilarity. Every day for the last two years, she'd thought about the night that ended her marriage here. Now, she remembered what she'd loved about the restaurant before that.

'Table for Gwen,' her friend told the hostess, a young woman Ailish didn't recognise. It had always been Alicia, and then Dario's ex-wife, Nicky, who greeted new arrivals. Just another changing of the times.

Ailish could feel a little swagger in her step that hadn't been there at any point in her life before the moment that Chanel had zipped up this utterly fabulous frock, and she walked a little taller, a little prouder, a little sexier... until she spotted a little lady sitting right there staring at her.

'Minnie!' Ailish gasped, a rush of joy and heartache and too many other things almost knocking her off the sparkly shoes she'd also borrowed from Gwen. 'Oh, Minnie, it's so lovely to see you here,' she told her truthfully, then tried to bend down to hug her but the dress wouldn't allow it. Instead, she reached over and lifted Minnie's hand from the table and gave it a heartfelt squeeze.

One of the hardest struggles of the divorce was how it had changed her relationship with her mother-in-law. Their love hadn't diminished in the least, but the logistics of their time together had been altered. Now she called to check the coast was clear before visiting. She still took Minnie for her shopping every week, but the subject of Eric was off limits. And the special occasions they'd always enjoyed together were now spent apart. Well, not tonight. And that made Ailish's heart swell.

Gwen and Rhonda stepped in to exchange greetings too, having adopted Minnie as the entire group's honorary mother-in-law when Ailish married Eric. Ailish knew Minnie loved them just as much as they adored her.

'I'm so proud of you for coming here tonight,' Ailish told her, meaning every word. They'd all seen how Minnie had been lost over the last year since Henry had so tragically passed away only two days into January. 'Are you alone?' Ailish glanced around, trying to see if there was anyone she recognised, a sudden rush of dread consuming her. Bugger. Don't say Minnie was here with Eric and his girlfriend? Noooooo. Not tonight. Not when she was just starting to find her way back to the twinkly lights of normal life.

Minnie must have sensed her concern because she answered quickly. 'Yes, dear, all on my lonesome. Well, apart from Henry, who'll be here somewhere.'

Ailish could have cried, with both relief and with the gut-wrenching sorrow for Minnie's loss. She was dealing with it in the way only Minnie would – she still chatted to Henry as if he was in the room, still told him everything she wanted him to know and she drew comfort from the unwavering conviction that he was still right by her side, looking out for her, just as he had for the last sixty years.

'He sure will,' Ailish went along with it, as she always did, because she truly believed that Minnie might just be right. She had no doubt that if there was any way for those that had passed to look out for the people they'd left behind, her devoted, loving father-in-law would have found it. Shame his son didn't inherit that sense of loyalty and care.

'Why don't you come sit with us?' Ailish said, with Gwen and Rhonda immediately jumping in to affirm the suggestion. But Minnie was having none of it and as Ailish followed the moving eyeline of Minnie's gaze, she saw why. Gino Moretti, her mother and father-in-law's lifelong friend was making his way back from the bar with two glasses of something Ailish was pretty sure would be sherry.

'Thank you, Ailish, but my friend is going to sit with me for a moment.'

'Ah, my favourite ladies!' Gino bellowed the greeting he gave to all of his guests, and no one minded because they all adored him.

His arrival kicked off another round of greetings, although, as Ailish hugged the man she'd known for more than half her life, her heart hurt for him too. Despite his extroverted bonhomie, his smile no longer quite reached his eyes. He'd never been the same since he lost the wonderful Alicia.

Ailish squeezed Minnie's hand again. 'Okay, well we'll be over there, and we'll keep a seat for you just in case you change your mind later.'

As they left Minnie's table, a memory tugged at Ailish's mind, so she urged the other two to go ahead, while she sidestepped into the alcove beside her – choosing not to acknowledge that it was exactly where Eric had proposed all those years ago – and pulled her phone out of her bag. She was sure Emmy had said earlier that she was going to drop in on Minnie tonight. Strange. Best fire off a quick text to check.

> Just got to Gino's and your gran is here. She's come alone but seems quite happy. Anyway, hope you're good. Will call you at midnight. Love you. xx

Popping her phone back in her bag, she caught up with the others at the table, but she didn't have time to fill them in on what she'd been doing because there, walking towards them, was one of her favourite people. With arms wide and a face that was still far too handsome, Dario Moretti welcomed them like they were his very favourite people too.

'Well, if there was a table I hoped I'd see tonight, this is it.' Dario had always had the same perfect blend of charm and humour as his father, and as he hugged each of them in turn, Ailish felt another rush of gratitude that Gwen had forced her to scrub up today. She felt strong. She felt happy. She felt like the woman she was the very first time she laid eyes on this man. Although, maybe slightly more sober.

Meanwhile, Dario appeared to jump on to the same nostalgia train that they'd been on all day.

'You know, I see you lot and I feel like I'm twenty again.'

'Ah, we wish!' Rhonda chuckled. 'Although, after all that plastic surgery I had after my second divorce, I'm pretty sure half of me is still in my twenties.'

'Tell us then, Dario,' Gwen asked, chuckling. 'If you could speak to your twenty-year-old self, what would you say?'

Ailish knew that was supposed to be a cute, jokey question, but their suave, confident friend was suddenly a rabbit in the headlights. Ailish wondered if this was the first time she'd ever seen him flushed, as he clearly struggled for an answer, his eyes darting from person to person, before finally admitting...

'I think I'd tell my twenty-year-old self that he shouldn't have been afraid to go for what he wanted.'

26

EMMY

Emmy had been talking to herself ever since she'd driven her car out of the hospital car park and steered it onto the road towards the fire station.

'Please be there. Please be there. Please be there.'

And yes, she was aware that she sounded just like Minnie, chatting away to the universe, hoping that someone could hear her.

At first, from a medical point of view, her gran's otherworldly communications with Grandad had worried Emmy, but she'd soon realised it wasn't a delusion – Minnie didn't actually see Grandad sitting in the chair every night. No, it was just her gran's way of soothing the pain and keeping the loneliness at bay and, actually, Emmy was glad of it. If Minnie was singing along to a favourite old song on the radio, and it made her happy to think Grandad could hear it too, then there was no harm in it. Besides, as she said, he'd always been a man of few words.

A bit like Cormac, really. He'd never been one of those blokes who chattered away all day long, or wasted breath talking about stuff that didn't matter. But like her grandad, he was funny, and smart, and a decent man. At least, that was what she'd thought. Now, she was about to find out if she should strike 'honest' off his list of qualities.

Urgh, she was starting to feel seriously nauseous. What the hell was she doing? Just after eight o'clock on New Year's Eve and she was trawling Glasgow streets that were thronging with revellers gearing up for midnight, on her way to check out her boyfriend because her suspicions were refusing to die. And yes, they were founded on some pretty weird behaviour on Cormac's part, but shouldn't she be better than this? Shouldn't she trust in his love for her?

But then, hadn't her mum trusted in her dad?

Fuck it, she was going, and she'd just have to live with herself later, one way or another, but at least she'd know the truth.

In the distance, she saw the fire station on her right-hand side and leaned forward, peering through the windscreen, anxious to get a closer look. Cormac's car – or rather, his truck – was usually parked in the car park at the front of the station. That had been something else she'd loved about him. None of that flash sports car energy with this guy – he had a slightly battered old white pick-up truck that he refused to change because he loved it so much. Surely that had to be an indicator of loyalty, right there?

Eyes flicking like a metronome between the car park in the distance and the road straight ahead, anxiety began to twist her insides. Yes! There was a white vehicle in the car park. She could see it. 'Thank you. Thank you. Thank you.' Bugger, she was doing the talking out loud thing again. *But thank you anyway. Thank you. Thank...*

Shit. She'd got close enough to see that it wasn't Cormac's white truck, but a small transit with 'Barry's Bakery' emblazoned on the side, next to a logo that showed a design that resembled the Olympics symbol, but was made out of intertwining doughnuts. If she wasn't so stressed, she'd find the whole scenario funny, but her sense of humour was clearly as lost as Cormac's location.

No, she chided herself. *Don't draw conclusions just yet. Stick with it. Believe in him.*

There was a car park round at the back of the building, so maybe his truck was there. Slowing down, she switched on her indicator as she approached the building. The doors were up, and she could see that one of the engines was out. Perhaps he was out with it. But if that was the case, his vehicle should definitely still be here.

Turning right into the entrance, she followed the road around to the back parking area. No pick-up there either. Hope fading, she drove into a space and pulled on the handbrake. He wasn't here – and suddenly she felt like she shouldn't have come because now she had the answer to a question she hadn't been brave enough to ask outright.

Or maybe now was the time for a more direct approach.

With clammy hands, she picked up her phone and checked the location again.

Be here. Just be here.

Nope. Cormac Sweeney still wasn't sharing his location.

Emmy closed her eyes, inhaled, exhaled.

Okay, do this.

Text. Cormac. Type.

> Hey love, how's your day going. Busy?

Send.

She waited, drumming her fingers on the steering wheel, counting the passing seconds in her head. When she got to 100, she couldn't stand it any more. Sod it. He came to her work earlier, so surely there shouldn't be an issue with her dropping by to say hello? It wasn't something she did often, but she'd occasionally stopped in with a hot meal or his favourite coffee if he was on a double shift.

Anxiety crackling under her skin, she switched off the engine and jumped out, barely registering the bitter cold of the evening.

Was this it? Was she about to find out, for absolutely definite, that two of the three men she'd loved the most in life were liars? Was Grandad Henry the only one who wasn't in the Lying Hall of Shame?

She was about to press the entrance buzzer, when a bloke she didn't recognise came out and held the door open for her to pass. She thanked him and veered around him, eyes scanning the back reception area and immediately spotting Jake, one of the officers who usually worked the opposite shift to Cormac.

Her instant smile was her very best attempt to act like nothing was wrong. 'Jake! How are you doing?'

In his fifties and planning to retire soon, Jake had one of those slow, languid, Matthew McConaughey smiles that told of someone who didn't get too flustered about the small things in life.

'Hey Emmy, I'm good. How about you? And why don't you have a jacket on? You'll get pneumonia out there.'

'I've got an inner glow that keeps me toasty,' Emmy joked with him, like she would on any other day. Any other day that she wasn't absolutely fricking terrified about the rest of her life. Right now, the risk of developing pneumonia was the least of her worries. 'Listen, I was just passing and wanted so see if Cormac's here by any chance?'

She left that one deliberately ambiguous. Even if he was on shift, he might not be here because he was out on a job. Although, Jake didn't need the additional detail of the missing pick-up truck.

With every fibre of her being, she wanted him to say, 'Sure, hold on and I'll buzz him.' She was praying for it. Manifesting it. Thinking it into existence until...

'Nope, it's Shift Two and Shift Three that's covering today. Shift One are off now until the third because they covered Christmas.' Suddenly, his eyes narrowed, as if it had just occurred to him that she should have known that, so she went straight for the bluff.

'Yes, but he'd said he might drop in because he'd left his gym bag here. I was just over this way and thought I'd try to catch him. No worries, Jake,' she said breezily as she began to back out of the building. 'Give my love to Caron...' Emmy had met Jake's wife at a couple of station functions. 'And Happy New Year.'

'You too, Emmy. And tell Cormac the same.' That was delivered with that slow, languid grin again.

Emmy managed to keep her smile up all the way back to the door, and had just burst back out into the cold when it cracked spectacularly, replaced by a weight on her chest that was making it hard to breathe.

Fuck. Fuck. Fuck. Fuck. He was lying. He'd been lying the whole time. For how long? Since the start of their relationship? Or was this something new? And who was she? Who was the woman he was texting, seeing, shagging so often she smelled her perfume on his clothes?

Some women might want to scream. To howl. To smash windows and slash tyres and Emmy didn't blame them, but right now, all she wanted to do was to speak to him, to confront him. She checked her phone again, hoping with every fibre of her soul that he'd replied to her message with some kind of answer that would clear the whole thing up, make this all an innocent misunderstanding. She couldn't even think what that would be, but she also couldn't bear to accept the reality. They were over. Done. This was how her mum had felt two years ago and oh, the shit coincidence that they'd both had their worlds shattered at the same time of the year.

The phone screen was blank. No reply. No explanation.

Before she really processed what she was doing, she hit a button to speak to one of the only people who could make her feel better right now. Yvie's number rang five or six times, then diverted to her voicemail. Strange. Yvie was usually joined at the hip to her phone when she was off duty. Must be in the shower or something. Emmy didn't bother to leave a message.

Her finger hovered over the screen again. Her mum would be arriving at Gino's about now. And her gran would either be enjoying her movie, or already in bed. Minnie turned in any time between 7 p.m. and 3 a.m., depending on her mood. 'One of the perks of being old, my love,' she would say. 'I can do absolutely anything I please.'

Emmy slouched back in the seat, head against the headrest, utterly deflated, sad and devastated... and there was not a single person she could call to talk about it. And the one person she wanted to speak to above everyone else? She had no idea where he was.

Another thought assaulted her. He'd told her he wouldn't be back until morning. Did that mean he was... Oh crap, deep breath. Her heart was starting to beat out of her chest as she realised that it meant he must be with someone right now, preparing to bring in the New Year, and then spending the whole night with them afterwards. Was he staying at her house? Or were they away in a romantic hotel somewhere, sipping champagne and swapping chocolate fucking strawberries?

Her phone suddenly buzzed to life and she yelped as she jumped. Damn, her nerves were shot.

Please make it be Cormac.

Please make it be Yvie.

Please make it be anyone who could listen to her while her heart broke.

Her gaze went to the screen. DAD.

Bollocks. The one person she definitely didn't want to speak to, especially not today. Not now. A tiny part of her longed for the dad that she'd grown up with, the one who would hug her when she was upset, make her laugh when she was sad. What happened to him? How could he have gone from that great father and husband to this train wreck of a person? She didn't know the answer and right now she didn't care to ask. Her dad could solve his own problems today. She was going to go home and lie in a bath and...

Another buzz. If it was her dad again, she decided she was putting the phone out the window.

It was a huge relief when the screen announced that it was Mum.

As she opened the message, she hoped it was going to say they'd had a change of heart and decided to stay in at Aunt Gwen's place. If that was the case, Emmy could head there now and let three lovely women shower her with support. Actually two. Aunt Rhonda would probably go hunting for Cormac with a sharp object.

She read the text. Then read it again because it took a moment to absorb what it was actually saying.

> Just got to Gino's and your gran is here. She's come alone but seems quite happy. Anyway, hope you're good. Will call you at midnight. Love you. xx

Emmy still didn't get it. Gran had absolutely, definitely, 100 per cent assured her that she was staying home tonight. Emmy had even felt sorry for her and worried that she'd be sad, but now it seemed maybe Gran was being economical with the truth too? Emmy dismissed that thought immediately. Minnie had never told a fib in her life. Something else had to be going on with her.

Her dad. Cormac. Her mum. Now Minnie. Everyone was shocking her today.

This was unbelievable. Unreal. Was there a full moon or some other weird thing going on? Or was she being pranked? That was it. Any minute now, a comedian and a camera crew would pop out of the bushes beside her.

She waited for a moment just to see if that happened.

Nope, this was all real. This was her life. Fricking spectacular. And there was only one way to deal with it. Her thumbs flew across the screen.

I'm on my way.

27

DARIO

Dario had spotted her the moment she'd walked in and for the first time today, he felt a tiny shred of happiness. Last time she was here was two years ago, and it had been a total shitshow, so he wasn't surprised that they hadn't come back last year. But here she was now, and on any other night, he'd be thinking the heavens were smiling on him, especially when he spotted the way her gaze flicked to him when he greeted them. Tonight, he just figured the heavens were playing some cruel, twisted joke. Not that he thought for a second that anything was going to happen between them. If it had, it would have been a long time ago. Nope, he'd resigned himself to the fact that she'd always just see him as a friend, and, well, it was better than nothing.

'You know, I always thought she had a thing for you,' Nicky said, nodding in the direction of his gaze.

He rolled his eyes, then took a step round to the side so that he was facing her. 'Do you always sneak up on people like that?' he asked her, feigning irritation.

It wasn't lost on either of them that the minute they decided to call time on their marriage, they ceased to view the other as the most annoying person that ever lived, and went back to just being best mates. Expectations, that was the difference. She no longer expected him to prioritise her over his job – something he saw now that she had every right to want. And at the same time, he no longer expected her to understand that all he'd ever known was working fourteen-hour days in the restaurant, and he had been unable to change that.

'Only when they're my ex-husband and I like to mess with his emotional well-being,' Nicky said with a wink, putting a tray of empty glasses back on the bar, and sliding a new drinks order over to Carlo, who was rattling them up like he'd been doing it forever. Which he actually had. 'By the way, the four bottles of lager and the vodka and lemonade on this order are for Sonya over on table six. Her Ollie has some pals back from uni and she's brought them all in to celebrate. They've said they'll sneak Sonya into their student accommodation to live with them when she gets evicted. Which is, of course, the craziest thing you've ever heard... so she'll probably do it. God, I'll miss her.'

It struck him again how he felt exactly the same. Nicky. Sonya. Matty. His dad. All of it. He was going to miss having a reason to get up in the morning. Even if it was only to give his ex-wife someone to take the piss out of.

'Me too. Can you comp that round of drinks for her, please?' he said to Nicky, as she went off with the tray Carlo had already prepared for her, holding it above her head as she dodged through the tables.

They were almost full now, just three or four parties still to come in. The night always followed the same format. Food, drink, then as soon as service was over, about 10 p.m., his dad would crank up the volume on the music. Then just before midnight, he'd climb up onto a chair and make a speech, then count down to the bells. Afterwards, he'd start singing one of his favourite songs, maybe 'That's Amore'. By the end of that tune, everyone would be joining in and then, over the course of the early hours of the morning, they'd get through all Gino's Greatest Hits – a natty selection of Italian and Scottish tunes that invariably included 'Caledonia', 'The Bonnie Banks of Loch Lomond', 'Volare', 'O Sole Mio' and 'Shout' by Lulu. It was an eclectic compilation that always got the customers up on their feet, singing, dancing and revelling in the party atmosphere.

Dario had taken the order Nicky had left behind, and was now holding a glass under the vodka optic, while Carlo worked another order, doing the work of two men without blinking. He was currently uncorking a new bottle of red, while simultaneously sliding out wine glasses from the brass rack above their heads. As soon as he started to pour, Carlo caught Dario's attention. 'Listen, I've been thinking about everything we were talking about earlier.'

Dario pulled out four bottles of Peroni from the fridge and put them on a tray next to Sonya's vodka. 'And now you're as depressed as me?' he quipped, conveying a sense of humour that he definitely wasn't feeling right now.

'Yeah, that too,' Carlo agreed with a rueful smile. 'But something else. Look, this probably isn't the best place to talk about this, but given the time crunch, I want to lay it out there.' He continued to work, putting a tray of drinks together as he spoke, nothing breaking his rhythm. They'd been doing this for so long that they could walk, chew chewing gum, hold a conversation and pour a martini all at the same time, without breaking a sweat.

Dario popped the tops off the Peroni bottles as he listened to what Carlo had to say.

'I know I said earlier that I would always have a job for Matty in the kitchen over at the café, and that I'd welcome Dad playing a role on whatever terms he wanted to...'

'And I appreciate that, I really do. It might just take a little bit of the sting out of this whole crap show for them. Although, looking at Dad's face now, I wouldn't bet on it.'

They both glanced over to where Gino was having dinner with his old friend Henry's wife and even from here, they could see that he was just oozing sorrow and sadness. Neither of them was surprised. The two couples had a history that went back to the seventies. Mum and Minnie had adored each other, and Dad and Henry had a bond like brothers. Dario always thought Henry's passing back in January had aged Dad ten years, and he wasn't sure he'd recovered even now.

Carlo sighed, and Dario felt for him, because he knew his baby brother worried about Dad just as much as he did. Carlo took the two glasses of red wine and put them on the tray in front of him. 'Okay, so I haven't got to the bit I wanted to talk to you about yet.'

'I'm listening,' Dario told him, picking up another waiting order and tossing a slice of lime into a glass for a gin & tonic for table number 2.

'Look, I just want to give you something to consider. You know I was saying earlier about the café being packed... sorry to rub that in...'

'Don't worry, I can take it,' Dario assured him, full of jest, but he'd be lying if he didn't wish this place was doing that well every day of the week too.

'Well,' Carlo went on. 'One of the things I've got planned for this coming year is to open another one. Maybe two more.'

It was the first Dario had heard of it, but he couldn't help feeling a wave of pride. With such a big age gap, their relationship had always sat between paternal and fraternal. This was like seeing your kid was about to rule the world and being so fricking happy for him. But then he paused... tonic half poured.

'Carlo, you're not about to suggest you take over this place, are you? Because, brother, that's not the move. The rates and the bills here are sky-high, and the building needs so much work. And you know we're not getting anywhere near the volume of people that we used to.'

It was a relief when Carlo shook his head. 'No, no... God, no. For all the reasons you just said, and for a few more too. This just isn't my business model. I look for places next to high-occupancy venues – that's why I took the unit next to the hospital – but where there's very little competition nearby. We'd get swallowed in this part of the city centre. Too many other options doing similar things.'

Dario nodded. 'You're not wrong. So where are you looking at?'

Carlo was onto three glasses of white wine and a porn star martini now. 'That's the thing, I haven't found the right place yet, because I don't have time to scout. The café is taking up all of my time and leaving nothing for development. So that's what I wanted to talk to you about. I know this is out of the blue, and I'm not expecting an answer now, but I want you to consider coming into business with me. A partnership. Between the two of us, we can run the current location, and that will also free up time to focus on expansion. When we get the second place open, you can use that one as your base, while we search for a third. Maybe by that time, Matty will take one, and we'll move on to the next. I'm not saying all this is going to happen tomorrow, but I'm definitely seeing it as something that starts now and stretches over the next few years. I can't do it on my own, and there's no one I trust more, either in business or in life.'

Dario didn't know if it was shock or intense gratitude that was suddenly making him feel emotional. This day, man. Just when he thought he was getting some grip in the sand, a big bloody wave came right for him. And it was the kindness again. Got him every time.

'Carlo, I can't even begin to tell you how much of an honour it is that you're asking me this.' For the second time today, he wondered if his mother was seeing how cool a guy her youngest son had turned out to be.

Carlo shrugged, as if it were nothing. 'You'd honestly be helping me out too. I think we could achieve something special if we did this together.'

Dario didn't disagree. Their temperaments had always complemented each other perfectly and what Dario had in experience, Carlo had in energy and ideas. They would make a pretty good team. 'I think we could too...'

But then... His gaze went back to his dad. How could he be making plans to move on to a whole new chapter when he hadn't closed this one yet? Especially when he knew that the ending of this story was going to wring out his heart?

Until his dad gave his blessing for this deal, then Dario couldn't even begin to think about what came next.

'Look, let me think about it, is that okay? I need to sort things out here first.'

Carlo was in no rush. 'Of course. Take all the time you need. I just wanted to raise it now so you know you could have something at the end of this. Maybe take the pressure off a bit. You've helped me all my life, Dario. Not to do all that mushy shite, but it's time I paid you back.'

'You owe me nothing,' Dario began to object, but Nicky slid back into the space in front of the bar.

'What doesn't he owe you?' she asked, eyes narrowing in mock suspicion. 'Whatever it is, I should have got half of it in the divorce.'

As he'd just been thinking, he'd miss her. Her boyfriend, Scott, was a lucky guy.

She barely paused for breath as she slid another tray of empties onto the counter, followed by an order for Carlo. 'Table number 12. Gwen, Ailish and Rhonda would like three Slippery Nipples and I swear I didn't put them up to that. They're saying they're the menopause version of Charlie's Angels and, apparently, they're reliving their twenties, so I might clock off early and go join them so we can all moan about how men couldn't find the tickly bit back then.'

'Nicky, we were married when you were in your twenties,' Dario retorted, full of indignation.

'Exactly,' she giggled, before grabbing the tray with Sonya's order and going back on her merry way, leaving Dario shaking his head and Carlo howling with laughter.

She'd only got a few feet away when she stopped, turned... 'Oh and by the way...' She nodded back over to the table where Ailish, Gwen and Rhonda were deep in conversation with his mate, Brodie, who'd known them almost as long as Carlo had. 'I always thought you had a thing for her too. You should go tell her. You've got nothing to lose, and what's the worst that can happen?'

28

MINNIE

Minnie was barely aware of the revelry and the happy buzz of the guests at the tables around her, too engrossed in her conversation with Gino. She'd been waiting for the right time to tell him why she was here, but she hadn't quite got to that yet because they'd had so much to talk about.

As soon as he'd spotted her being seated at her usual table, he'd come straight to her side, and as she'd stood up, he'd wrapped her in the warmest embrace. 'Ah Minnie, my friend.' That was all he'd managed before his voice cracked, and Minnie understood. Gino was just like her Henry in so many ways. Neither of them showed vulnerability – probably a generational thing, she'd always thought – so when they got emotional, they would hold back, pause, wait until they'd composed themselves before going on.

'Sit, sit, please,' he'd beckoned, before gesturing to the seat opposite her.

She took in his appearance, not to judge, but to get an indication of how he was doing. On the surface of it, as always, he gave the appearance of a very dapper gent, with his beautifully cut suit and his silk cravat. But closer scrutiny hinted at a different story. He'd lost weight and his cheeks were a little sunken, his eyes were heavy with tiredness, the shadows under them as grey as rain-clouds. He wasn't tall but he'd always given the impression of size, his huge personality filling every room. Today, he seemed smaller. Almost shrunken. And she could see that there were a couple of creases in his suit that must have been missed when it was pressed. Alicia would never have let him out of the house like that. Whether they were rich or poor, she'd always insisted that Gino and the boys were impeccably dressed.

'Have you come with a friend?' he'd asked warmly.

'No, Gino,' she'd responded, and she was sure she'd seen a flicker of relief on his face. 'I've just come to see you.' It would be difficult to talk properly if she'd brought a stranger with her. Only two people truly understood the history of their friendship, and they were both here now.

'Then it would be my pleasure to eat with you,' he'd said, to her surprise. Gino rarely sat down on Hogmanay. Just another thing that was different this year. 'Let me get you a drink. A sherry, I think?' he'd offered.

'That would be lovely, thank you.'

He'd glanced around, but all of the waiting staff were busy, and he'd never been known for his patience. The next thing she knew, he was on his feet and on his way to the bar to pour the drinks himself. She'd been watching him, thinking that she'd seen him do that very same thing a million times before, when she noticed that Ailish, Gwen and Rhonda had arrived, and were about to pass her on the way to their table. What a lovely surprise that was and, of course, Ailish had spotted her immediately. Although, Minnie had almost had to look twice because her daughter-in-law was simply ravishing. What a fool that son of hers had been. Not that appearances were everything, mind you, but they already knew how beautiful Ailish was on the inside too. The fact that she still took such lovely care of Minnie, even after everything that had happened, said so much about her character.

When the girls had gone off to their table, she and Gino had ordered their meals, then nursed their sherries. There was so much to say to him, that Minnie wasn't sure where to start, so she'd decided to go back to the beginning of the year and work forward from there.

'Thank you for coming to Henry's funeral. That would have meant so much to him, Gino.' For every moment of that day, Minnie had wondered what Henry would have been thinking of those who came to pay their respects. The sight of Gino would have pleased him. The sight of Eric, sitting with his girlfriend on one side of the aisle, and Ailish and Emmy on the other side, would have bitterly disappointed him. Like her, Henry had loved Ailish like a daughter, and Emmy had been the apple of his eye.

'I wouldn't have missed it. I'm only sorry that...' She'd seen that he was suddenly emotional again and struggling for the words. 'I'm sorry that I didn't come to see you again since then.'

Minnie had reached over and put her hand on one of his. 'You've had your own grief to deal with, without adding on mine.' Minnie and Henry had both been heartsore for him after he lost Alicia, because she was his very world.

'You know, shortly after Alicia died, Henry came to my home,' Gino had said. 'And that was not how it was with us...'

Minnie knew what he was saying. The two families came together every Hogmanay, and perhaps a few other times in the year, but they weren't in the habit of visiting each other's homes. As far as she could remember, Gino had only been in their house that one time, decades ago, on the Hogmanay that they were all sick and hadn't gone out. The Morettis had a restaurant to run, and the Ryans were busy working and bringing up children. And besides, it was a rare treat to go out to eat in those days. It was only in the last twenty years or so that Henry would suggest they go out for the occasional meal on a Friday night, and of course they always came here.

'I was broken with sadness, and I had refused to spend time with anyone else since she passed. Not even my sons.' Gino had gone on. 'I'd decided that there was no point to life, if I couldn't wake up every morning to see Alicia there. But Henry... That day, he reminded me that she was not my only love. There was my family. My restaurant. Henry talked to me long into the night, and we worked out a plan that I could live with. A small life. Nothing like the one that I'd lived with my wife, but at least I would be here to watch over my sons, to see my restaurant every day. The next week, I handed over everything to Dario, but I started coming here again when I was ready. Henry came to me when I needed him and I should have come to you.'

Minnie had shaken her head, then paused as their meals were served to them, before going on. 'Please don't feel guilty. We all handle grief in different ways.' She knew that was true. 'I keep Henry with me by talking to him all day long. I find a comfort in that. I'm sure his ears must be bleeding.'

That had made Gino laugh and they'd spent the next hour or so eating and chatting over old times.

Only now that their plates had been cleared, and a second round of sherries delivered, did she feel ready to share the reason she was here. She reached for the box that she'd put on the other chair beside her, tried to formulate the words, took a breath, when...

'Gran!' The interruption was sudden, abrupt, and brought with it a swift curl of her toes. Of course, when she'd bumped into Ailish she should have considered the possibility that word of her appearance here might get back to her granddaughter. The same granddaughter that she'd outright lied to and who was now standing here, eyebrows raised in question.

'Would you believe me if I told you that I had a last-minute change of mind?' Minnie asked tentatively.

'No.'

Emmy must have noticed that Gino was watching the discussion with amusement, because she broke off from being outraged to reach down and give him a kiss and a hug. 'Hello, Gino, it's lovely to see you. I'll be right back with you once I've got some answers from the runaway granny over here.'

His face creased with laughter and Minnie thought for the first time that he looked just a little bit like his old self.

'I'm sorry, love,' Minnie began. 'But I had something I wanted to talk to Gino about so I decided to just come here myself.'

'But why didn't you say?'

'Because I know the last time you were here was the night that ended your parents' marriage, and I didn't want to upset you or your mum by bringing it up.' She glanced over to her right. 'Although, your mother seems to be dealing with it very well at the moment.' Emmy turned her head, so they could both see that Ailish was wiping away tears of laughter. 'And while we're on the subject of untruths, me and your grandad came here last year too, after we told you we were staying home.' Minnie brought her gaze back to Gino. 'I'm as well getting all the fibs off my chest when I'm already in trouble anyway.'

Emmy was shaking her head now, and Minnie spotted that the edges of her mouth were twitching. 'Lies. Deceit. Minnie Ryan, I don't think I even recognise you any more,' Emmy said, milking it now, but she didn't get any further, because the next thing, her friend, Yvie, had appeared beside her. 'Emmy! What are you doing here? I thought you said you were going home for an early night?'

Minnie was now the one with the raised eyebrows. 'Like
Granny, like granddaughter it would seem.'

Even Emmy saw the funny side. 'I'll deal with you later,
Minnie Ryan,' she said, before taking her friend's hand and
leading her away.

When Minnie's gaze returned to Gino, she could see that he
was eyeing her questioningly, intrigued, perhaps, about what
she'd come to talk to him about.

Right. Now was the time to get back to the purpose of tonight
and come clean with Gino. If Henry was watching her now, he'd
be rolling his eyes and shaking his head. He was always saying she
could never get to the point.

But yet again, her plan was foiled, when Gino checked his
watch, and said, 'Minnie, there is so much more I want to say, but
I have to leave you for a moment or two.' He made a sweeping
gesture to the rest of the room. 'It's time to sing, to dance. All of
these people, they have come to celebrate, and I have to deliver
the party. Even if it's for the last time.'

That threw her. 'Why would it be for the last time?' she asked.

She had a grip of fear that maybe he'd been having dark
thoughts. When Henry had visited him that day shortly after
Alicia died, he'd come home and told her that he was having
those concerns too, because Gino had repeatedly said he didn't
want to live without his wife. Thank goodness they'd been
unfounded, but now?

Gino began to explain, and she felt weak with relief when she
realised that she'd got the wrong end of the stick. Although, the
other end of the stick wasn't a great place to be either. He told her
about the troubles at the restaurant, about the offer they'd
received to buy them out, about Dario's wish to accept it.

'And you?' she asked, knowing what the answer would be.

His angst was almost palpable. 'It's all I have left. What else would I have to wake up for?'

Okay, this was it. Her chance to tell him. She heard Henry's voice. *Right, Minnie, go.*

'Well, Gino...' she began, finally ready to lay it all out.

But before she could say anything else, Dario interrupted them and asked to speak to his father in private for a moment.

Gino stood up, lifted her hand, kissed the back of it, the way he'd done since she was a twenty-four-year-old mother of young kids, living in the third-floor tenement flat next door.

'I'll be back shortly, my friend,' he said, before heading off in the direction of the back office.

Minnie realised with a sigh how the next couple of hours would go. The restaurant was so busy, that from now until midnight Gino would be distracted by interruptions from his family and staff, his duties as the host, and his inherent need to make sure everyone had a great time.

'Minnie! I thought that was you. Och, lovely, I'm so sorry about Henry. I was just saying to my Ollie what a great man he was...' Sonya slipped into the seat Gino had just vacated, and Minnie felt so touched that she'd come over. Sonya had always been one of her favourite people to catch up with here every year. As they began to chat, she decided that she'd just have to accept that the conversation she'd come to have with Gino would need to wait a little bit longer.

She couldn't help but glance heavenwards again. *I know what you're thinking, Henry Ryan, but you'll just have to be patient because I'll get to it, don't worry.*

10 P.M. – ALMOST MIDNIGHT

29

AILISH

Ailish couldn't remember the last time she'd laughed so much in one night. Probably the last time she was here with this same crowd – although the caveat to that was that it all went tits up later on that particular night after her husband was caught out the back door with his mistress and her whole life had been shredded. Tonight, she had no such fears, because it was just delicious food, great cocktails, wonderful friends and absolutely, definitely no impending heart-wrenching betrayal.

Now, as the minutes ticked down towards midnight, their table was more alive than ever with conversation and laughter. To the right of her banquet seat in the huge round booth, Gwen and Rhonda were deliberating the best movies of the nineties (*Titanic, Independence Day, Armageddon* – they were leaning slightly towards doom and disaster) with Brodie, who'd been coming here for as long as they had. He'd been at the bar earlier and Rhonda had dragged him over here in what could only be described as a kidnap attempt. Not that Ailish minded, because Brodie had always been one of those men who added great chat to any table.

Ailish remembered when he used to come here with his wife, Crystal, who ran off with his business partner a few years back, but he seemed to be over that, because he was currently locked in heated debate with Rhonda and there were gales of laughter coming from their direction.

'I think we might be witnessing the sweet bud of a new romance,' came the whispered comment from the right of her. 'Or, at least, a mad, potentially kinky one-night stand, because it is Auntie Rhonda.'

A giggle escaped, before Ailish could stop it. 'Emmy Minette Ryan, that's a scandalous thing to say about my lifelong friend.'

Emmy picked the cherry off the top of Ailish's cocktail and popped it into her mouth, but she still managed to murmur, 'True, though.'

There was an edge to Emmy's tone that made Ailish give her daughter a sideways glance. 'Are you sure you're okay, darling?'

Emmy's arrival had been the absolute cherry on top of tonight's celebration cake, but Ailish couldn't shake the feeling that something was wrong. Emmy seemed too... flat. That was the best way to describe it. And a couple of times, she'd spotted her daughter biting her lip, the way she'd always done when she was worried or upset. When she was six and lost her cabbage patch doll, she'd chewed it for days.

'I'm fine, Mum, really,' Emmy assured her.

It might convince someone else, but not Ailish. No point in pressing the matter though, because Emmy clearly didn't want to talk about it here. Maybe it was a work thing, Ailish decided. Working on the elderly ward came with such sadness sometimes. Yes, that must be it, because everything else in her daughter's life seemed to be going so well. She had a lovely group of friends, a job she loved, a wonderful boyfriend.

'Honestly, Mum, don't worry,' Emmy continued to reassure

her. 'Just you get on with having a fab night because you deserve it, especially after... after...'

Now Ailish was really worried. Emmy had suddenly paled, lost her words, closed her eyes and now she was making the most peculiar groan.

'Oh... hell... no.'

Panicked, Ailish immediately reached for her hand. 'Emms, are you having some kind of medical issue? Are you feeling faint? Dizzy?'

Emmy managed to lift her eyelids. 'Sorry, Mum, I should have warned you.'

'Warned me of what?' Ailish felt her worry escalating. 'Are you sick?' A sudden thought. 'Emmy, are you... pregnant? That would be amazing. Oh, my goodness!'

'Mum, I'm not pregnant!' Emmy hissed. 'I'm... absolutely fricking raging! I told him not to come here but apparently he couldn't help himself.'

Ah, that gave Ailish her answer as to why Emmy was out of sorts. She must have had a fight with Cormac, and told him she didn't want to see him tonight. In her mind, she put her fictional grandchild's baby-grows back in their drawer.

'I'm so sorry,' Emmy said for the second time, confusing Ailish even further. Why would Emmy be apologising about fighting with her boyfriend? What was she missing here?

'Sorry about what, honey?'

Emmy was staring right past her now. 'Sorry about him.'

Ailish slowly turned her head, focused her gaze, blinked. Then blinked again. And again. Nope, he was still there. Eric Ryan was headed straight for her.

'Aw bugger, someone give me a fork and bail money,' Rhonda demanded beside her, and Ailish guessed she'd just spotted him too.

Unlike Rhonda, she was momentarily speechless, so she was glad when Emmy took the lead. 'Seriously, Dad? Did I not make you promise not to do this tonight?'

'I know, I'm so sorry, Em. But I just need to speak to your mum for two minutes.'

Ailish felt like she was in some other realm, watching this unfold with detached curiosity. Eric. Her Eric. But he wasn't that, any more, was he? This Eric's hair was different, longer, swept back off the face that she'd kissed goodnight every night for three decades. He was unshaven, which was unusual, but somehow it worked on him. If she was being objective, she'd say it gave him a bit of a sexy, rugged edge. But she wasn't objective because this was the man who'd broken her heart.

'Ails, can I talk to you for a moment? Maybe outside?'

'Nope,' Rhonda answered for her.

Ailish's questioning gaze immediately went to Emmy, who gave a helpless shrug. 'Whatever you think, Mum. Up to you.'

No, Ailish decided firmly. She didn't owe him anything. Not a minute more of her life.

'Please, Ails,' he said again, and she felt a chisel start to chip away at her defences. He reached his hand out towards her, and she was painfully aware that everyone at the table – Rhonda, Gwen, Brodie, Emmy – was frozen in time, waiting for her response.

Before she could give it, like some kind of rapid response unit, Dario appeared out of nowhere. With their parents all being so close, Dario and Eric had always rubbed along just fine, so she was surprised by the disgusted glare he was firing Eric's way now as he asked, 'All okay, Ailish?'

She wanted to say no, but her deep-rooted, conflict-avoidance habit had programmed her differently. 'I'm fine, Dario. Eric just... popped in to see me.'

She could see from Dario's shifting gaze that he was being protective, but didn't want to overstep his mark. 'Okay, well shout me if you need anything at all,' he said, pointedly, before switching attention to his friend. 'Brodie, can I have a quick word in the office?'

Brodie nodded, and slid out of the booth. They both headed away from the table in the direction of the kitchen, but not before Dario threw Eric another piercing stare.

On any other day, Ailish would ponder the reason for that, but right now she was already up to her neck in an ex-husband confrontation.

And the ex-husband's hand was still outstretched, waiting for hers. Almost without conscious thought, her own hand rose towards it, and as they touched, she felt a charge of electricity that almost undid all the spectacular work that Roxy had put into her hair.

As she rose, she heard Gwen ask, 'Are you sure, Ails?' Ailish managed a nod that said yes. Maybe. No. Yes. Possibly.

Gwen took it as a yes, but Ailish could feel several sets of eyes on them as she followed Eric to the nearby alcove, which contained a dessert trolley and the banjo that Gino often played after midnight, so they sidestepped those.

Eric turned to face her, and she realised his hand was still holding on to hers, and meanwhile, her hand was ignoring all commands from her brain to pull away. Eventually, her brain gave up and diverted to the memory section, throwing up images of the times they'd been here before. Eric had asked her to marry him right in this spot, and they'd kissed in this little alcove until Gino interrupted them because he needed two tiramisu and his banjo. On the night she'd told him she was pregnant with Emmy, they'd stood in here and he'd promised to be the best dad he could be to their child. And only a few years ago, shortly after she'd turned fifty, he'd gently pulled her in here at midnight, told her that marrying her was the best thing he'd ever done and that he couldn't wait to grow old with her. Exactly two years later he had a mistress who told her differently.

'Thank you for speaking to me,' he said earnestly. 'You look amazing, Ails. Stunning.'

'I haven't got long,' Ailish immediately countered, quietly chuffed at the compliment, but playing it cool while trying to make sure he knew this wasn't all on his terms and that she wasn't just jumping because he snapped his fingers.

'Okay, I'll be quick. The thing is...' He took a deep breath and then his exhalation brought a torrent of words with it. 'Ailish, I'm so sorry. For everything. I've been such a prick and so bloody stupid. I've known almost from the start that I'd made a huge mistake, but then it just all exploded and it was too late to fix it. Next thing I knew, we were over and I was with Donna and...'

What was he saying? That he'd never wanted them to split up? That he regretted the whole affair?

'You've been with her for over two years, Eric,' she challenged him, drily. 'That doesn't sound like a brief error of judgement.'

'You're right. I think it just all got out of control and then I'd made my bed...'

'Her bed,' she said cattily. Jesus, she sounded like Rhonda.

'Yes,' he conceded, clearly embarrassed. Her unusually confrontational manner was pushing him right on to the back foot. 'But like I said, it was a mistake. I can't do it any more. I've ended it. Moved out. It's over.'

Wow, she almost reeled from the shock of that. In no world had she seen that coming.

'And I know I messed up so badly, but if we can put the last two years to one side, just for a second...'

Ailish's mind was still on the news of his break-up. How did she feel about that? Relieved? Vindicated? Actually, just really, really fricking furious. Although, maybe a bit vindicated too.

He was still speaking. '...Then you can't deny that we had thirty really happy years together. That has to say something?' he implored.

'It says you shouldn't have left me for someone else,' Ailish blurted, unable to stop herself from pointing out the obvious.

'You're right! And if I could go back, I swear, Ailish, I would change that. I honestly don't know what the hell happened to me. I can't expect you to forgive me, but all I'm asking is that you could find a way to at least be open to talking again and see where we go from there. I'll do whatever you need me to, just to get you back. Please. I love you, Ailish. I always did. I just screwed up and forgot it for a minute. But I truly do. I love you.'

He loved her. He loved her. He. Loved. Her. Oh dear God, what were her insides doing? Her heart was thudding so fast, she was feeling giddy. Wasn't this what she had thought about for two solid years now?

Rhonda's question from earlier replayed in her mind.

'What about Eric? If he ever came knocking on your door again, how would you feel? Would you consider taking him back?'

She now knew at least part of the answer. Stunned. That's how she'd feel. As well as shocked and scared and all over the place.

All her intelligent, profound, meaningful words were stuck in her windpipe, so she could only manage, 'I need... to... to... think about it.'

'I totally understand. Take your time. Think about it. I saw Mum on my way in, so I'm going to go sit with her for a bit. But, Ailish, I want to start the new year with you. New page. New chapter. Please say yes.'

As she walked back towards her table, her thoughts were exploding like the fireworks that would light the city sky at midnight. Did she want him back? She'd loved him so, so much for all of those years.

They'd had a life together. A history.

And she couldn't ignore the tiny part of her that wanted to make it their future too.

30

EMMY

Back in the red leather booth, Emmy watched her parents in deep conversation over in the alcove, unsure as to whether or not she should intervene. She'd much rather go check on Gran, but she could see that Gino's chair was still being occupied by Sonya, who was chatting away to Minnie.

She focused back on her parents again.

'Should I go over there?' she wondered aloud, in earshot of Rhonda and Gwen, who were also watching intently.

'Only if you have a gun,' Rhonda sniped, then climbed down a rung. 'Sorry, I know it's your dad, but I bear a grudge.'

Gwen leaned forward on her elbows and Emmy noticed that she was beginning to look a little tired. Maybe tonight was too much, too soon, after all she'd been through.

'But that's the thing, Rhonda, maybe Ailish doesn't bear a grudge the way you do,' Gwen countered. 'And maybe life is too short not to forgive someone you love when they make a mistake.'

Rhonda didn't seem impressed by this perspective. 'Okay, Dalai Lama, pipe down. I preferred you before you got into all this karmic spiritual stuff. Please go back to being a stroppy cow so we can be friends again.'

Even though her whole world was crumbling around her, that made Emmy laugh. No wonder these three friends had got though everything life had thrown at them – cancer, divorces, heartache, sorrow and Aunt Rhonda's compulsive shopping habit. They just stuck together and found some kind of humour in even the worst of things. Emmy saw the same spirit on her ward all the time and she was convinced it could be the difference between giving up and fighting on.

Too anxious to watch, her gaze went from there, over to the bar, where Yvie was chatting to her fiancé, Carlo. There was a couple who wouldn't be having a midlife crisis at fifty. Both of them were equally devoted to each other and Emmy couldn't suppress the pang of pain that pinged her heart. She'd thought the same about herself and Cormac. Thought they were forever. That she knew him inside and out. Yet she'd been wrong.

Despite vowing that she wouldn't, she picked her phone back up and flicked to the location app again.

Cormac Sweeney's location is unavailable.

She wanted to drop her phone into Aunt Rhonda's Slippery Nipple.

Instead, she made idle chit-chat with her aunts until they saw her mum coming back towards them. They all smiled at her as she approached, but under their breath, and trying not to move their lips, there was a whole conversation going on.

'Brace, brace, brace...' That came from Rhonda.

'No matter what's happened, be nice. I repeat: Be. Fricking. Nice.' That was Gwen.

Her mum slid back into the booth, clearly a bit shaken but trying her best to act calm and unfussed.

'Well?' Rhonda asked, cracking first, then making a circle motion with her index finger as it pointed to her own face. 'And I just want to point out that this is my non-judgemental face. They made me put my furious, murderous one in my bag.'

Her mum replied, 'Nothing really,' with a casual shrug, but she was kidding no one. Although, maybe it was for the benefit of her dad, who had replaced Sonya and was now sitting with Gran, but staring over this way.

Emmy shook her head. She officially had the most dysfunctional family in this restaurant tonight.

Her mum was the second one in sixty seconds to crack. 'Okay!' she exclaimed, but in hushed tones. 'He basically said he's left Donna because he's known almost since the start that it was a big mistake, and he's really sorry for being an idiot and wants me back because he still loves me and would I please, *please*, give him another chance.' All that was uttered without stopping for breath.

'I knew it,' Aunt Rhonda said, clearly disgusted.

Everyone else took a beat, before Aunt Gwen asked, 'And what did you say to that? How do you feel?'

Her mum shrugged helplessly. 'I said I need to think about it because I don't know. It's all such a shock.'

Emmy felt her face begin to heat up, and just like every single time in her life when she'd got caught out in something, her mum sensed it.

'You knew all this already, Em?'

Crack number three coming up.

'I did,' she admitted wearily. 'He showed up at my door first thing this morning, borderline deranged, telling me how he'd been a fool and that he wanted you back. But I didn't want to tell you because I wasn't sure if he was going to speak to you or not and I was wary. There would have been nothing worse than sharing all this with you, only for him to change his mind and go back to Donna by dinner time. And, to be honest, I didn't want to get involved. I'm meant to be the kid... Okay, so I'm twenty-nine, but you know what I mean. I don't want to be in the middle of my parents' marriage.'

She squinted with one eye to see how her mum had taken that news, but, of course, Ailish was nothing but love and understanding. Her dad was a total arse for letting her go – a fact that had been pretty well established but was nonetheless true.

'I'm sorry you were put in that position, darling. He should have known better.'

'Story of his life,' Rhonda muttered, slipping off her temporary visit to the diplomatic high ground.

Undistracted, her mum remained focused on Emmy. 'Does that mean you don't have an opinion on this? I'd love to know what you think. I know you don't want to be involved, but it affects you too. Do you think I should try again?'

Emmy managed to buy some time to think, because at that point, the music suddenly stopped and over at the bar, Carlo had come out from behind the marble counter, climbed up onto a chair and was calling for attention. 'Ladies and gentlemen, it's ten minutes until midnight, so if any of you lovely people don't have a drink to toast the bells, please grab one from the nice lady...'

He pointed to his former sister-in-law, Nicky, who was holding a tray of about twenty short glasses – Emmy guessed whisky – above her head, and who shouted back, 'Gorgeous! You were supposed to say, GORGEOUS LADY!'

Everyone in the restaurant cheered at that and Nicky took an elaborate bow, almost spilling the drinks, but righting the tray just in time. The music started up again and the party resumed, and for just a second Emmy experienced the same feelings she'd had every year of her younger life, when she'd been brought here by her parents and grandparents, and they'd had the happiest, most treasured of times.

It would be so great to have those moments again. Grandad had gone, but Gran, Mum, Dad, her and Cormac...

The bubble of happiness was burst by that thought. No. Not her and Cormac, because she'd never be able to forgive whatever he was doing today, or whoever he was doing it with.

And that led Emmy to her answer. Because how could she ask her mum to forgive her dad when she wasn't prepared to do the same in her own relationship?

'I think you have to do whatever you feel is right, Mum. But don't do anything because you feel obliged to. Or because it's easy. Or because he wants you to. He has to deserve you because you're worth so much more than the way you've been treated by him. Just do what's in your heart. And if that means going back to Dad, I'll support that too because even though he's been a complete moron, I still love him. Although if you reject him, the two of you aren't getting me on alternative weekends,' she tagged on, trying to lighten the mood, because she could feel her chin begin to wobble.

All night, it had felt weird being here, and she'd tried to join in the spirit of it, but she was too consumed by devastation. On top of that, there were just so many memories, both good and bad. And now, Cormac's absence had added another one, a crushing weight in her chest that was making it difficult to breathe.

All this emotion, and the prospect of the midnight celebration, was unravelling her. She couldn't do this. Couldn't be here.

'I'll be back in a second,' she said, but her mum immediately objected.

'Emmy, wait. It's almost midnight. You'll miss the bells! Hang on—'

'I'll be back, Mum. I just need to quickly grab something from the car and give Cormac a call to wish him Happy New Year.' It was all she could come up with, and the last words she got out before her throat clammed shut. She wouldn't be back and she wasn't going to call him either. She just couldn't be here. Couldn't stand to watch all the happiness, all the love, all the joy, when her life was exploding around her.

Dodging staff and diners, all rushing to get into position for the bells, she crossed the restaurant in seconds, making her way to the front door, trying desperately not to attract attention and make sure Minnie didn't spot her either. The last thing she needed was her gran haring out after her and slipping or stressing.

Almost there. Katie at the hostess stand at the door gave her a quizzical smile, but Emmy ignored it.

Almost there. She reached the front door.

Almost there. Slammed it open and...

He was there.

Cormac.

Standing right there in front of her.

Huddled together with Yvie.

And Emmy thought her heart was about to stop.

Her eyes went from one to the other, desperate to be mistaken.

Yvie was the first one to spot her and let out a strangled yelp of, 'Nooooooo.'

And from somewhere inside, Emmy heard the sound of Carlo hushing the crowd again.

It was almost midnight.

31

DARIO

Brodie was leaning against the wall of Dario's office, phone in his hand, ready to make the call.

And Dario still couldn't pull the trigger.

He was slumped on the sofa, Nicky next to him, and Matty was perched on the desk, all of them looking to him for a decision. One that he couldn't bring himself to make.

The last couple of hours had been excruciating. He'd interrupted his dad just after his dinner with Minnie and asked him to come talk to him one more time to plead his case.

Gino had reluctantly agreed, and as he'd walked to the office, Dario had felt a stab of grief for what he was doing to the elderly man beside him, a father who seemed to have aged even since this morning. Pain did that. Sadness did that. And Dario knew that, because he was feeling all those things too.

For a brief interlude earlier, he'd managed to forget that the walls were closing in. When Ailish, Gwen and Rhonda had arrived, they'd made him feel human and hopeful for the first time in weeks, but the sight of his father, lowering himself into the chair, had slammed the door shut on any happiness he could possibly feel.

For the second time today, he'd told Gino the facts, the pros, the cons of the deal. The list of pros was long – clearing their debts, escaping the burden of a restaurant that had become unprofitable, saving them from ruin and giving them financial security going forward. But the cons? Now that Carlo had offered to take on Matty, and Dario had agreed to make sure Sonya would be taken care of, there was only really one – he would be ripping out his old man's heart, destroying Gino's life's work, quite literally bulldozing his memories to the ground.

When he'd gone through it all again, his dad had raised his eyes and Dario had seen tears there. The man who had never cried in public in his life, not even when Mum died. Back then, he'd just locked himself away, and then shocked them all by giving the restaurant to Dario. He'd never understood what led his dad to that point, but whatever it was, now he was repaying that gift with a whole world of pain.

'There's no way out of this, Dad. I need to know that I have your blessing. I beg you. Please.' In desperation, Dario had even gone low, dug right into the depths of the barrel with the one thing that might just sway him. 'Mum wouldn't have wanted this, Dad. She wouldn't have wanted us to keep killing ourselves to keep this place alive, and she'd never have stood by and watched us sink further and further into debt, until there was nothing left. And that's the only way that this ends if we don't take the deal. Mum would have let this go, because she knew that we, our family, were more important that the bricks in these walls.'

That had lit a fire, but not the one that Dario had hoped for.

His dad had slowly raised his head, fixed his dark, glistening eyes on Dario, and spoke in a voice that sounded almost haunted. 'Don't you dare tell me what your mother would have done. I knew my Alicia so much better than you. She lived for this, for our dream.' In pretty much a repetition of what had happened this afternoon, his dad had risen from his chair and eyed Dario with such disdain that he'd felt like he was a child again. 'I haven't changed my mind,' he'd said. 'When your mother died, I gave this business to you. I gave it to you because I trusted you with its care. And because I gave it to you, I now have no power. So you need to be the one to decide its fate, Dario. It's in your hands. But don't ask me for my blessing, because as I told you earlier, I won't give it.'

Dario had watched as the most stubborn man who had ever lived walked out of the room.

Fuck.

That was when he'd gone out into the restaurant and over to his friends' table. He'd have given anything to have been able to sit down with them, have a glass of good red wine and pass the rest of the night in laughter and happiness. That was what life should be about and he'd been missing that for far too long. When he got out of this mess, that had to change. *He* had to change. He just hoped there was still time for him to find the joy he was looking for.

Ailish had just been leaving the table with that tosser, Eric, when he'd got there. Dario had always tolerated him, but she should be with someone who was worthy of her and treated her with the respect she deserved. Dario could see in her eyes that she knew that. He just hoped that she listened to her heart.

In the meantime, he'd had other issues to deal with.

'Brodie, can I have a quick word in the office?' They'd made their way back through the thronging, jubilant crowd to the cold deathly silence of the office.

'Well?' Brodie had asked him.

'My dad is still not on board, so I don't know if I can do it. I mean, maybe there's another way. Maybe I can find something,

anything, to turn this round. There has to be another solution.'
How many times over the last few months had he said the same
thing? How many times had he wrangled with the same dilemma?
They had talked through everything they'd tried, everything they
hadn't tried, and they'd come up with nothing.

'We both know there's no other way to solve this,' Brodie had
told him, as gently as he could. 'But if you want to try, I'll loan you
everything I've got, pal. Whatever you need, it's yours.'

Argh, the fucking kindness again. For maybe the first time
outside of weddings, funerals, and midnight at decades of
Hogmanay parties, Dario had hugged his friend and didn't want
to let go.

'Damn, I always suspected!' Nicky had joked, as she'd burst in
the door to be greeted by the sight of their embrace, before stopping, sensing the atmosphere. 'I never could read a room,' she'd
muttered, as the two men separated. 'Okay, everyone next door
has got their drinks for the bells and my lovely boyfriend, Scott,
who, quite frankly deserves a medal for putting up with this
messed-up family dynamic, is proving his love for me by minding
the bar because Carlo's going to start the countdown in a few
minutes. Your dad asked him to do it tonight.'

Dario hadn't had a chance to comment on that, to say that it
was the first time in the history of the restaurant, because right
behind his ex-wife, his son had followed and, strangely, he
seemed to have lost the thunderous expression he had been
wearing all day. Dario had sat down on the couch, Nicky next
to him.

'We have five minutes left before the clock on this deal runs
out and I need to know where everyone is,' he'd told them.

Brodie had pulled out his phone. 'Ready to go.'

Nicky had taken his hand. 'I don't think we have a choice,
Dario. And I want to go marry Scott, eat carbs and let myself go...

Sorry, not reading the room again,' she'd said, with an apologetic shrug, before tightening her fingers around his. 'I say sell.'

Matty had been the next to speak. 'I've just been speaking to Uncle Carlo and he's offered me a job. A partnership actually. Maybe my own place. He told me about your conversation earlier, about expanding his business with you, and offered to cut me in too.' He'd pushed his hand through the long dark hair that had been taken out of its band now that he'd finished in the kitchen. 'I think it could be a good move, Dad. And I'm sorry about earlier. Just... you know, a hot head.'

Once again, Dario was reminded that his son had inherited Gino's stubbornness, his passion, his talent and his quickness to forgive.

'Apology accepted, son. So, just to be clear, you're saying...?'

'I say sell.'

So everyone was in agreement.

Everyone except the man that mattered most.

That's where they were right now and the clock was still ticking.

'Make the call, Brodie.'

It answered on the second ring. 'This is Brodie Moore, acting on behalf of Dario Moretti and Gino's Trattoria.'

Dario felt his hands begin to tremble. He could still stop it. Still change his mind and signal to Brodie to hang up.

Brodie must have been having the same thoughts because he was staring at him now, eyebrows raised in question.

Dario nodded, then stretched over and signed the contract that was sitting on his desk.

Brodie relayed the message. 'We accept your offer. We'll send the paperwork over in the next couple of minutes.' He hung up, reached out and shook Dario's hand. 'I'll send the contract now. You did the right thing, pal.'

'Thank you for everything, Brodie.'

'That's more of a thanks than I got when we divorced,' Nicky quipped, refusing to read the room again.

Dario kissed her cheek anyway, then got up and hugged his son.

Out in the restaurant, Dario could hear Carlo hushing the crowd. It was almost time.

He would speak to his dad and tell him what he'd done later. That wasn't for now.

Right at this moment, there was only one conversation that he wanted to have.

When he'd briefly sat with his friends earlier, he'd had a realisation that was still stuck in the front of his mind.

This year, Ailish had got divorced and yet she'd found the strength to start a new life. He just prayed Eric hadn't changed her mind. At the same table, Gwen had faced death, and yet she was still optimistic about her future. And Rhonda... well, she just woke up and made the most of every day.

That's what he wanted. That determination to live his best life. And if he could do it with someone special by his side? Well, he wasn't going to waste any more time.

He'd taken a couple of steps towards the door, when Nicky interrupted his thoughts.

'Hey, where are you off to? Not waiting to hug me at midnight?' she asked, hamming up some fake outrage. 'After Scott, of course. You're way down my midnight snog list now.'

Dario shook his head, a nervous smile reflecting the genuine hope he was feeling for the first time today. 'You said earlier that she had feelings for me. I'm going to find it out if you're right.'

32

MINNIE

After Gino had finished speaking to Dario in the office, Minnie had watched as he'd begun his rounds of the restaurant, chatting animatedly to his guests, serving them drinks and generally whipping up the party. All the while, she could see the strain behind the forced smile on his tired face.

Sonya had joined her while Gino was away, and then Eric had taken her place. She'd been shocked to bits when he'd charged in the door. He'd spotted her immediately, then given her a brief kiss, and said, 'I'll be back over to see you, Mum. I just need to have a quick chat to Ailish first.' He was off before Minnie could say a word. Just as well really, because if he'd given her a chance to speak, she'd have issued a stern warning that he'd better not be here to upset anyone. Especially Ailish or Emmy. As it was, he seemed to be the one who'd ended up having his feathers ruffled.

She'd watched him go over and speak to Ailish and Emmy, and then he and Ailish had gone off to have a tête-à-tête in the alcove. As that conversation ended, Sonya had left to rejoin her grandson, so Eric had taken her place across from Minnie, but, to be honest, he wasn't much company, too preoccupied by what was going on over at Ailish's table. He'd yet to divulge what had been discussed and Minnie didn't like to pry. She'd find out later from Ailish, and then report back to Henry to keep him in the loop.

By the time Gino had finally made his way back over to her, there were more pressing matters to attend to. Minnie had checked her watch and cursed in a voice that only Henry could hear. Damn, she was running out of time. It wouldn't be long until they would start getting ready for the countdown to the bells, although, strangely, Gino wasn't showing any signs of kicking off the preparations.

After Gino, polite as ever, had welcomed Eric and chatted to him for a few minutes, Minnie had cleared her throat. 'Eric, dear, I wonder if you wouldn't mind leaving Gino and I for a few moments. There's something rather private that I'd like to discuss with him.'

Well, Eric's eyes had been like saucers, and she could tell he was wondering what secrets she had that she didn't want him to hear. Rich, really. This was the same boy who had been a secret smoker for years in his teens. And also the man who'd had an extra-marital affair and hoodwinked them all.

When he'd left, she'd immediately tried to get a gauge of whether they'd have time for the conversation she'd been planning to have with Gino all night.

'Do you have to start preparing for the countdown to the bells, Gino?' He'd usually be organising the music, making sure everyone had drinks, checking the microphone, preparing what he was going to say.

To her surprise, he'd shaken his head. 'No. I've asked Carlo to do it tonight. He's the only one in our family with something to look forward to this year.'

Minnie had, quite frankly, felt her sympathies begin to waver. Gino was here. She was here. But Henry and Alicia were not and she was quite sure that if either of them was given more precious time on this earth, they certainly wouldn't be spending it brooding like this.

She'd been about to point this out, when he'd launched into a long, blow-by-blow account of the discussion he'd just had with Dario, and Minnie had put her own agenda to one side yet again to listen to him, despite the sand in the egg timer of today running quickly to the bottom.

And yes, her heart had ached for him when he'd recounted his response to Dario's suggestion that they sell up, and she'd seen the emotion and the pain he had at the prospect of letting everything go. But then, she'd swayed back to her earlier thought about Henry and Alicia. That was true loss. Everlasting. Permanent. This? There was life after this, if the man could only see it.

'And do you know what Dario had the audacity to say?' he'd ranted, his Italian accent always thicker when he was speaking with passion. He hadn't even given Minnie a second to respond. Not that she had any idea anyway. 'He said that Alicia would agree to selling!'

Full of ire, he'd slapped the table when he said that, causing many people around them to glance over. Minnie had felt her cheeks burning and it fired her on. She hadn't had a near-death experience at the shops this morning, then spent all day preparing to come here, only to fall at the last hurdle of her mission. But first she had to de-escalate his temper down to a point where he'd listen, and begin to try to pave the way for what she had to say.

He'd opened his mouth to resume his rant, but she'd put her hand up to stop him and uttered a sharp, 'Gino!'

His surprise at the gesture had been evident by the way he seemed to swallow his words and lose his train of thought.

She'd gently removed the napkin that had been on her lap,

and placed it rather delicately in front of her, sending the subliminal message that the banging of tables was not acceptable. Then
she'd waited until she felt his blood pressure may have subsided
from 'explosive', before speaking in a firm but loving voice.

'Gino, first of all, I warn you that you may not like all that I
have to say, but please stick with me because it's very important
and I truly think you need to hear it.'

He'd said nothing, but he hadn't disagreed, so at least that was
something.

'First of all, I have to tell you that I feel Alicia would indeed
agree to sell the restaurant if there was no viable alternative and if
she felt it would release pressure on you or your sons.'

His eyes had narrowed, and she could see he was about to
interrupt her, so she'd put her hand up again to make it clear that
wasn't an option. Two thoughts had struck her at the same time.
The first was that there was something quite energising about
speaking her mind like this. The second was more a feeling than a
thought. In the place in her mind where she saw Henry, now she
could imagine that she saw Alicia too. Her friend had been in the
very fabric of these walls, and now Minnie had an unequivocal
sense that Alicia was listening in and that she would be standing
behind Minnie now, hands on hips, telling her to do what must be
done.

Now, time had caught up with them. Dario had given the ten-
minute warning and Nicky had passed out drams of whisky for
the toast. As midnight came almost upon them, Minnie knew she
had to get to the point.

An air of anticipation was sweeping around the room, and
behind Gino, she saw Carlo prepare to climb back up onto the
chair for the final countdown, the way his father had done for
over fifty years. It was now or never. And Minnie Ryan wasn't
giving up.

'Gino, the thing I've come to understand since losing Henry is that time moves on. And if you're so busy clutching on to the past, then all you do is destroy any chance for a happy future. I know how much you love this restaurant, but it's time to let it go. And I say that as a friend who loves you and wants the best for you too. And as the wife of a man who viewed you as a brother.'

There was a split second when she wondered if he was going to storm off and leave her sitting there alone, but, of course, he would never do that because, for all his temper and his stubbornness, he was a good and decent man.

Her gaze met his, and the tenderness and love in his eyes told her that her words were hitting home.

'Gino, the reason that I came here tonight, was because, before he died, Henry asked me to do something for him.' Minnie almost gasped, as the act of mentioning Henry's death threatened to steal her breath.

An internal monologue began to calm her heart and encourage her to go on. It was Henry's voice, as always, that she heard. *Come on now, Minnie, you know you can do this, ma darling.*

Her greatest love. Last year, they'd danced the night away in this very room, and only two days later, his heart had failed for the first time. The skill of the paramedics had brought him back to her, but only for a bittersweet evening. That's when he'd beckoned her close and told her what she must do if the heavens were to claim him.

'Go to Gino, ma darling. And tell him...'

The memory of Henry's words was interrupted by Carlo, who was now banging a glass with a spoon and calling for hush.

'Ladies and gentlemen, it's almost midnight...' A roar of excitement made the floor tremble. 'So if you'd all like to grab your drinks, I'd like to say something...'

Minnie forced herself to carry on, all too aware that if she didn't do this now, her words would be drowned out in the chaos. From the chair beside her, she lifted the box that she'd collected from the jewellers this morning.

'Before Henry passed, he asked me to have this made for you. And he asked me to deliver it to you tonight, with a message...'

Once again, she was back in the hospital, holding Henry's hand, listening to him say. 'Wait until next New Year, ma darling, because I'll want you to be strong and to be ready to laugh again.'

So, here she was...

'I'd like to propose a toast,' Carlo was saying now. 'To the wonderful people who would tell us every year about how they danced in the street outside this restaurant on the first Hogmanay it was open, because there were no customers inside. And how the music brought them friends that would last all of their lives.' Carlo held his glass high. 'To my father, Gino. To my mother, Alicia. Who created this world for us. And to all of you for sharing it with us.'

Another deafening roar of appreciation shook the room and as soon as it was over, Carlo checked the clock, and then beckoned to his audience.

'Friends, let's say goodbye to the year behind us and welcome the wonders to come. Please raise your glasses and count down with me.'

Everyone in the room did exactly as he asked, beginning with a rousing chorus of, 'Ten...'

33

MIDNIGHT

As the crowd bellowed out that first number...

Ailish rose from her seat and glanced around the room, searching for the person she wanted to speak to. It was time to tell the man she had loved what she wanted to do.

Outside, while Carlo had been speaking, Yvie had just finished explaining that Emmy had been so wrong about everything today. That the reason she couldn't find Cormac all day was because he had been finalising the surprise that Yvie had been helping him plan for months. And now, Cormac was stepping forward towards Emmy with the strangest expression on his beautiful face.

In the corner of the restaurant, Dario watched Ailish stand up, and knew the time to make his move was now. He began walking towards her.

At her table, Minnie handed over the gift that her beloved Henry had asked her to bring.

'NINE...'

Ailish walked towards him, her eyes finding him, every step taking her closer.

Cormac dropped to one knee, and pulled a small blue velvet box from his pocket.

Dario's heart began to race as he saw that she'd fixed her eyes on him now.

Minnie watched as her oldest friend pulled open the bow and flicked open the wrapping paper underneath, before lifting the lid of the box.

'EIGHT...'

Ailish tried to steady her heart as she asked herself one last time if she was sure about the decision she was about to make.

Emmy gasped as Cormac opened the box and she saw a beautiful diamond solitaire glistening there.

Dario reached Ailish and he held out his hand to her.

Minnie watched Gino's surprised reaction when he saw the flask, then his lips move as he read the inscription aloud... *Friendships last long after midnight.*

'SEVEN...'

Ailish saw Dario's hand and reached out to him.

Emmy's hand went to her mouth as Cormac raised the box towards her.

Dario and Ailish's fingers slowly touched – she was the friend he had known since she was twenty-one years old, when she'd kissed the man who would become her husband right in front of him at midnight.

Minnie looked into Gino's tear-filled eyes, and whispered, 'Henry knew that we would both be alone...'

'SIX...'

Ailish met Dario's gaze and smiled as she had a sudden hunch as to what he was about to do.

Over the sounds of the countdown inside, Cormac said, 'Emmy Ryan, you always have been everything...'

Dario let his fingers trail away from Ailish, who nodded to him as he kept on walking.

Minnie put her hand over Gino's and went on, 'And he wanted the two people he loved to take care of each other...'

'FIVE...'

Ailish reached her ex-husband and put her hand up to touch his cheek.

Emmy listened to her love saying, 'I don't ever want to live a day of my life without you.'

Dario took several more steps towards the woman that he'd thought about for years.

Minnie prayed Henry was right as she said, 'Gino, you're lonely, and I am too...'

'FOUR...'

Ailish swallowed, found the words and the courage to say them. 'I'm sorry, Eric. It's over for us.'

Emmy thought of how she'd dreamed of this moment since she'd met Cormac.

Dario reached the woman he had feelings for, whispered into her ear, 'A million years ago, you kissed me...'

Minnie leaned across the table, to make sure he could hear her. 'So what do you say, Gino...'

'THREE...'

Ailish saw Eric's crestfallen expression as he said, 'You're rejecting me?'

Voice oozing emotion, Cormac asked, 'Emmy, will you marry me?'

Dario went on, 'And I know it was only because you felt sorry for me, because Ailish had done a runner with Eric.'

Minnie finally, *finally*, got to the point, 'I have a spare room waiting for you. Shall we team up and do what's left of this life together?'

'TWO...'

Ailish thought about Eric's question, then watched his puzzled frown when she replied...

Emmy's heart told her this was so right. But a voice in her head told her it was all so wrong.

Dario said, 'So I thought I'd like to kiss you again. If that's okay with you?' And then he watched as she lifted her lips to his.

Gino's fingers wrapped around Minnie's as he nodded slowly, saying, 'Yes. But, Minnie, what if it's too late?'

'ONE...'

Ailish watched Eric's puzzled frown as she replied, 'It's not that I'm rejecting you, Eric. I'm just choosing myself instead.'

Emmy opened her mouth, and whispered her answer. Just one word. 'No.'

Dario kissed the woman he thought may be his future. And Gwen kissed him right back.

Minnie heard Henry responding to Gino's fear, and she spoke his words aloud. 'It's never too late, Gino. It's only midnight.'

And as the bells rang out in Gino's Trattoria, and in the streets outside, and on the televisions of people across the country, four people knew that the year ahead was going to be very different from the one they'd just left behind.

MIDNIGHT – MORNING

34

AILISH

All around them, the restaurant was a carnival of celebration, as people kissed their loved ones, raised toasts to absent friends, and danced with the children who'd been allowed to stay up late enough to welcome the bells. Carlo was leading a rousing, heartfelt rendition of 'Auld Lang Syne', Robert Burns' lament to bygone times, the anthem that was sewn into the very fabric of the nation.

Ailish slipped her hand through the arm of the man who'd instigated the divorce papers that had dropped through her door this morning, thinking she could feel his sadness. On any given day in the last two years, she'd have relished a bit of discomfort thrown the way of Eric Ryan, but not today. Not any more. It was time to move on and she surprised herself as she realised she now felt the power inside her to do that. She didn't need Eric. She just had to start showing up for herself.

As they sang, Ailish cast her gaze around, searching for the people she loved. She spotted Gwen and Dario locked in an embrace and the sight of it made her heart soar.

They'd finally got there.

Over the years, Ailish had always hoped that they would. After she'd split with Eric, Rhonda had hinted that Dario might be a great option for her, but the truth was that Ailish's feelings for him had never run deeper than friendship. And besides, over the many New Year's Eve parties they'd had here, she'd spotted Gwen's eyes following Dario too many times to count. She just hoped that, on both sides, this could be more than a tipsy kiss at midnight.

However, a tipsy kiss at midnight was definitely the option that Rhonda had taken, as she was currently locking lips with Dario's son, Matty, who was possibly the most handsome man Ailish had ever seen, and, at thirty, twenty-four years younger than her pal. Not that Ailish was judging. A fifty-four-year-old man kissing a thirty-year-old woman wouldn't so much as raise an eyebrow. Not that Rhonda's Botox actually allowed her eyebrows to move. However, Ailish did have a fleeting thought that if both those matches led to long-term relationships, their family Christmas dinners were going to have a pretty unusual dynamic.

Ailish decided to find the others on her midnight hug list before going to interrupt love's young dream. She scanned the room for Emmy, but there was no sign of her. Must still be outside on the phone to Cormac.

'Come on, Eric, let's go see your mum,' she said, spotting Minnie and Gino hugging at their table.

Minnie saw them coming together and her eyes widened with surprise as she opened her arms to Ailish, leaving the men to shake hands. 'Happy New Year, darling Ailish! Does this mean...?' she asked, as their heads met, both of them understanding the unspoken question.

Ailish kissed her beautiful now-ex-mother-in-law on the cheek and decided to reframe that terminology. Minnie was the mother she didn't have. Through thick, thin, and divorce, that remained the essence of who they were to each other. 'No, Mum,' she gave Minnie her answer. 'But it does mean we can all be together again, and I think that's a good place to start.'

Minnie's delighted expression told her that was good enough.

'Happy New Year, Gino,' Ailish said, as she hugged the elderly man, marvelling as always at the happiness he had created here. So many years, and so many people had seen in the bells with joy and surrounded by love, thanks to a dream that he'd made into a reality. As she left his embrace, she noticed the beautiful silver flask on the table and squinted to read the inscription that was carved into the gleaming metal.

Friendships last long after midnight.

The two women who were making their way through the crowds to them now, bringing their midnight kisses with them, had proved that time after time.

Rhonda reached her first, and with a shriek of, 'Happy New Year,' wrapped her in the tightest of bear hugs. 'It's going to be the best year ever,' her wild friend promised, out of earshot of the others. 'I'm already in love.'

'And you're already fricking fabulous, so you're sorted,' Ailish giggled.

'If you've taken the Adulterous Arse back, I might have to kill you though,' Rhonda chirped, her words a hilarious contrast to the jubilation in her tone.

'Still single,' Ailish assured her, laughing. 'This dress was too good to waste on him. Thanks, Rhonda. I love you more than you know.'

'Ah, bugger, you'll wreck my lashes!' Rhonda sobbed, frantically fanning her face so the tears didn't dislodge the glue that held her diamond-edged, mink masterpieces in place.

The celebratory jig of changing partners continued with Dario, then Matty, until finally Ailish embraced Gwen gently, careful not to bruise the thin skin that was covering her bones.

Her friend would get her strength back, and the happiness in her squeal of, 'Happy New Year, Ails!' told her that Gwen's illness might have sapped her strength, but it had left her spirit intact.

Ailish's eyes were crying, but her grin was beaming as she embraced her.

They held their clinch, as Gwen's mouth reached Ailish's ear. 'I kissed Dario,' she whispered, the words oozing pure joy.

'I saw!' Ailish murmured in return.

'He's the biggest reason I wanted to come here tonight and why I planned this weeks ago,' she confessed. 'I've thought about him for years, and just decided that if I didn't tell him this year, then I might not get the chance. He just told me he feels the same. I can't believe it, Ails.'

'Believe it, my love. I'm so happy for you, Gwen. You deserve this.'

'I do. You know what?' she said, still just the two of them in their own world.

Ailish gulped. 'Tell me.'

'Fuck cancer.'

Ailish could barely breathe through the tears now. 'Fuck cancer,' she repeated, because right now, with all of them together, it felt like there was nothing that could beat them.

In fact, it felt like nothing could ever spoil this perfect moment... Until her daughter raced towards her and fell into her arms.

35

EMMY

'No.'

She'd only said one word, but it had been enough to crush their whole relationship to dust.

Still on one knee, Cormac had let his hands fall, the ring he was holding no longer required. 'No?'

Emmy's head was shaking slowly from side to side, her eyes wide, hand over her mouth as if to stop it uttering another lethal blow.

A few feet away, Yvie had been stunned into silence, her face a mask of shock and bewilderment, a stark contrast to the crowds of people who were celebrating in the streets around them. Fireworks soared above them, cheers rang out, music blared from windows that had been opened despite the cold, to let the New Year in.

Emmy had barely even registered that any of it was there.

'No. I can't, Cormac. I'm so sorry.'

Cormac had risen to his feet, fuelled by confusion and horror. 'I don't get it,' he'd said, and there was no challenge or aggression there, just hurt, dripping from every word. 'I thought this was what you wanted. What *we* wanted. Emmy, I meant what I said – from the day I met you, all I've wanted is to do life with you. All of it. Just me and you. I thought you did too.'

'I did,' she'd said honestly. 'But now I just don't...' she'd paused, then changed tack. Stick with honesty. The least he deserved was the truth. 'Cormac, all day I've been freaking out because I thought you were having an affair. You've been acting so weird for weeks now and I didn't understand, so I made up my own story. And that's where my mind went.'

'I was organising this. Shopping for the ring. Yvie helped me choose it.' He'd gestured to Yvie, who was still speechless as she gave a conciliatory shrug. 'And today I had to go collect it. I told you I was working because I wanted this to be a surprise tonight. I was waiting to find out where you would be. I thought I would find you at your mum's place. Then it changed to your gran's house and then Yvie called to say you were here. The plan was always to propose at midnight, wherever you were, whoever you were with. I was just about to come inside and do it in front of all the people that you love.' A scenario had obviously dawned on him and he'd groaned. 'Fuck, I'm glad that didn't work out. I'd be standing in there like an idiot right now.'

Emmy had felt like the worst person on the entire planet. And still people around them were bloody celebrating. 'I'm so sorry, Cormac. I love you, but I just can't do this.'

'But why? I still don't understand.'

Emmy had bitten her lip, scared to say it because it said more about her than him. This wasn't Cormac's fault. It was hers. She'd felt herself begin to crumble as sorrow swept in.

'I. Can't. Marry. You,' she'd said, squeezing the words out through sobs. She'd taken a breath. *Say it. Tell him the truth.* 'Because you deserve better than someone who is going to think the worst of you. You deserve someone who will never doubt you. And I don't think I can be that person any more. I'm so sorry.'

Overwhelmed, she hadn't stuck around for his reply, because she couldn't bear to hear it. Instead, she'd about-turned, run back into Gino's and straight into Ailish's arms.

'Emmy! What is it? Oh, sweetheart,' her mum was murmuring now as she held her, and Emmy didn't care that they were surrounded by the concerned, curious expressions of just about everyone she called family: Gran. Dad. Aunt Gwen. Aunt Rhonda. And then the friends – Dario, Matty, Gino – that she'd known all her life too.

'Emmy, are you okay?' That was from her dad. A bit clueless and hopeless as usual, but she could hear the worry in his voice.

She lifted her head, dried her cheeks with the cuffs of her jumper, nodded hesitantly. 'I'm sorry. I'm okay. Just...' Her words got stuck there, because she didn't know what to say next. I've just blown my relationship? I'm a terrible person? I've just trashed my boyfriend in the street?

Before the silence grew, her mum stepped right in and took charge. 'You don't have to explain a thing, sweetheart. Just come with me and we'll talk somewhere a bit quieter.'

'You can use my office,' Dario offered. 'It's out past the toilets on the left. Here's a key.'

Emmy felt a toe-curling mix of gratitude and embarrassment. She kept her head down, hiding her tear-soaked face as her mum took her hand, and led her through the restaurant to the small room at the back of the building. On the way, they passed Nicky and her boyfriend, Scott, who were talking to Dario's friend, Brodie, but her mum avoided subjecting her to an uncomfortable encounter by giving them a cheery, 'Happy New Year! Just borrowing the office – we have a make-up emergency,' as she swept Emmy right past them.

As soon as the door closed behind them, her mum steered her to the couch. 'Okay, tell me from the start. What's happened?'

Emmy spilled it all out. The suspicions that had been rising over the last month or so. The fears that had been niggling at her, but that had overwhelmed her this morning. How she'd tracked him, found he wasn't where he should be, caught him in a lie. And then, the biggest kicker, how she'd just found out the reason behind it all. He hadn't been having an affair at all. He'd been planning the most special moment for her. She'd found him outside, and he'd gone down on one knee and asked her to share the rest of her life with him. And...

'You said no,' Ailish finished the story for her, then went to the natural conclusion. 'Oh, Emmy, I'm sorry. But if you don't love him enough, or you're not sure, then it's best to be honest with him. It's the right thing to do, even though it doesn't feel like that right now.'

'But that's the thing, Mum, I do love him enough. But today, I convinced myself that he'd done something awful. Why would I do that?'

Her mum tried to cushion that one. 'Well, there was some evidence that would make you think that...'

'But why didn't I just ask him? Why didn't I trust him? What is wrong with me?'

That seemed to snap something in her mum because, all of a sudden, she reached over and lifted Emmy's chin and she was totally giving pissed-off vibes. 'Now you wait a minute, Emmy Ryan. There is absolutely nothing wrong with you.' Her shoulders slumped, as she went on, 'Aaaargh, I could bloody murder him.'

'Who, Cormac?' Emmy was confused. 'Because he doesn't deserve that. He's a really good guy.' Why did Emmy feel like she was losing her grip on this conversation?

'No, not Cormac. Your bloody dad.' After blowing out a really irritated breath of air, she went on. 'I'm no psychologist, Emmy, but it's not difficult to see how you got there. Your entire life, you've always been so trusting, always seen the best in people, especially your dad. You trusted in his honesty, and then you found out in the most brutal way that he'd lied to you, to me, to all of us. A shock like that leaves its mark. It's only natural that it shifts something in you, makes you lose faith in people, in your own judgement, maybe even in love. It makes you protect your heart and push danger away. It's why I've shut down every feeling since it happened. Your dad's affair didn't just affect me though, it broke our family and that leaves a scar. It has to, because we're human. But you can't give into it, sweetheart, because that damage will fade, I promise. It might just take a bit of time, but you'll get there.'

Emmy took in what she was saying, processed it, ran it back and forwards in her mind, and then recognised the truth of it. Damn, it made total sense. Why had she not thought that through before now? And why had she just stormed right in and screwed everything up? Her groan came right up from her boots. 'But if I do get there, I'll be fricking alone because I just blew it with Cormac.'

'Well, maybe you should go speak to him and see if he'll understand too. And if he's the man you think he is...'

Her mum didn't even finish the sentence before Emmy was on her feet and running.

36

DARIO

Dario stared at his dad, trying to take in what he'd just told him. He took a step towards him, trying to block out the cacophony of sound coming from every corner of the room, as Carlo had moved on to a new musical number and now led the crowd in an enthusiastic chorus of 'The Bonnie Banks of Loch Lomond'.

'You're going to have to say that again to me, Dad, because I need to make sure I'm hearing you right...'

The last fifteen minutes of his life had been insane. Selling his family's company. Then finding the connection he'd always felt with Gwen was real.

But now two ropes were pulling him in different directions, and it felt like they were ripping him apart. Gwen. The crazy crush that had lasted over thirty years and now she'd told him that she'd felt the same. How did he get so lucky? And how did he get so unlucky that it fell on the same day that he committed a betrayal that his father would never forgive?

Or was he telling him something different now?

To the side of his dad, he saw Minnie Ryan nod to Gino, as if spurring him on, and Dario realised he had seen that dynamic before, when his mum would cajole his dad into something that Gino was reluctant to do. And she was always right.

'I said, I've changed my mind,' his dad repeated, and yes, Dario had heard it correctly the first time. He wouldn't have been more surprised if Gino had punched him in the face. 'I agree to sell the business. It's the right thing to do.'

Dario wondered if his dad was drunk, but he sounded perfectly lucid.

'I know that the deal expired at midnight...' his dad was saying, 'but if you go now and call them, maybe you can still get them to honour their offer.'

Dario needed more information to absorb this.

'But, Dad, are you sure? Why the change of heart?'

His dad glanced over to Minnie and returned her smile. 'Because maybe I'm a foolish old man who needs to be reminded that it's the people we love that matter, nothing else. And life is too short to lose them before the choice is taken out of our hands. So I'm sorry, Dario. I should have listened to you. Now go make the phone call.'

Stunned, Dario didn't know whether to confess to what he'd done, or quit while he was ahead and avoid risking upsetting Gino all over again. It was one thing being given the go-ahead now, but would his father be furious that he'd gone against his wishes?

Sod it. He had to tell him. He couldn't bring himself to be dishonest, even by omission.

Through clenched teeth, he winced as he admitted, 'Dad, I already made the call. I sold the business.'

Gino froze, stared at him, and Dario saw a thousand emotions run through the eyes of a face as still as stone. This was Gino's dream. His heart and soul. And Dario had taken that away without his consent. He braced himself, waiting for the retribution, the wrath...

But it didn't come. Instead, Gino's words were slow and deliberate. 'Then you did the right thing. I was wise to give you the business, Dario, because you did what we needed to do even when I refused. That takes courage.'

Dario's feet were glued to the floor, every sense blocked by both shock and gratitude.

That was when Minnie stepped forward and hugged him. 'Well done, Dario. Your mum would be so proud of you.'

'Thank you,' he croaked, overcome with affection for the friend his mother had adored. He wasn't sure he would hold it together long enough to say any more than that, so he was grateful when a diversion took Minnie's focus off him and on to something else. Or, rather, someone else.

'Emmy! Are you all right, my darling?'

Ailish and Emmy had rejoined them and now Minnie was speaking to her granddaughter, clearly full of concern.

'I am, Gran. I just need to sort something and... Cormac!'

Everyone in their group now stopped their conversations and turned all eyes to Emmy and then to the guy who was standing at the bar with Carlo's fiancée, Yvie. The same man who had just turned and was now walking towards them. He stopped a few feet in front of Emmy and didn't shrivel at all under the gaze of the now-silent audience in this corner of the room. Instead, he remained silent, waiting for Emmy to speak. Dario felt Gwen's hand slipping into his as they watched Emmy step forward.

'Please ask me again.'

Silence.

'Please. Ask me again,' she repeated. 'I made a mistake. You said you wanted to ask me in front of the people I love, and here we are,' she said with a nod to the crowd. 'So if you truly do love me enough to spend the rest of your life with me, please ask me again.'

She didn't need to say it a fourth time.

Cormac pulled a box out of his pocket, and then opened it and took out a beautiful diamond ring. He took one more step towards her and held it out to her.

'Emmy Ryan, will you please, please put this ring on and say that you'll marry me?'

'Cormac Sweeney...' Emmy replied, with the widest smile in the room. 'I most definitely will.'

The celebration that erupted in that corner rivalled the one they'd had at midnight, as Cormac lifted her up, swung her around and then kissed her in front of a standing ovation. They all swarmed around them, giving congratulations, good wishes, kisses, and promises of an all-expenses-paid honeymoon in Ibiza. That came from Rhonda. And only on the condition that they could all go with them.

Dario dashed to the bar, where Nicky and Scott were now chatting to Yvie, Brodie and Sonya, and in two minutes, all of them were on the way back with bottles of champagne and trays of glasses. When the drinks had been poured, the toasts had been given, and the love had been shared, he reached again for Gwen's hand and realised that it wasn't there.

Casting around, he spotted her leaving through the front door and wondered if this had all just been too much for her. Handing his glass over to Ailish, he kept his smile on his face as he excused himself and went after her.

Outside, he found her leaning against the wall of the restaurant, head back, eyes closed.

'Gwen? Are you okay? Are you sick? Do you need a—'

Her eyes opened as she shook her head slowly. 'I don't need anything. Maybe just you.'

Heart melting, he went to her, slid his arms around her waist. 'I'm right here. Although I still can't quite believe that you're here with me.'

He wondered if he'd got this wrong, because for him, this was the happiest of moments, yet she was staring at him with such sorrow.

'Is this a thing, Dario?' she asked quietly, searching his face for answers. 'I mean, a real thing?'

'I think so.' Shit, he had got it wrong. She was obviously doubtful. Unsure.

'I think so too. But if it is, then you need to know something first.'

Fear now overruled everything else. He'd waited thirty years for this woman and now there was something that could stop them exploring what they could be.

'Tell me.'

'I lied this morning. I told everyone that my scans were clear, because I wanted this day. I couldn't bear to let it go by in case I never got another chance to see you, to be with you at midnight. The truth is, I have no idea what my results will say, but you need to know what could be ahead, because you can walk away now. I would understand, I promise.'

He put his fingers up to her lips and stopped her. 'I'm not walking.'

'But it could be—'

This time, it was his lips that hushed her as he kissed her. There were so many possibilities, so much potential for heartache, so many things that could go wrong. But right now he wasn't going to think about any of them, because if he'd learned anything today, it was that the past didn't matter. Neither did what lay ahead. So, from now on, all he was going to worry about was today.

'It will be what it is,' he told her softly. 'And we'll find out together.'

37

MINNIE

Inside her front door, Minnie kicked off her shoes, and gave silent thanks that she'd managed to last the whole night without the kind of incident that had felled her twice yesterday. She put that down to good shoes, great company and the beautiful meal at Gino's restaurant. For someone who regularly forgot to eat, that had been such a treat.

And there would be more of them to come. She and Gino had talked long after the party had ended and they'd set out a plan – the same one that Henry had in mind in the moments before he left her.

Gino's sons were going to help him move his things over here and into her spare room tomorrow.

No one could replace Henry, and no one could replace Alicia, but they could share a house, and share their days, and it would make both their lives so much better. Company mattered, didn't it? Life was so much better when the joys were shared too.

They'd already planned a few things that they might like to do. Day jaunts to the coast. Maybe one of those bus trips up north.

And Gino had even suggested that they might visit Italy, to see the village he'd grown up in.

And Minnie had agreed to it all, because if they didn't do it now, well... They both knew what the alternative could be.

They were going to live every single day as if it was their last and they were going to enjoy every minute of it.

Most of all, they were going to take care of each other. And that was what Henry and Alicia would have wanted.

Minnie went through to the living room, switched on her record player and put the needle on the start of the record.

She was exhausted, her skint knees were stinging, and her hip was beginning to ache again, but as the opening bars of 'Moon River' filled the room, her ailments were forgotten as she began to sway, and as always, felt Henry's cheek touch hers.

'My darling, I have so much to tell you,' she said to him, without speaking the words. 'Ailish and Eric have mended fences, but only as friends. Eric wanted more, but, well, there was no going back for Ailish, and nor should there be. Eric is just going to have to find a different happiness. And going by the sparkle in Ailish's eyes tonight, I think she's already there. You've always loved her like I do, Henry, so I know you'll be pleased about that. And, Henry, your darling granddaughter got engaged to Cormac. Oh, to be that age again. There was a slight hitch getting there, but when they sorted it out, the joy on their faces made me weep with happiness for them. I'll only admit to you that I so wish it was us. Imagine starting all over again, Henry. Another lifetime with you. I'd give anything for that to be true.'

The bars of the music wrapped around her heart, and she knew that he'd give anything to have that too. But for a little while longer, she had to live in the real world.

For the first time since the music started, she whispered words aloud, just to make sure he heard them. 'And, Henry, I spoke to

Gino, and everything went just as planned, my darling. So you can go rest now, because I'm going to be fine.' She knew he could see her smile and hear the soft words she was saying now. 'Henry, my love, you'll always have my whole heart. I'll see you when I get there...'

And with that, Henry Ryan kissed her and then began to walk away.

'You will, ma darling,' she heard him say. 'I'll be waiting.'

EPILOGUE
ONE YEAR LATER

Carlo's Cafe was closed for business. At least, to the outside world.

However, inside, there was a private party, and the glasses were being refilled, ready to toast the dawn of another year.

Yvie and Emmy were circulating with two bottles of champagne, but as Emmy passed Cormac, he pulled her down on to his knee and kissed her. 'Hey, wife...'

He'd been doing that a lot since they'd tied the knot right here the week before. They'd chosen Christmas Eve to say, 'I do,' because, well, they both knew Hogmanay was just too unpredictable.

'Would you mind putting my daughter down, only my glass is empty,' came a man's amused voice from the next table.

Cormac immediately put his hands up, doing as he was asked. 'Apologies, Eric.'

Emmy feigned outrage. 'Father, your drink will be topped up when you grab a tray of those sausage rolls and whip them around to everyone too.'

Happy to oblige, Eric leaned over and kissed the woman beside him. 'She gets that bossiness from her mother,' he quipped to his new girlfriend, Colette. He'd met her when he'd joined a gym at the start of the year and so far, so good. Although, his knees were starting to ache because she could outrun him every day of the week on the treadmill. But at least she was in the same age bracket as him so she could remember the eighties.

'Erm, Eric Ryan, I heard that!' Ailish shouted from the corner table, where she was delivering Slippery Nipples to Rhonda and Matty, who'd surprised everyone by lasting longer than the tiramisu at last year's party. Rhonda was well aware that people raised an eyebrow about the age difference, but she couldn't care less because, as she always said, thanks to a few cosmetic nips, tucks, and enhancements, there were definitely parts of her that were only twenty-nine.

'I'll have two of those sausage rolls over here, please, waiter,' Sonya chirped, then cleared a space in front of her to make room for them. She'd just been telling Nicky and Scott that she was starting her diet tomorrow. Or maybe next weekend. Her Ollie hadn't come home from university because he'd fallen madly in love with an astrophysics student and was being taken home to meet his boyfriend's family for the first time. Sonya was going to join them tomorrow. She'd already batch-cooked a full week's worth of dinners for Gino and Minnie, but she knew they'd probably go to waste because those two were never home. Taking care of them as their live-in housekeeper was the best job ever though, so she didn't mind in the least.

'Five minutes to go!' Carlo bellowed, then got thoroughly distracted because Yvie was now dancing with her tray, and he knew it could all go wrong at any second. She was a wonderful nurse, but a terrible waitress. She was also the most laid-back girlfriend in the world and didn't mind that he'd been working longer hours than ever this year, opening two new cafés with Matty and Dario. There was a fourth on the way, and the first event at that one would be their wedding. She'd already told him she wanted four kids, and they'd all be allowed to go into the family business.

He'd need new partners by then anyway, because Dario was already semi-retired. He only worked a couple of days a week, because he spent the rest of the time making up for the fact that he'd worked far too many hours in his lifetime already. Besides, there was so much life out there to enjoy, and Dario felt truly lucky to be experiencing it all with Gwen. Her scan results last January had been clear, and all the tests she'd had since then had continued to show she was cancer-free, so they were planning a three-month tour around Europe in the summer. Gwen had already invited Minnie and Gino on the Italian leg of the trip, and they were excited to help Gino finally revisit his homeland and the village of his youth.

Dario switched on the large TV on the wall and turned it to the countdown that was shown live from Edinburgh Castle every year.

They all saw that it would shortly begin, so Gino stood up, banjo in hand, and raised a silver flask, the one inscribed with a message from an absent friend.

'I would like to propose a toast,' he told them, to a raucous cheer. 'To the people who are no longer with us... We miss you...'

Another cheer.

Minnie raised her eyes heavenwards and murmured, 'That's you, Henry, love.' She would always be grateful for his love both before and after he died. Sharing the house with Gino had been the wonderful chapter that she hadn't expected, and she was in no hurry for their story to come to an end.

'Minnie, are you listening?' Gino teased, much to the amusement of the others.

'Just waiting for you to get to the point, my friend,' she replied sassily, earning a round of whoops and applause.

Gino took the hint. 'And to the people who are still here by our sides. Let us love and laugh from this year to the next. Because, as a very special man once told me, friendships last long after midnight. To friendship!'

'To friendship!' came the response, everyone on their feet now to bring in the bells.

On the television, the countdown began, and the whole room joined in.

'Ten... Nine...'

In the middle of the throng, Ailish's boyfriend stood behind her, wrapped his arm around her waist and whispered into her ear. Brodie had asked her to dance with him after all the drama at Gino's had calmed down last year. They'd taken it slow, because Ailish was in no hurry to rush into love again. Although, lately her heart had been telling her something different.

'Eight... Seven... Six...'

'I know there's so much history here...' Brodie whispered.

'Five... Four... Three...'

'So can I just check when would be a good time to tell you I'm in love with you?'

'Three... Two... One...'

In the first second of the brand new year, as the bells rang out across the city, Ailish turned around and kissed him.

'Happy New Year, Brodie. You can tell me right now. Because this feels like a good time to tell you that I love you too.'

ABOUT THE AUTHOR

Shari Low is the #1, million-copy bestselling author of over 30 novels, including One Day With You and One Moment in Time and a collection of parenthood memories called *Because Mummy Said So*. She lives near Glasgow.

Sign up to Shari Low's mailing list for news, competitions and updates on future books.

Visit Shari's website: www.sharilow.com

Follow Shari on social media:

 facebook.com/sharilowbooks

x.com/sharilow

instagram.com/sharilowbooks

bookbub.com/authors/shari-low

ALSO BY SHARI LOW

My One Month Marriage

One Day In Summer

One Summer Sunrise

The Story of Our Secrets

One Last Day of Summer

One Day With You

One Moment in Time

One Christmas Eve

One Year After You

One Long Weekend

One Midnight With You

The Carly Cooper Series

What If?

What Now?

What Next?

The Hollywood Trilogy (with Ross King)

The Rise

The Catch

The Fall

Boldwood

Boldwood Books is an award-winning fiction publishing company seeking out the best stories from around the world.

Find out more at www.boldwoodbooks.com

Join our reader community for brilliant books, competitions and offers!

Follow us

@BoldwoodBooks

@TheBoldBookClub

Sign up to our weekly deals newsletter

https://bit.ly/BoldwoodBNewsletter

Printed in Great Britain
by Amazon